# INCUBUS OF BOURBON STREET

## JADE CALHOUN SERIES, BOOK 6

## DEANNA CHASE

# ABOUT THIS BOOK

Newlyweds Jade Calhoun and Kane Rouquette have barely said "I do" when there's a disturbance in the shadow world that's draining the energy of angels. As shadow walkers, Jade and Kane are pressed into service, tasked with the impossible mission of solving the mystery before any angels are lost… until Kane's accused of poisoning the shadows with his incubus energy and his power is stripped.

Life goes from bad to worse when a lesser Goddess shows up, hell-bent on stealing the spirits of mortals in pursuit of a fountain of youth. Now it's up to Jade and her coven to keep their friends safe, clear Kane's name, and fix the shadows before one of them is lost forever.

# CHAPTER 1

"*D*o you ever call on your magic during sex?" my best friend, Kat, asked as she tipped her glass of chardonnay to her lips.

I sputtered mid-sip and coughed. "What?"

"Oh, come on, Jade. Are you really telling me you never spice things up with a spell?" Her bright blue eyes gleamed in the soft lighting of the restaurant.

"Well…" How was I supposed to answer that? My husband was an incubus, so magic was just a part of things now, but I wasn't sure I wanted to talk about it. And not in the middle of Muriel's, sandwiched between two tables occupied by conservative-looking old-world New Orleans couples. "Umm, there might be some magic involved, but I don't cast any spells." I gave her a sly glance. "What about you? Does Lucien unleash his magic on your girly parts?"

She clasped her hand over her mouth as she giggled. "He'll kill me if he finds out I told you…he does this thing where he trails a magical current over my skin that drives me crazy. But last night he took it a little further and...uh, it wasn't along my skin, it was—" she lowered her voice, "—inside me."

"Whoa, Lucien." I raised my eyebrows in curious surprise. "I didn't know he had it in him."

She frowned and put her glass down. "What's that supposed to mean? Lucien's hot."

Oops. "That's not... Um, I know he's good looking. I just think of him as more of a brother type."

Her irritated expression vanished. "Well, that's probably a good thing." Then she laughed. "It's somewhat intimidating talking about this with someone who lives with an incubus. I might be feeling a little out-sexed."

Chuckling, I shook my head. "I don't think magical orgasms are anything to feel insecure about."

"Magical orgasms?" Pyper echoed too loudly as she slid into an empty chair. She wore silver pants and a tank top that matched the electric blue stripe in her dark hair. The older couple to our right both turned and gave us disapproving looks. Pyper smiled at them, her eyes dancing with mischief. "Sounds awesome, doesn't it?" she said to them in a conspiratorial tone. "All that magic prolonging the release? Who wouldn't—"

"Pyper!" I stared at her with amused horror. "Stop."

She winked at the woman. "Well, I'm sure you get my meaning."

The woman's outrage slammed into me, nearly knocking me over.

"Oh, jeez." I sucked down a quarter of my margarita, silently cursing my empath ability. I'd donate a kidney in exchange for a life free of other peoples' emotions. "We can't take you anywhere."

"Please. I keep things interesting." She waved the waiter down and ordered a mojito. "What's everyone having?"

"Duck," Kat said. "And crepes. I've been waiting for this all day."

I scanned the menu. "Tuna. Definitely."

"I'm starving," Pyper said. "Maybe the pork chop. Or the beef medallions or—"

My phone started playing "Stairway to Heaven." I grimaced as my friends frowned at me.

"Don't even think about answering it," Pyper said. "This is girls' night. No witch business, got it?"

"But it's Lailah."

Kat plucked the phone from me and hit Decline. "She can leave a message."

"Yeah, okay," I said.

We'd been trying to have a night out together for more than two months, and every time we scheduled something, plans were either interrupted or cancelled by one thing or another. Lailah was a friend, but she was also an angel and my soul guardian. Unfortunately, more often than not her calls came with orders from the angel council. A ball of foreboding weighed heavily in my gut. What had happened now?

My phone buzzed with an incoming text. I reached for it, but Kat grabbed it and then switched it off. "No phone. The world can wait until you eat."

I eyed her, somewhat irritated by her heavy-handedness. But mostly I was relieved. The angel council had imposed on Kane and me far too often lately. If I had to slip into the shadow world to check one more lost soul, I was going to scream. So far we'd rescued half a dozen ghosts and destroyed half a dozen more in the last four weeks. The ones we saved were shuffled into the angel realm. The ones we destroyed had been bound for Hell to be used by the demons for...well, no one really knew what the demons wanted the souls for. No doubt it wasn't anything good. The work was satisfying, but extremely intrusive.

With my phone confiscated, I sat back, feeling relaxed for the first time all day. Girls' night out was looking better and better.

Or it was until Pyper's phone started ringing. She looked at the screen. "It's Kane." With a swipe of her finger, she answered it. "You know we're at dinner. What's so important it couldn't wait?" she said by way of greeting. Then she grimaced. "Seriously?"

"What's wrong?" I held my hand out to Kat for my phone. She didn't fight me on it this time.

As I turned it back on, Pyper said, "There's a disturbance in the shadows. You've been summoned."

I threw a twenty down on the table for my drink. "Tell him I'll be right there."

She relayed my message to Kane as I took off out of the restaurant, listening to Lailah's voicemail, which said, "There's an emergency council meeting convening right now. The energy coming from the shadows is tainted with evil. Your presence is required."

Kane was standing on the sidewalk, waiting for me in front of our house a few blocks over. The early evening sun shone down on his dark hair, and he squinted in my direction, holding out his hand. "They're waiting."

I glanced down at the dagger strapped to his belt. "The Brotherhood hasn't called on you?" Kane and his incubus Brotherhood were demon hunters. They walked the shadows as they slipped in and out of our world all the time. A disturbance would be high on their radar.

"They did, but the angel council overruled them. And for some reason, Maximus let them." Kane's brow wrinkled in confusion.

"That seems...unusual," I said, slipping my hand into his. Maximus was the leader of the Brotherhood and didn't much care for the high angel ordering around one of his demon hunters. Kane and I didn't have a choice, though. We'd signed a contract with the angels in order to protect my soul. But Maximus was under no obligation to the angels and often refused Kane's services when it interfered with demon-hunter missions. Since angels were in constant danger of demons, the high angel relented more often than not.

"Very." He tugged me inside and as soon as the door shut behind us, a bright light streamed from the ceiling.

Taking a deep breath, I nodded to Kane and together, the pair of us stepped into the light.

The world spun, flashes of white light making my eyes water. Then my feet slammed into a hard surface and for once, I managed to stay upright. Blinking hard, my vision cleared and the stark white-and-gold sanctuary came into focus. We were standing in the angel realm's version of the Saint Louis Cathedral. The floors were white and gold checkered tiles and the murals on the walls were washed out, void of the vibrant colors I was used to. I rubbed my arms, trying to stave off the sudden chill.

The angel council stood in a line up on the dais, their expressions somber.

Chessandra, the high angel, stepped forward and gestured for us to come closer. She was dressed impeccably as always in her sleek cream pants suit, but there was something harried in her tight expression and wary onyx eyes.

I glanced around, noting the empty chairs. Usually when we were summoned, all of the angels of the realm were in attendance. Not this time.

My biological father, Drake, moved gracefully to Chessandra's side, concern radiating from his gaze. His

5

straight white-blond hair fell forward as he leaned in and whispered something to her.

"What's going on?" I asked.

An elder council member in the back scowled at me. It was customary to not speak until spoken to, but I didn't care about any of their arcane rules. I'd just been plucked from girls' night. Someone needed to start explaining.

Kane slipped his fingers through mine, and a tingle of his humor warmed my skin. Clearly he was just as tired of their ridiculous formalities as I was.

Chessandra pretended as if I hadn't insulted the entire council and said, "There was an incident earlier today when one of our angels went into the shadow world."

"Nasty business," a white-haired older woman of the council said in disgust.

Chessandra cast her an irritated glance. Her expression cleared as she focused on me again. "She was doing a routine check for viable souls when her magical abilities were suddenly severed. She said she felt as if she'd suffered a demon attack, but she saw nothing. The only reason she was able to return to us is because I recalled her when she didn't report back at her expected time. You both are tasked with investigating the matter. This is of the highest importance."

"Just us? We don't get any help from the council?" I asked.

Chessandra gave me a stern look. "Ms. Calhoun, I just told you an angel suffered an invisible attack. It should be obvious to you we can't risk any of our own getting trapped in the shadows."

Deep-seated frustration tightened in my gut. There were warnings about making deals with the devil. No one ever cautioned against dealing with the high angel, though. Of course they wouldn't risk one of their own. Why should they when they had a white witch and an incubus demon hunter at their beck and call?

Kane squeezed my hand, a silent show of solidarity. He was just as irritated as I was that we had to jump every time they called. Especially when it involved demons. Not that we weren't equipped to deal with them. Kane was a demon hunter, after all.

"Right," I said to Chessandra, my tone clipped. "But I was referring to other shadow walkers. You know, people with power who might be able to help." I was the leader of the New Orleans' coven, but none of my fellow witches were shadow walkers. That skill had been bestowed upon me not too long ago as part of my contract to work for the council.

"And what about the demon hunters?" Kane asked. "Will you be working with them on this? In other words, can I brief my superior on my mission?"

His question seemed like a no brainer. The angels and the Brotherhood had the same mission: to keep people safe from demons. Only, the angels were more concerned with people's souls, and the hunters were more interested in destroying demons. The two went hand in hand, but neither party was very fond of the other. All of our shadow world missions were classified. If Kane didn't tell the Brotherhood about our orders, he could be called into a demon battle at any time, leaving me to deal with the mission on my own.

Chessandra studied him carefully. Then with a flick of her wrist, a door to the right swung open. "Follow me. Both of you."

I stared at Drake, who stepped back into line with the other angels. He wouldn't meet my gaze. Damn, that wasn't a good sign.

Kane and I followed Chessandra into her private office.

"Have a seat," she said and perched on the edge of her desk.

I had a sense of déjà vu from the last time we'd been there. She had the same contemplative expression on her face and the same authoritative air about her.

We did as we were told and waited while she flipped through an old leather-bound notebook. "Maximus isn't sympathetic to our cause."

Kane and I looked at each other. Then he turned to her. "I'm not sure I understand. Maximus is fully dedicated to ridding our world of demons."

She nodded. "Yes. He is. But he also has a grudge against us. He resents the fact that we don't fight the demons ourselves. That we employ witches and lower-level angels to do that work for us. He believes we think too highly of ourselves and that we're the reason demons exist in the first place."

I had to admit, I kind of agreed with him. The angels of the angel realm saw the world in black and white and held little compassion for those beneath them. They only cared about whether or not a soul was safe and useful to their cause. I still wasn't sure what their end game was. All I knew was that when I'd been sharing my soul with Meri, a former fallen angel, they'd voted to give my soul to her because they thought she'd be more valuable than I was, even though it was mine and always had been. In the end, taking it from me had proven to be a lot more difficult than they'd thought and it had torn in half. Thanks to my aunt and a deal with the not-so-angelic Chessandra, my soul had been repaired, but it hadn't been pleasant.

"With all due respect, Chessandra," Kane said, "I don't think it matters how Maximus feels about the angel council. What matters is my ability to do my job. I think it would be far more advantageous to everyone if I'm able to share information."

"It matters what Maximus thinks," the high angel said. "Far more than you know. But considering the circumstances, I'll allow you to inform your superior of my orders. That is all you're allowed to divulge, however."

"What else would we say?" So far, all we knew was one angel had been mysteriously attacked by...something. While I agreed the incident was alarming, we still didn't have any solid information and what if the angel was mixed up in some dark forces of her own? Despite their name, not every angel was in fact, always one hundred percent saintly.

Chessandra let out a deep sigh. Frowning, she waved her hand. Behind her desk, the wall shimmered and then seemed to disappear as if a veil were lifted, revealing a hospital-like room. Inside were half a dozen young women lying down, hooked up to IVs. Each one was pale and gaunt in appearance. "The incident wasn't just one angel. It was all of them."

# CHAPTER 2

*I* let out a tiny gasp as I stared through the magical veil at the recovering angels. At least, I hoped they were recovering. It was hard to tell, since none of them appeared to be awake.

"How did this happen?" Kane asked, his voice low and controlled.

Chessandra waved her hand again, closing the veil. "They were all caught in the shadows today, but no one else knows their energy was drained except Drake and my personal physician. As far as the rest of the council is concerned, only one angel was trapped and lost her powers. It's imperative that we keep this development quiet. Otherwise, all the angels, including the low-level ones, will be in danger. One angel losing her powers is easily explained—I can say a spell backfired or a demon attacked her or she fell ill. But if word gets out that six collapsed due to the conditions of the shadow world, then evil beings will start planning attacks."

I sat straight up, my back rigid as the implications of what she'd just said hit me hard. Only really powerful beings could shadow walk: sex witches, white witches who'd been granted the ability, incubi, angels, and demons. But all spirits could. It was unlikely a witch or incubus would go after an angel. But a demon? Definitely.

And if an evil spirit or entity managed to trap an angel in the shadows with this new disruption, the angel's soul would be in serious danger. Shadow walking wasn't difficult for those of us who had the gift. It wouldn't be hard to take an angel with you. All one had to do was grab hold of an angel and imagine the shadows until the fabric between the two worlds faded away. Then the shadow walker and angel could cross over. Chessandra had good reason to be worried.

"If I hadn't sent them out in a group," Chessandra continued and started pacing, "we might have lost someone. When no one returned, I knew there was a problem and summoned them back. Had they not been under my direct command, they would've been trapped there. Lost for good." Her hands started to shake. She glanced down at them and then hastily clasped them together. "That's why this is top secret. The shadow world is too dangerous for us now. And too many beings have access. We're vulnerable. I won't have that. I need you to figure out the problem and come up with a plan to fix it before any souls are lost. And I'm not just talking about angels here. If we're attacked, humans will be next, and we won't be able to do anything about it."

I sat back in the chair, processing. Chessandra was freaking out. I'd never seen the high angel lose her cool like this before. Not even when talking about angels being taken into Hell, which was by far the worst thing for an angel. But this was different—an unknown. She clearly had no idea what to do to keep her angels safe, other than send a white witch and an incubus in to investigate while trying to keep the news under wraps.

"All right," Kane said. "We'll investigate tonight and report back in the morning after I talk with Maximus."

"Be sure you do not divulge what I just told you about my angels, Mr. Rouquette. I don't distrust the Brotherhood, but in organizations there are always leaks. Remember, one angel was affected and that's it."

Kane's expression didn't change. "Understood."

"And you, Ms. Calhoun…" Chessandra paused and eyed me.

Kane's hand tightened around mine when she said Calhoun. It was the second time she'd used my maiden name. I still hadn't changed my last name despite the fact that Kane and I had been married for two months. I knew he wanted me to, but I hadn't gotten around to it yet.

"Yes?" I asked.

She crossed her arms over her chest. "Use of your coven is off limits."

"You do realize that'll weaken my magical abilities, right?" I couldn't call on the coven's collective when I was in the shadows anyway, but that didn't mean they couldn't be useful for other spells I might need to get the job done.

"It's too risky. You're powerful enough."

I swallowed a frustrated grunt. I was glad she thought so. I wasn't so sure.

Kane stood up and tugged on my hand for me to join him. "We'll be in touch," he told Chessandra.

I rose and asked, "Will they be all right? The angels?"

Chessandra nodded slowly. "They're recovering. The physician expects them to be back on their feet within a week or so."

"Good." The image of our resident angel Lailah lying in a hospital bed, the life nearly drained out of her, rushed through my head. A chill rippled over my spine, making the vision feel all too real. I'd seen enough of my friends injured by mystical forces to know what that felt like. Sympathy for Chessandra hit me hard, and I reached out, taking her hand in mine. "We'll do our best."

She stared at our connection for a moment, then pulled her hand back. Her expression turned hard. "You'll do better than your best. You'll fix the shadows or you'll die trying."

I opened my mouth, ready to tell her exactly what she could do with her orders, but was cutoff when she waved her hand once again.

This time, my entire world blurred into shades of white. And when everything cleared, Kane and I were once again standing in our living room.

"What a bitch," I said, my heart pounding with anger.

Kane stood still beside me, a calm expression on his face as frustration streamed off him. If I hadn't been an empath and felt the tension coating my skin, I never would have known. "Try not to let her get to you, love."

I gave him a side-eye glance. "You've got to be kidding me. Don't act like she didn't get under your skin, 'cause you can't hide from me." I wrapped my arms around him and gazed up into his handsome face. My lips twitched into a small teasing smile. "Come on, Kane. Tell me how you really feel, just this once."

He shook his head slowly. "No. It'll only encourage you."

"To do what?"

"Feed your irritation. And since you already know I agree with you that she's a bitch, why don't we move on to something more important. Like dinner?" He slipped out of my embrace and tugged me toward the kitchen.

"Dinner." I sighed. I was supposed to have crepes and tuna. Now I was probably looking at toast. I couldn't even remember the last time one of us went shopping. "Is there anything in the fridge?"

Kane pulled the stainless steel door open and grinned.

I peeked over his shoulder and spotted take-out containers that hadn't been there earlier. "Where'd those come from?"

He reached in, grabbed the containers, and handed me a note that had been taped to the top one.

"Pyper! Oh, man, I love that girl." Pyper was Kane's best friend and business partner. While she didn't make it a habit of just walking into our house, she did have a key in case of emergencies. And having to run out during dinner definitely qualified. At least, tonight it did. I was starving. "What'd she get us?"

Kane flipped the tops on the containers. "Crepes, tuna, and steak." He opened another smaller Styrofoam bowl. "And gumbo."

"God, now I love her more."

Kane chuckled and gave me a mischievous grin.

"Stop." I swatted his arm. Pyper was bisexual, and he never missed a chance to make some inappropriate innuendo when the opportunity arose.

He laughed and went to work on heating up the food.

I skipped the wine we usually had with dinner and filled two water glasses. After placing them on the table, I sat and texted Pyper, *Thank you!*

She replied with an emoticon happy face.

We really did have great friends.

Kane brought the food over, giving me the crepes and the tuna, while he took the gumbo and the beef. I smiled at him, loving that he knew what I wanted without even having to ask. He kissed the top of my head and then sat next to me. He raised his water glass. "To enjoying dinner."

I mimicked his motion and said, "To spending quality time with my husband."

His expression softened as he took my hand and kissed my

palm.

We ate in silence, both pretending we were a normal couple who hadn't been ordered to fix a whole other dimension.

❦

WE'D JUST FINISHED EATING dinner when the doorbell rang. "I got it," I called to Kane and headed to the front of our shotgun double home. Before I even opened the door, the angel's refreshing energy washed over me. I smiled and pulled the door open.

Lailah stood on our front porch, her honey-blond hair piled high on her head. Her eye makeup was smoky and her lips bright red.

"Where are you headed off to tonight?" I asked, waving her in.

"I had a date to see the new production *Witches Don't Cry* at the theatre, but then orders came down to check on you and Kane." She swept past me and headed into the kitchen without waiting for me to answer.

"Alrighty then." I closed the door and followed her.

She had her head buried in the fridge while Kane finished loading the dishwasher. The scene was so domesticated it was ridiculous. Usually Kane was off hunting demons and I was busy with the coven. And on other nights, Kane was at his strip club overseeing business, and I was in my glass studio making glass beads to sell to jewelry designers. I couldn't even remember the last time we'd eaten dinner at home.

Lailah pulled a bottle of lemonade out of the fridge and then slumped against the counter. She took a long drink before asking, "When are you going to investigate the shadows?"

"We were going to go just as soon as we finished cleaning up." I waved toward Kane, who was wiping down the counter.

"Where?" she asked.

I glanced at Kane.

He shrugged.

"I guess at the club." I hated walking into the shadows from our house. It just felt too invasive to do that from our sanctuary. Plus, there was a portal beneath the club, and had anything breached it, we'd be able to tell.

"That's what I figured." She took another long drink. "I've been ordered to keep tabs on what you two are up to, but to stay away from the investigation. Want to tell me why?" Her big blue eyes were bright with suspicion.

"Guh!" I couldn't help the outburst. What was wrong with Chessandra? If she didn't want us to talk about the investigation, she shouldn't have said anything to Lailah.

Kane gave me a slight warning glance. "Did she tell you what happened today?"

"Something about an angel passing out in the shadows." She eyed me, and I had the suspicion she could read my mind. She'd been able to before when a spell had gone wrong, but as far as I knew that particular ability had faded away.

"Right," Kane said. "She was attacked, and we're going to investigate. Chessandra doesn't want to risk any more of her angels getting hurt."

Lailah never took her eyes from me while Kane was talking. "There's more going on."

I nodded. I couldn't help it. After being able to read my mind, Lailah understood my nonverbal communication better than most people did. "Yes, but we've been ordered to not say anything about it."

She frowned. "Well, in that case, I won't press you. But this does make my job harder. Will you tell me if there's anything I need to know? Like if a demon is on the loose? I have souls to protect." Her eyes met mine. "Including yours."

Lailah was my soul guardian and she took her job very seriously. Unlike my last guardian, she wasn't going to let a demon get my soul. Not on her watch. I didn't know how to answer that, so I just nodded. If the shit hit the fan, we'd probably need all the help we could get, no matter what Chessandra had said. Not to mention Lailah was one of my most trusted friends.

"Okay. So you're going to investigate the shadows now. Can you call me after you're done?" she asked.

"Sure," I said, despite the warning glare Kane was giving me. Ever since he'd become a demon hunter, he'd taken honoring his word to a whole new level. If he wasn't supposed to talk about a mission, he wouldn't. That was fine for him. But I wasn't going to leave my friends in the dark if I thought they were in danger. I doubted he would either, but he'd rather not make promises he couldn't keep. I, on the other hand, hadn't exactly promised anything. I'd been given orders I didn't agree with and hadn't had a chance to compromise.

"Thanks." She grabbed the lemonade bottle and gave us a short nod before heading back out the front door.

After we heard the door close with a soft click, Kane nodded toward the door. "She wasn't just in the area, was she?"

"Maybe. But we both know that's not why she stopped by." She'd come in person because she knew she was being left in the dark and wanted to see my reaction. She had what she needed now.

He nodded. "I suppose we do. That's what makes her good at her job."

"And now it's time for us to get to work." I moved to stand in front of him and slipped my arms around his waist. "Ready to go see some strippers?"

He chuckled. "I'd rather watch you strip."

I laughed. "I bet you would."

# CHAPTER 3

*K*ane and I stood outside Wicked, the strip club he owned, staring at the patrons waiting to get in. They were lined up down the block and around the corner.

"What the heck is going on in there?" I asked. "You're not having an event night, are you?" Every now and then the club hosted theme parties, such as bachelorette night, or cowgirl night, or even dominatrix night, but the draw was never this good.

"No. Not that I'm aware of." Kane tightened his hold on my hand and led me to the front door. A couple of drunken assholes protested until someone else recognized us and shouted for them to shut up. Kane ignored them all. He nodded to the bouncer as we slid past him into the packed club.

My body came alive with familiar lust as soon as we crossed the threshold. Kane's fresh rain scent intensified, overwhelming me. He stopped half a step in front of me, his shoulder muscles rippling deliciously beneath his form-fitting cotton shirt. My pulse quickened as my body lit with electric desire. I moved forward and instinctively pressed my body up against Kane, needing to touch him. Raising my free arm, I trailed my hand down his neck and fixated on his lips as I ached to kiss him.

"Jade," Kane said carefully. "What are you doing?" His tone held a note of confusion.

I glanced up into his searching eyes and then stepped back, shaking my head. I wasn't in the habit of throwing myself at him in the middle of his club. "I..." Swallowing, I took another step back, trying to put distance between us. His incubus allure was in full effect. "You might want to rein the magic in."

He frowned. "What are you talking about?"

I grabbed his hand and tugged him through the lust-filled crowd. The patrons—men and women alike—as well as the dancers and employees, paused to watch him. As we neared his office, he stopped and scanned the crowd. They collectively moved toward us.

"Inside," I commanded and yanked him through the doorway. The door slammed closed with a satisfying click.

"Jade—" he started.

"Wait," I said. "Do you not even know you're doing it?"

"Doing what?"

I threw my hands up. "Stop being so dense. Your incubus allure is affecting not just me, but everyone in the club. The electricity in there is off the charts."

He jerked back in surprise at my words. "I'm not putting anything out there."

"But..." I tilted my head to the side and really studied him. He was tall and dark-haired with rich chocolate-brown eyes, a chiseled face, and a narrowed waist. Freakin' gorgeous. Ever since Kane had been turned into an incubus, his already good looks had somehow turned him into something resembling a

Greek god. There was no denying practically everyone who met him was awed by his mere presence.

"What do you see, love?" Kane asked.

"Just you. You're right. No incubus energy in sight." I sat on the edge of his desk and thought that through. His incubus energy had hit me full-force as soon as we'd walked through the door. The place was overcharged with his sexual energy. That made no sense whatsoever. Kane didn't even spend that much time at the club these days. Charlie was the manager, and Kane came in during the day to help with the admin side of things.

"Wait here," I said and moved toward the door.

"Where are you going?"

"Just out into the club. I'll be right back." Slipping through the door, I deliberately closed it behind me. The incubus allure tingled down my spine, making me sway with pent-up sexual energy. "Holy shit."

Kane's energy was filtering through the club, charging everyone with more than they bargained for. I steeled myself, trying to shake off the sensation. But since everything about Kane excited me, it wasn't exactly working. A sheen of sweat coated my face as I heated from the inside out.

"Jade?" a familiar voice called over the music.

I spun, nearly running directly into Charlie. "Oh, hey. I was looking for you."

Her lips twisted into a sexy half smile as she ran her hand down my bare arm. Ripples of pleasure coated my skin making me shiver. "Well, you've found me. What can I do for you, gorgeous?"

I stared at her, transfixed by the connection.

She chuckled.

Her laugh ripped me from the lust-state that made me

stupid, and I shook my head, clearing my brain fog. "How long has it been like this?"

She glanced around the club. "Like what?"

"Uh, a line wrapped around the block and everyone so hopped up on pheromones the place feels more like a sex club than a strip club."

"Oh, that." She laughed. "It started last night. I thought you guys put a spell on the place or something. If so, it's cool and all, but I had to call in extra help to keep the fiends watered." Jabbing her head toward the bar, she pointed at two extra servers. "You're saying it isn't a spell?"

I shook my head. "At least not one either of us knew about."

"Damn." Charlie glanced around the club and then shivered. "That's kind of creepy."

"Yeah," I agreed. "Well, there's nothing to do about it now. Maybe we should ask Kane what he wants to do."

She eyed the group of men crowding the stage. So far, they were keeping their distance from the dancer. "I'll call in extra muscle just in case."

"Good idea." I nodded toward the office. "Kane and I can't stay, but if anything goes down that you don't like, give Pyper a call. She'll know what to do."

"You got it." She leaned in for a quick hug, but stopped and held up her hands in a surrender motion. "Maybe not tonight."

I chuckled. "Maybe not."

The battle to fight Kane's incubus energy was a real struggle. My senses became fuzzy and all I wanted to do was go back into that office and climb on top of him. *Get a grip, Jade.* I stood at the door, holding the handle for at least a full minute, trying to erect my glass silo in order to block out everything around me.

Finally, when the walls slid into place, I took a deep breath and retreated back into the office.

Kane was sitting at the desk, his head in his hands.

"Hey," I said and placed my hand on his back. "You okay?"

He lifted his head, his brow knit in a pained expression. "Headache. It came on suddenly, as if my energy's being leeched out of me."

I dropped my barriers instantly and ran my fingers lightly over his forehead, leaving a whisper of my magic behind.

Kane let out a tiny moan of relief. As I was pulling my hand away, he caught it in his and kissed the tips of my fingers. "Thanks."

I smiled down at him. "You're welcome."

He gazed up at me, his features smoothing out. "Did you find what you were looking for when you went out there?"

"Yes. The club is charged with your energy for some unknown reason. The people are lined up around the block because of your incubus pheromones. What we don't know is why. Charlie said it's been this way since last night. She thought we spelled the place to be sexually charged in order to boost business or something."

His eyes went wide with surprise. "Damn."

"Yeah."

He stood up and stared at the closed door.

"There's not really anything we can do about it right now," I said. "Tomorrow, after everyone's left, we'll check into it. Maybe get the advice of the other incubi."

"Maybe." But the way he said it made it sound as if telling any of the Brotherhood was the last thing he wanted to do.

"We can worry about it tomorrow. For now, Charlie has it under control, and I told her to call Pyper if anything gets out of hand. She'll be able to contact Bea or Lucien." My solution for Charlie wasn't the ideal plan, but it was better than nothing. Kane and I had a job to do.

He retreated from the door and walked to the middle of the office. "I'm ready when you are."

I positioned myself beside him, slipped my hand into his, and held my breath when our world tilted. The soft glow of the office light winked out, replaced by pure darkness. Wind rushed in my ears, and then, still holding Kane's hand, my feet slammed into the ground. I didn't even stumble.

"We're getting better at this," I said to Kane as my eyes adjusted to the lack of light.

He didn't respond and was so silent that had my fingers not been wrapped around his, I might have thought we'd been separated. Anger and hatred crawled over my skin, and my heart slammed against my ribs. "Who's here?"

Kane shifted, tightening his hold on my hand. "Jade?" His voice was strained.

"What's wrong? What's going on?" I twisted, craning to look up at him, but the shadows were too dark. I couldn't see anything except his outline.

"Everything feels… off," he said so low I barely heard him.

"It is off. Someone or something is here." I leaned in closer and whispered, "Whoever it is, is full of hatred."

"Jade?" Kane said again.

"Kane?" Had he not heard me at all? Alarm took over, making my head spin. "What's happening?"

He swayed next to me and before I could do anything to stop him, he lurched to the side and fell, landing hard on his shoulder.

"Kane!"I cried again and dropped to my knees, rolling him onto his back. Finally my vision had adjusted enough to make out his features. His eyes were closed and a trickle of what appeared to be blood ran from a small gash on his cheek. "No, no, no. Not now."

It suddenly dawned on me that he was reacting the exact

same way the angels had. Whatever the evil was that lingered here was draining all of his energy. If I didn't get him out of here... I didn't even want to contemplate the consequences. It was too awful.

Clutching his hand with both of mine, I closed my eyes and imagined the pair of us walking back into the club's office. The thought should have been enough, but nothing happened. The world didn't spin and when I opened my eyes, we were still in the desolate grayness that was the shadows.

Except this place was filled with hatred. Anger. Desperation. The air pulsed with it. And as I concentrated on the evil trying to worm its way into my consciousness, my limbs became heavy and the world started to fade. The problem was we weren't headed back to the club. We weren't headed anywhere.

My defensive walls shot up in a last-ditch effort to shield myself from whatever was stealing our energy. Instantly, my head cleared and the shadows came into focus. What was usually a mirror of our world, cast in shades of gray, was now a crumbling ruin. We were sprawled across a room that resembled Kane's office, with peeling walls and rotting floors. The ceiling was caved in, and crumbled paper and garbage lay strewn across the floor.

An image of Kane and Lailah trapped in an old ruin came back to me. Purgatory? Is that where we were? Or a remote part of Hell? Kane and I had been there once. It hadn't looked like this, but it had been full of destruction and despair.

We had to leave. One way or another, we were getting out of here. If I couldn't walk Kane out, I'd just have to use my magic.

"Kane?" I said as I gripped his right arm. "Can you hear me?"

His eyelids fluttered, but he didn't open them.

"I'm going to cast a spell tied to home. When I start to speak, just imagine our home and that we're back there. I'll do the rest."

He didn't make any indication that he'd heard me, and panic started to crawl through my veins.

I forced it down, focusing on the magic that pulsed just below my heart. It was fainter than it usually was, but I pushed away the doubts trying to claim my mind. I was a white witch, leader of the New Orleans coven. Nothing was going to keep me here in this hellish place.

Magic warmed my chest and spread, fortifying my weakened state. I gazed down at Kane, waiting for the magic to build. He was completely still, his chest barely rising.

A gasp caught in my throat and tears blurred my vision. "No, damn you. Don't even think of leaving me." Reaching down, I let the magic spark over his chest and pushed some of my own energy into him.

His body bowed as he sucked in a sharp breath. Groaning, his eyes flickered open.

"Kane?"

"Jade?" he said through cracked lips.

"We're going home now, you understand?" My words came out in short, choked sobs. "Home. Just picture us at home, and we'll be there in a few moments."

"Home," he said, his eyes closing again.

My insides were churning with raw, desperate fear, something I'd never experienced before, even after all the battles we'd suffered through. And something I never wanted to experience again.

Clasping both of Kane's forearms, I chanted, "From one to three and three to one, carry us home, thy will be done."

Magic sparked over me, engulfing my hands, and spread over Kane's bare skin.

A tiny bit of relief thread its way into my heart, but then the magic retreated and started to crawl up my arms.

"No!" I steeled myself and forced the magic back onto Kane, imagined it engulfing his entire body and forming an invisible barrier so it couldn't attach itself to me again. "Kane!"

He blinked, his eyes clear as he stared up at me.

"Imagine our home. Do it now."

His gaze searched mine, seemingly hesitant.

"Now!"

The shock of my bark seemed to startle him into action, because he gave me a small nod and closed his eyes. A second later, his body vanished, leaving me alone in the ruins of the shadows.

# CHAPTER 4

"*H*ome!" I cried and imagined our living room, but my magic flickered like a dying lightbulb and winked out. *Dammit!* Plan B. Imagining the office in the club, I took a step and nearly sighed in relief when the world tilted.

A second later, I was sprawled on the office floor, my ability to walk through the shadows still intact even if my coordination wasn't. Scrambling to my feet, I pulled my phone out of my pocket and hit Kane's name. The phone rang once and went to voicemail.

"Double damn!" I shot through the office door and fought to block out the intense sexual energy pulsing through the club. The tension was so thick my limbs became heavy and my head swam with hazy confusion, but I kept moving. I had to find Kane.

Bursting through the front door, the warm night hit me in a wave of redemption as all the raw energy from the club faded away. Sure, the excitement from the nightlifers on the street still invaded my senses, but it was nothing like being in the club. Without looking back, I picked up the pace and ran the few blocks to our house.

"Kane?" I called as I burst through the door.

Silence.

"Kane!" Sprinting to the back of the house, I rounded the corner to the hall and smacked right into the solid form of my incubus.

"Whoa." His arms came around my waist, steadying me. "What took you so long?"

"What are you talking about? It's only been a few minutes." I curled my fists and punched him lightly in the shoulders as he smiled down at me, humor lighting his eyes. "Are you laughing at me?"

He shook his head. "Never." Then he dipped his head and covered my mouth with his. A tiny spark of magic danced between us, just enough to calm the remaining panic.

I pulled back, scanning his body from head to toe. "Are you all right?"

He was a little pale but appeared fully functional. Nodding, he walked us backward into our bedroom. "I will be."

Stopping in the middle of the room, I cupped his cheek. "What happened?"

He chuckled. "I passed out. You were there."

I pursed my lips. "Yes, I remember that part. Did you just black out, or did you feel something stealing your energy?"

Unbuttoning his shirt, he sat on the edge of the bed. "Come here."

"Kane." The fight went out of my body as I gazed at him waiting for me, his eyes lidded with fatigue.

"Kiss me," he said, tugging me down so I was straddling him. He ran his hands up my thighs, taking his time as if savoring every inch. His firm, yet gentle touch sent shivers of anticipation up my spine.

I reached up and brushed a stray lock of his dark hair out of his eyes, reveling in the faint trace of his fresh rain scent. His hands tightened on my legs as he seemed to breathe me in. We sat there, suspended in the moment, all traces of magic and incubus allure gone. It was just the two of us, reconnecting.

"I love you, Jade," Kane said, his voice low and full of emotion.

It was enough to bring tears to my eyes. "I love you, too." Tilting my head, I cupped both of his cheeks and kissed him softly, barely brushing my lips over his.

"I never doubted you'd get us out of the shadows, you know," he said against my lips. "You're the strongest person I've ever met."

"No stronger than you are," I mumbled, running my hands over his shoulders.

He pressed his forehead to mine and placed his hand over my heart. "I meant in here. The love you carry for those of us lucky enough to be in your life is greater than anything I've ever known."

I chuckled. "I think you're a little punch drunk from the energy zap you got when I transported you home."

"Maybe. But that doesn't mean I'm not speaking the truth." He snaked his arms around me and slid his hands up under my shirt, caressing gently.

I closed my eyes, luxuriating in his touch. Ever since he'd turned incubus, our lovemaking had been intense. Frantic even at times. Overwhelming. But this, the pair of us sitting together, just enjoying each other, was rare. "This is lovely," I said, brushing my lips over his cheek bone.

"You're lovely." He pulled my shirt up further, his warm breath tickling my neck.

I lifted my arms as he tugged the shirt over my head, leaving me in my black lace bra.

"And so are these." He grazed the tips of his fingers over the crest of my breast while trailing kisses down my neck. Pausing at my throat, he gently pushed my bra straps over my shoulders, chasing the fabric with his lips.

The gentle sensation of his touch warmed my heart, and the love pulsing between us seemed to swell and grow, filling all the tiny cracks left by our trip into the shadows.

"Kane?"

"Yes, love," he murmured across my tingling skin.

My fingers found the top button of his shirt. "I need to feel all of you. To know you're real. That we're real. That the shadows didn't take even one tiny inch of you."

"I'm all yours, pretty witch."

"And don't you forget it."

He gave me a small smile as I pushed his shirt off his shoulders. I took a moment to caress his bare skin, the cuts of his well-defined muscles, the two-inch scar just below his collar bone, and the ridges of his abs.

He sucked in a small breath, his stomach quivering under my touch. Then, with his eyes smoldering, he stood, lifting me easily. My legs automatically went around his waist as he spun us around and then crawled onto the bed, lowering me beneath him. He hovered over me, his hungry gaze heating me all over.

I trailed my fingers over his chest. "Now what do you have planned?"

Humor flashed in his dark eyes, followed by a spark of heat. "My plans include a lot less clothing."

In answer, I unfastened the button on my jeans.

Kane watched me for a moment and shifted down to help me shimmy out of them, removing my underwear with them. He quickly divested himself of the rest of his clothes, while I freed myself from the lace bra.

A moment later, Kane crawled back on top of me, cupping my breasts. The magic sparked deep in my belly as my nipples hardened, aching for his touch. But he didn't oblige. Instead, he ran his hand down my side until he reached my hip. He was being deliberately slow, taking his time to torture me.

I wasn't having it, though. I needed him. To feel him. To touch him. To have him inside me. Hooking one leg around his, I rolled us both over and straddled him. "I can't wait," I said, tears of emotion burning the backs of my eyes.

Kane sat up, repositioning me so my legs were wrapped around his waist. And when his lips claimed my right nipple, I let out a low moan and lifted my hips, catching the tip of his hard shaft at my center.

"Yes," he whispered against my skin, holding himself completely still.

My breath caught and then ever so slowly, I lowered myself, taking him inside me. A deep, contented sigh escaped from my parted lips.

Kane pulled back slightly, his hands loosely gripping my hips as he filled me up, stretching me.

Then, as we watched each other, we both started to move, slowly, deliberately, savoring the moment. Love-filled magic blossomed around us, consumed our bodies, and as my power built, I felt his love touch me deep in my soul.

I let out a tiny whimper and pressed closer, trying to relish every last inch of him.

"You're mine," Kane said into my neck. "Now and forever."

"Forever," I echoed as the tension built deep in my core.

Suddenly Kane's hands were everywhere, my neck, my breasts, the sensitive flesh where my hip and thigh met. Each stroke matched his thrust and just when I was certain I'd never get enough of him, his teeth scraped over my nipple as his thumb found that sensitive bundle of nerves at my center.

"Oh." I moaned, my muscles tensing around him.

"That's it, Jade. Come for me, baby." Powerful magic burst from deep inside me, crackling around us as Kane's strong hands gripped me and he thrust up hard. Once. Twice. And with one last stroke, we both cried out, coming undone together, powerful magic crackling around us.

Kane clutched me to him, burying his head in my neck as I held on, riding out the ripples of pleasure and tiny magical aftershocks.

"Wow," I said a few minutes later, kissing his temple.

I felt his lips curve into a satisfied smile against my collar bone. "That was…"

"Amazing?"

He pulled back. Using one finger, he gently tucked a strand of my hair behind my ear. "I was going to say intense."

"That, too," I said and slipped off him, tugging him down to the bed.

Kane rolled onto his back, cradling me in his arms. "Are you okay?"

I rested my head on his chest, content to listen to his heart beating. He was asking about the magic transfer. As an incubus, Kane now attained his power from me and after being drained in the shadow world, he'd needed more than usual. "I'm fine."

He lifted his head and gazed down at me. "Really?"

I smiled up at him. "I might need an extra vitamin supplement in the morning, but really, I'm okay."

"Good." He pressed his lips to the top of my head, giving me the sweetest, most tender kiss.

My heart swelled. The love between us was overwhelming. All consuming. But also deep and mature and full of meaning. It was more than I could've ever asked for.

Silence closed in around us, our bodies entwined. And as

we lay there in the quiet of the dark, I couldn't help the night's events flashing through my mind: Kane almost unconscious in the shadow world, me not able to walk him out of the shadows, and then the magic used to bring him home and the fact that through our touch we were able to make each other whole again.

The reality of what we could accomplish together made my heart swell with gratitude and pride. I snuggled in closer to Kane and just hung on, grateful to be in his arms.

Kane's breathing became deeper and regulated. I pulled the blanket from the end of the bed, tucking it around us, and then curled up, joining my incubus in the oblivion of sleep.

The dreamwalk hit me the moment I slipped under. I found myself in Pyper's apartment above The Grind. Kane was standing next to her near the ceiling-to-floor windows, their heads bent together in confidence.

Neither noticed me, and for the first time in over a year, I felt like an intruder in Kane's dream. I cleared my throat, not wanting to interrupt but not wanting to eavesdrop either.

Kane's head came up and he glanced around, but he seemed to look right through me. Pyper glanced at him, cast a confused look around the room, and then continued talking, her expression intense.

"Whoa," I said. I'd assumed they were whispering, but now that I could see their faces, it was obvious that wasn't the case. And I couldn't hear a thing. I waved a hand, trying to get their attention, but once again neither noticed. "You can't see or hear me, can you?"

Pyper shifted and stared out the window. Kane frowned and scanned the room again, his brow wrinkled in confusion. It was clear he didn't see me. Shaking his head, he turned and stood next to Pyper. After a moment, she slipped her arm around his waist and leaned into him.

He absently stroked her hair, and a small dart of... something shot through me. Jealousy? Not quite. More like an uneasy ache. I swallowed the emotion, ashamed I felt left out.

But then, right there before my eyes, Pyper lifted her right hand and trailed her fingers tenderly over his jawline.

I froze, my eyes wide and my heart thundering in my chest. Kane froze, too, seemingly shocked by her actions.

I saw her mouth the word *Kane*. Moonlight filtered in through the tall window and shone on her hopeful gaze.

My stomach rolled. No. This wasn't happening. Pyper was not making a pass at Kane in his dream. One that I was shut out of, but was forced to watch.

Pyper reached up higher, cupping Kane's cheek.

"Oh, hell no!" I took off in their direction, determined to stop this dreamwalk madness, by force if necessary.

But before I could get there, Kane jerked back, scowling down at Pyper. I still couldn't hear his words, but his meaning was clear. He grabbed her wrists and pushed her away from him, a mixture of confusion and anger in his dark eyes.

Pyper shook her head, her expression clouded with frustration. She took a step forward and—

I woke with a start and sat straight up in bed, taking the covers with me. "What the hell was that?" I asked, turning my gaze on Kane as I tried my best to tamp down the outrage trying to seize me. Pyper had just made a pass at my husband. The only reason I wasn't losing my mind was because Kane had clearly been an unwilling participant.

He stared at me for a long moment, then sat up, running a hand through his thick hair. "I have no idea."

Clenching my fists, I scowled. "You were just dreamwalking Pyper and if she'd had her way—"

"You were there?" he asked, cutting me off.

"Yes. Only you shut me out." I knew I sounded like a

petulant child, but as much as I wanted to calm down, I was having trouble turning the other cheek after seeing Pyper try to kiss my man.

He shook his head slowly. "No. I didn't. *I* didn't do anything."

"Well, I know you didn't. I saw Pyper come on to you. I saw you pull away from her. But how else could I have been shut out of your dreamwalk if you didn't do it?" My voice shook with anger.

"No, Jade." He turned to me, his eyes flashing. "You don't understand. I wasn't dreamwalking. It was as if *I* was being dreamwalked."

That statement shocked me into silence. I opened my mouth to respond then shut it. Kane had told me once before that he used to dreamwalk Pyper fairly regularly in college. He said when he was close to someone, he had trouble controlling it. As he'd gotten older, he'd gained a better command of his gift and then after he became an incubus, control had no longer been an issue. His power had fixed that. Finally I asked, "How is that possible?"

He shook his head, foreboding streaming off him. "I have no idea."

# CHAPTER 5

"*A*re you saying Pyper pulled you into a dreamwalk?" I asked Kane.

He got up, shook his head, and started pacing. "How could she? She's not a dreamwalker."

I sat in the middle of the bed, watching him. My chest started to ache from Pyper's betrayal even as my head tried in vain to come up with a plausible explanation. Had she been spelled? Possessed? On drugs? "No. She isn't."

"Everything about it was wrong." He stared at me. "You said you were there? I thought I felt you, but couldn't see you. Why didn't you say anything?"

"I did. You couldn't hear me."

He shook his head again. "It was just wrong. All of it. I didn't control the setting, couldn't see you, and Pyper was... off. It was as if—"

"Someone else had the power," I supplied, selfishly praying that was true. If it wasn't, I didn't think our friendship could survive. Not after what I saw.

He nodded and moved to sit next to me on the bed. "We have to call Pyper."

My face ached from my perma-frown. It was well past two a.m. Exhaustion claimed me and all I wanted to do was bury myself back in the covers and pretend none of this had happened. I shook my head and clasped my hand around his. "Do you think it could wait until the morning?"

He frowned, a worry crease lining his forehead. "But what if she's in trouble?"

Damn. He had a point. The world we lived in was full of mystical anomalies, and no matter how much I just wanted to curl up next to him and block the rest of the world out, if Pyper really was spelled or possessed somehow, I'd hate myself. Nodding, I grabbed my phone from the nightstand and handed it to him.

"Thanks, love." He took the phone and scrolled through my contacts until he found her name.

I climbed off the bed, pulled a T-shirt on, and then headed into the kitchen for a glass of water. When I returned, Kane was sitting on the edge of the bed, staring at the phone.

"Hey." I handed him the glass. "What did she say?"

He put the phone back on the nightstand. "She says she hasn't even been to sleep yet."

The tension that had been coiling in my gut ever since I'd seen Pyper try to kiss him eased. I felt equal parts relief and concern. If she hadn't been sleeping, there was no way she'd been in a dreamwalk. But if it wasn't her, someone or something else had used Pyper's image.

"A witch?" I asked.

He thinned his lips and shook his head. "I don't know. I really thought it was her. The person had her voice, used the same words she does, and even felt like her presence."

I climbed back into the bed and pulled the covers up over my bare legs. "Come here," I said softly.

Kane glanced back at me. "Something invaded my dream state."

I nodded. "I know. But the good news is Pyper's safe. And whoever or whatever it was didn't have a strong enough hold to hurt either you or me. In fact, I think I was there in the dream because of you, not whoever pulled you over. And now that you're aware of it, I'm betting you can stop someone else trying to gain control of you. Right?"

He raised one eyebrow and then shook his head, a small smile on his face. "How come you're so calm?"

I shrugged. "After battling demons, having our wedding interrupted by crazy angels, and dealing with black magic, a little dream meddling isn't going to take either of us down."

Without taking his eyes off me, he set the glass on the nightstand. "Beauty and brains. How'd I get this lucky?"

I grinned. "It must be your—"

"Masterful skills in bed?" That sexy grin of his was back.

"I was going to say your real estate, but sexual talent is a good second place." The jab was funny because there was a ring of truth to it. In addition to owning the French Quarter house we lived in, Kane also owned the buildings that housed Wicked and The Grind. Then there was the plantation house in Cypress Settlement, where we'd gotten married.

His eyes narrowed and then he pounced, grabbing me around the middle as he flattened me on the bed. "I knew it!"

Laughing, I lifted my head to kiss him. "You're the one who gave me a house as an engagement gift."

"And I don't regret it for a moment."

∼

I woke to the sound of my phone ringing. Groaning, I rolled over and grabbed it. "Hello?"

"Jade?"

I blinked, trying to get my eyes to focus in the bright morning light. "Gwen?"

My aunt let out a relieved sigh. "I'm so sorry to call this early, but I had a vision and…well, this couldn't wait."

My eyes finally focused on the white numbers of the alarm clock—7:01 a.m. That meant it was just past six in Idaho. "You have got to start staying up later," I said. "Six o'clock is ungodly."

"Jade? Did you hear me? I have some information."

The panic in her voice finally penetrated my hazy mind, and the rest of what she'd said sunk in. A vision? Gwen never told anyone the details of her visions. She believed the information usually made the situations worse. If she was willing to give me details, then whatever she'd seen was devastating. I sat up, tucking my feet under me. "What did you see?"

"You know I can't tell you that, honey."

Of course I did. I'd spent my teenage years under Gwen's care. The only time I was privy to them was when she spoke during one of the episodes, giving me a clue as to what she saw. "Right." I rubbed a hand over my forehead. "Then what is it you *can* tell me?"

She took a deep breath. Then she said, "When the time comes, look to the past."

I bit my lower lip. "What past? Whose?"

I could almost feel her struggle with what to tell me. Gwen and I had been very close and even though as an empath I usually needed to be in close proximity to feel someone's emotions, I swear right then, I felt her inner turmoil churn within my stomach as my limbs went cold with fear.

"Gwen?"

"Sorry, honey. I'm just flustered. You'll need to...um, do your research."

"Uh, okay. That doesn't give me a lot to go on." I glanced around the empty room, frowning. When had Kane gotten up?

"I know," Gwen said and sighed. "But it's the best I can do. Now I have to go. The horses need to be watered."

"Gwen?" I called before she could disconnect us.

"Yes?"

"How's Mom?"

My aunt paused, seeming to search for the right words.

"Gwen?" Mom and Gwen had been in New Orleans until Kane and I had gotten married. Then they'd gone back to Idaho. I'd heard from them once a week, but my calls with Mom had gotten shorter and shorter over the past month.

"She's doing okay. Just trying to find her footing again."

"Isn't she working on her healing herbs?"

"Oh, yes. That's going well. It's just...well, dang. She's dating again."

My eyebrows shot up. "Really? That's good, right?"

"Yes, darling. It's wonderful. I think she's just not sure how to tell you."

I frowned. "Tell me what? That she's dating? I think that's fantastic." I really had no idea what the problem was. Well, other than the fact that she'd been trapped in Purgatory for twelve years. That would make anyone rusty.

"Not what, Jade. Who." Gwen's tone lit with something that sounded suspiciously like joy.

"You can't say that and not tell me!" I cried into the phone. "That's just mean."

"You know it's not my place." She laughed. "I'll talk to you soon, Jade. Remember to do the research. You're going to need it."

The call ended, leaving me in a state of frustration. I loved my aunt, even when she was being evil. I thought about calling my mother, but she wasn't an early bird like my aunt. Chances were she'd only been in bed for a few hours. She was an earth witch and often stayed up late working on her magical herbs.

The door swung open, and Kane walked in, carrying a large red mug. "Morning," he said and handed me the steaming cup of coffee.

"Is that bacon I smell?"

He gave me a slight smile. "Might be. Breakfast is in five."

I took a long sip of the perfectly prepared latte and sat in the armchair under the window. "Any chance of breakfast in bed?"

He shook his head as he retreated to the door. "Sorry. With our track record, we'll end up very late. We have a meeting in forty-five minutes."

"What?" I stood and headed straight for the dresser. "What meeting?"

"Chessandra. She demands a report."

"Great," I said dryly. "This should go well."

He shrugged. "At least she's coming here this time."

"She is?" A shiver of unease filtered through me. The high angel seemed to only show up in person when there was a dire emergency.

"That's what the note says." He handed me a thick stock notecard. Inside it read, *The high angel will arrive at 7:45 a.m. Be prepared.*

Crap. I glanced at the bathroom, contemplating a shower, but the bacon scent filling the air won out.

～

I WAS SITTING cross-legged in one of the kitchen's wooden chairs, sipping my second latte, when the brilliant white light shone down inside our kitchen.

Neither Kane nor I moved. I hadn't even dressed for the meeting. All I'd done was pull on a pair of fresh underwear and a cotton skirt and then stuff my feet into flip-flops. Kane was in jeans, a T-shirt, and had bare feet. If the high angel was going to show up before eight, she'd just have to live with what she got.

Chessandra appeared in our kitchen. Her long golden hair was pulled back into a sleek ponytail and she wore a crisp white tailored suit. She looked every bit the high-powered business woman.

I raised a questioning eyebrow. "I hope you didn't get dressed up for us."

She barely glanced at me and focused on Kane. "What did you find?"

I hated when she did that, acted as if Kane was in charge, as if the man was the one who had all the answers. "He's not the only one who was there last night, you know."

This time she met my gaze and held it. "I'm aware, Ms. Calhoun. I'm also aware I'm more likely to get a straight answer from Mr. Rouquette, and as I have another appointment, I'd rather not waste any of my time." She flicked her gaze from mine to Kane's. "Report?"

Kane put his coffee mug down and stood. "We entered the shadows and as soon as we did, my energy was drained. If it wasn't for Jade, we'd still be there."

"I see." She rubbed her jaw, contemplating. "This is worse than I thought."

I stood up beside Kane. "I have to tell the coven. If I—"

She held her hand up. "That is unacceptable."

Clenching my fists, I resisted verbally lashing out at her. "If you want me to try to get to the bottom of things, I need my coven. I need to brainstorm with my mentor, Bea. I can't fight the entire shadows by myself."

Chessandra's expression turned stormy as she stared at me. "I do not appreciate your tone, Ms. Calhoun."

Dammit. I'd actually been trying to be reasonable. "And I don't appreciate you asking me to fix the entire shadow world without any help whatsoever."

We had a stare-down of epic proportions.

Finally I said, "Beatrice Kelton is the most trustworthy witch I've ever met. She has already proven she'd lay her own life down to save Lailah, our resident angel. And you're still not willing to take a chance by allowing me to work with her?"

The angel glanced from Kane to me. Then she said, "I never said you needed to fix the entire shadow world all on your own. Your mission is to find out what's causing the disturbance and then to report back without causing a mass panic."

I opened my mouth to reply, but she cut me off.

"I came to tell you that one of the angels has woken up. As soon as she's strong enough, you may interview her." Her eyes went flat as she added. "You may speak with Mrs. Kelton, but no one else."

She raised her arms and despite the absence of the white light she usually travelled through, she vanished into thin air.

"Whoa," I said and turned to Kane. "How did she do that?"

He shook his head. "Special high angel magic, I suppose."

"I guess so," I said, feeling awful about my exchange with Chessandra. She'd come to give us information, and I'd been nothing but hostile. Not to mention I'd misinterpreted the mission. Dang, I was an idiot.

"Jade?" Kane said.

"Huh?" I glanced up.

He was standing in front of me, holding his Demon Hunter dagger in one hand. The design in the hilt was glowing, indicating he was being summoned. "It's time to go."

I clutched his hand, wishing I'd thought to put a bra on as the dagger pulled us into the shadows.

# CHAPTER 6

*J* wanted to cry out, to somehow stop Kane from letting us travel through the shadows, but the magic wrapped around us and a tug pulled at my belly, sweeping me through the fabric of the other dimension.

The light was a blur of color and the next thing I knew, we were standing in front of the Brotherhood mansion in the Garden District. The trip had only lasted for a few seconds, but it had left me disoriented and slightly nauseated.

Kane squeezed my hand. "Hey, are you all right?"

I swallowed back the bile threatening to choke me. "Yeah. I'll be fine." Then I glanced up at him. He was pale, and fatigue shown in his eyes. "What about you?"

He straightened his shoulders, seeming to steel himself. "Fine."

But he wasn't fine. He was exhausted. The shadows had drained him and had the dagger not pulled us straight to the Brotherhood house, I was almost certain he would've gotten trapped again. The energy he'd gained from our lovemaking the night before was already drained. Squeezing his fingers, I tapped the power gently pulsing beneath my skin and pushed it into him.

Right before my eyes, his skin tone evened out and the weariness claiming him melted away.

"Jade." He pulled away from me, putting a foot between us. "You can't keep doing that."

"Why not?" I gave him a pointed look.

"Because if I keep taking your power, you'll be drained. Then what will you do?"

"I'm fine," I insisted. And I was. For now. But I wasn't going to let him go deal with Maximus looking like he was going to pass out. Demon hunters weren't weak. Especially not mine.

The double doors of the Antebellum home swung open, and Maximus himself appeared.

Kane and I shared a glance and then moved forward. Well, Kane did. I bounced off an invisible wall and stumbled backward.

"Whoa," I said and pressed my hands against the solid barrier. I'd always been able to enter the compound before.

Kane paused and glanced back, reaching for me.

"The witch isn't invited to this meeting," Maximus said, in an authoritative tone as he came to a stop beside Kane.

Kane dropped his hand, set his shoulders, and gave his leader his full attention. "I think you'll find her relevant to the issue I need to discuss with you."

"I'm afraid we'll have to agree to disagree." The leader stood tall and stiff, not meeting Kane's gaze.

"Maximus," I said, cautiously. "It's good to see you again."

"Likewise, Ms. Calhoun." He kept his gaze straight ahead, his tone even more formal than usual. "Unfortunately, we have classified Brotherhood business to discuss. I'm afraid I'm going to have to ask that you forgive our rudeness, but I can't invite you in today."

I forced a patient smile, trying to ignore the ball of unease forming in my gut. While Maximus had made noises about denying me entrance into the Brotherhood's proceedings, he'd never tried to leave me in the dark when anyone was in danger from supernatural forces. "I understand your position, but I have classified angel business to discuss with you."

He finally turned and looked me in the eye. "Classified?"

"Yes," Kane answered for me. "It's important."

Maximus inclined his head, relenting. "Very well. Please enter."

The air in front of me shimmered with foreign magic as the barrier disappeared. "Thank you," I said as I joined Kane.

"Don't thank me yet." Maximus retreated back into the house.

Kane and I shared a questioning glance but neither of us responded.

Inside the house, Maximus led us to his office. Two of the walls were lined with leather-bound books and a third had rows of daggers and swords.

"Have a seat." He pointed to the chairs across from his desk, sat in his leather chair and steepled his fingers together. "You have news?"

"It's classified." I settled into the chair as Kane took the one next to me.

Maximus pursed his lips. "So you've said."

"Right. The information doesn't leave this room."

"Understood."

This was uncomfortable. "There's a disturbance in the shadow world," I said. "The high angel has ordered us to investigate. No one knows yet what's going on."

"Last night Jade and I went into the shadows, and my energy was leeched or stolen. Jade brought me back out, but if she hadn't been there, I'd have been stuck," Kane said. "Obviously this is a concern for all incubi."

Maximus stood and crossed his arms over his chest. "Actually, Mr. Rouquette, it isn't. Two different teams have ventured into the shadows. One yesterday and another one early this morning. None of them were affected."

Unease spread from my gut and sent ripples of goosebumps over my skin. Why had the shadows weakened Kane and not any of the other incubi?

"No one?" Kane asked.

Maximus shook his head. "There's more."

"What did you find?" I asked.

Maximus picked up a file off his desk and tossed it to Kane. "The shadows are tainted with incubus energy."

"Huh?" I asked. "No, it isn't. I would've felt it."

He raised both his eyebrows and stared pointedly at Kane.

"Mine?" Kane flipped the file open and scanned the paperwork. Then he looked up at Maximus. "It says here it was tainted yesterday afternoon. How is that possible? We didn't go in until last night."

"You tell me." Maximus leaned against the desk, his expression revealing nothing.

"Wait a minute." My mind whirled. The club had been soaked in Kane's energy as well. Something was very wrong. I stood and placed my hands on my hips. "What do you mean, tainted?"

"It means, Ms. Calhoun, that the reason the angels were drained is because incubus energy stole it. Kane's energy. Somehow, the shadows are bursting with his magic, feeding off the angels."

Holy crap. He already knew about the angels. How?

"Don't look so surprised," Maximus said to me. "I knew about the attack before you did."

He had to have an informant from the angel realm. Chessandra had been clear very few people knew what happened.

Kane jumped to his feet, ignoring our exchange. "That's crazy. I haven't done anything to the shadows. And if you recall, we just told you I myself was drained."

Maximus picked up Kane's file, made a note, and then put it into one of his desk drawers. When he finally looked up again, he said, "The shadows are a strange, mystical place, Mr. Rouquette. Whatever was used clearly backfired. The shadows are hungry for more of your magic and will take it by force."

"But not mine? Or other incubi?" As I heard myself ask the question, I cringed internally at my omission. I had been weakened, though I'd been able to fight it. Since Kane and I shared magic, was it possible the shadows were feeding off the magic he'd shared with me?

"Incubi magic doesn't feed on other incubi magic. And as for you, I suspect your powers are strong enough to ward off the intrusion."

I nodded absently, acknowledging his explanation.

Kane sat back down, holding his head in his hands.

"You know Kane didn't do anything to the shadows," I said to Maximus as I eased back into my chair.

He stared at me, his expression blank. But then there was a tiny flash of frustration and he placed his elbows on his desk. "I'd like to think that's true. But right now, we don't have any solid answers. All we know is that Kane's energy is what's causing the disturbance and for that reason, he needs to be suspended."

Kane's head snapped up. "What?"

Maximus stood again. "Kane Rouquette, I am officially suspending you from the Brotherhood, pending an investigation. Please turn in your dagger." Maximus held his hand out and before Kane could grab the hilt, his dagger vanished from his hip and reappeared in Maximus's outstretched hand.

Kane stood there, his mouth partially open and his eyes wide.

"But he didn't do anything," I said quietly, my heart thrumming with anxiousness. His dagger was his connection to the Brotherhood. Without it, his power would be greatly diminished.

"That is entirely possible," Maximus said. "But until we find some answers, I think you'll agree we don't have much of a choice."

"Well, I don't—"

"Jade." Kane put his hand on my shoulder. "It's all right."

I gritted my teeth and looked up at him, trying to swallow my frustration. Maximus was treating Kane as if he was guilty until proven innocent. "It's not all right."

His resigned expression was more than I could take. I wanted to rail against Maximus. To force him to somehow see the goodness in the man beside me. Instead, I clamped my mouth shut, unwilling to make the situation worse.

Maximus crossed the room and opened the door. "You'll be notified after we've completed the investigation."

"What exactly does that entail?" Kane asked, not moving.

"The investigation?" Maximus asked.

Kane nodded.

"One of the hunters will be assigned your case. He'll investigate the magic used to taint the shadows. If he determines it was done by you, you'll be dealt with and erased. If there's another explanation, you'll be recalled."

"Erased!" I cried, unable to hold myself back. "You can't do that!"

A muscle in Kane's jaw twitched as he clenched his teeth.

Then he slipped his arm through mine and nodded at Maximus. "Very well."

Maximus was silent until we passed him. "Ms. Calhoun, regarding the shadows, I'd like to keep the lines of communication open between the Brotherhood and the Angel Council. Please tell the high angel I'd like to be informed of new developments, and I'll return the favor in kind."

I glared at him.

"We'll be in touch," Kane said and tugged me gently out of the office.

Neither of us said a word as we left the hallowed halls of the Brotherhood. But when we stepped through the front gate, Kane paused and glanced back at the house. His disappointment brushed up against me. I squeezed his arm in silent support. He stiffened at my touch, and the disappointment vanished instantly.

"What happens when one is erased?" I asked quietly.

"It just means removed from the Brotherhood. Memories, history, anything that I could use against them should I turn evil." He said the last part with an ironic smile. Then he sobered. "It's fine. Maximus is only doing what he has to. Just as you would if one of your witches was compromised."

He had a point. When Lucien had been cursed by a black magic user, he'd been suspended from the coven until we'd been able to figure out a solution. We hadn't treated him like a criminal, though. "Maybe. But I like to think we handle incidents with a little more understanding."

He gave me a wry smile. "It's not as if I've been incarcerated."

"No, but—"

"We'll work it out," he said with an air of finality.

Message received. He was done talking about it.

Kane stopped abruptly, scanning the street.

"What?"

"I can't feel the shadows." He glanced at me. "Can you?"

I shook my head. "No, but I'm not trying, either."

"Try."

Ever since we'd been granted the gift of shadow walking by the angels, Kane had never had trouble crossing into the other dimension. And once he'd been turned incubus, it had been second nature. For me, it was different. I had to focus and imagine the shadows before they appeared. "Can you not cross?"

"I don't feel them the way I usually do."

I raised my eyebrows. "The way you usually do? What's different?"

He shrugged. "I used to always feel them. Now I don't. And when I focus on them, it's just...odd."

"How?"

The large oak tree we stood under shaded us from the sun as Kane stared past me, appearing to be focusing on nothing. Finally he said, "It must just be because Maximus benched me. I'm sure it's nothing."

"Is it like it was before you were called to the order?"

"No. It's more intense than that and yet...not." His dark eyes found mine. "We have to go back in."

"To get back home, you mean?"

"To investigate the shadows, again." He pointed back at the house. "I need to feel what they do. To see what's going on." He was dead serious.

"But last night, the shadows drained you. I don't think—"

"Jade."

"What?" I asked, panic taking up residence in my chest.

"I'll be fine. I just need to understand what's happening."

"But what if the tainted energy drains you again? What if I can't get you out? I don't want to risk you."

"That's why I have you, pretty witch. I trust you." His eyes softened as he smiled down at me. Then he straightened his shoulders and waited for my answer.

He seemed so sure of himself. So sure of me. And it was clear by the expression on his face he wasn't taking no for an answer. "Fine. But if you so much as even wobble, I'll spell your ass back home so fast you won't even have time to blink."

His smile widened. "Just my ass?"

"Oh, shut up." I laughed. "Let's get this over with."

"If you insist." He winked and held out his hand.

I refrained from rolling my eyes as I wrapped my fingers around his. "Ready?"

"Ready."

We stepped together, and once again the world shifted.

# CHAPTER 7

"*D*id you walk us here?" I asked Kane as we stood in the shadows of his club, Wicked.

He tightened his grip on my hand. "No. I thought you did."

I shivered, but not because I was cold. Kane's energy was pressing in on me, scraping against my skin, clawing at me, trying to invade every one of my senses. My head spun from the intoxicating nature of it. I wanted to let him in, to give myself up to his incubus energy. I was all too happy to surrender to his seductive allure.

Swaying on my feet, I leaned in to him, wanting more. Needing more. But when my body brushed up against his, there was a small shift. Something almost immeasurable changed. The energy coming off him was a shade cooler. A tiny bit less intense.

Maximus had been right. The shadows were tainted with his energy. I could feel it now, but it was somewhat different than the energy coming directly off Kane.

"Let's go," Kane said. A second later, we were back in his real office, the soft glow of artificial light illuminating his desk.

I sank into a metal chair, holding my head. "That was… odd."

Kane slowly paced the room, staring at the worn carpet. His energy was completely normal again, comfortable. He came to an abrupt stop. "You felt it didn't you?"

I jerked my head up at his sharp tone. "I felt something."

"Me, right? My energy is tainting the shadows."

Hesitating for a moment, I grimaced and then nodded. "Did you feel it?" As an incubus, he was in tune to desire. Could sense it, but distinct energy signatures weren't his thing. That was mine.

"Maximus might have taken my dagger, but my incubus senses are still in full force."

That meant yes. He felt the allure lurking in the shadows. His allure. "But how is that possible?"

He shook his head. "I don't know."

Kane and I had slipped into the shadows from the club numerous times. I'd never felt that before. Not even the night before. Except I hadn't been listening to my own senses that much. Not after being in the charged club. Sexual tension had been everywhere.

The door to the office burst open. "Give me five minutes, will you? If I don't get this order in, all we're going to have to serve is tap water tomorrow night," Charlie called back into the club. She spun and then jumped back with a yelp. "Holy crap. Where'd you two come from?"

I smiled. "We just got in from a meeting."

Kane stood and waved for her to take his chair. "Don't let us get in your way. You appear to be busy."

She laughed. "Busy. You could say that again. Last night we

had record business. Like, three times as much income as a night during Mardi Gras."

"Whoa," I said softly.

"You can say that again." Charlie slid into Kane's chair and grabbed the phone receiver. After punching one of the speed dial buttons, she shook the computer's mouse, waking up the machine. "Can you do me a favor?" she asked Kane.

"Sure. What do you need?"

"Can you call everyone who isn't working tonight and ask them if they can come in?"

"Everyone?" I asked.

She held up a finger and spoke into the phone, placing an order for about four times as much alcohol as we normally needed.

Kane watched her with fascinated interest instead of going to work on calling in extra employees. When she hung up, he leaned over her shoulder and clicked on a spreadsheet. "This is last night's report?"

She grinned up at him. "Yes."

Kane scanned the document, then clicked another. And another. "All of these are accurate?"

Her grin faded as irritation lit her green eyes. "Yes, boss. I double and triple-checked. It's accurate. If you'd stuck around either of the last two nights, you wouldn't be surprised."

He turned his head to give her an amused glance. "Surprised isn't the word I'd use. Impressed is closer. Nice job, Charlie."

She shook her head. "Thanks, but it's not anything I'm doing. In fact, we were so short staffed the first night, I'm amazed anyone stuck around. The booze, dancers, and places to sit were in serious short supply."

I already knew why no one had left. The over-the-top sexual energy made it too hard to resist the pull. But unless someone was an incubus or witch, the person wouldn't be able to feel the magical charge. He or she would just be compelled to stay.

"What can I do to help?" I asked her.

She didn't even look up from her notes. "It'd be a huge help if you could restock the bar."

"Sure. I'm on it." I waved at Kane and slipped out of the room. The truth was, I could use something mundane to take my mind off the morning's events. Especially since I had no idea what to do about any of it. My first instinct was to call Bea. The second was Lucien. Both of them had years on me when it came to the supernatural world.

I'd spent my formative years with my mother, an earth witch, but I hadn't known I had power. I'd thought my only gift—if you want to call it that—was my empath ability. And once Mom disappeared, I'd shunned the witch community altogether. That was, until I'd moved to New Orleans and had been forced to face reality. Now I was the coven leader and couldn't go even a few months without some sort of major crisis. The only problem was, I'd missed years of learning my craft. I had a few books, but book learning was different than experiencing.

Walking over to the bar, I pulled out my phone and tapped Lucien's number.

"Morning, Jade," Lucien said after just one ring.

"Morning." I sat on one of the stools. "Hey, Kane and I have a situation, and I'm hoping you might be able to help us with some research. Do you have some time today to meet up? Maybe early afternoon?"

He hesitated. "Is it an emergency?"

Was it? I wasn't sure. "Not a dire one. Not yet, anyway."

He chuckled. "Right. I can meet you at one for lunch."

"Your place?" I asked. Lucien had reference material we

might need.

"Sounds good."

I shoved my phone back in my pocket and headed into the storage room. Lugging cases of alcohol was the perfect activity for working off my lingering frustration.

An hour later, I had the bar completely restocked and was breaking down boxes when Kane and Charlie reappeared. Charlie had her arm around Kane's waist and was leaning into him as they walked toward me. The scene startled me and I stood there just staring as she laughed at something he'd said. Then she patted his chest, her fingers lingering for maybe a second or two.

I didn't think I'd ever seen Charlie touch Kane quite that way before. It wasn't so much that she was being inappropriate. If she'd been Pyper or Kat, I wouldn't have even blinked. But this was Charlie. She was...flirting. Charlie never flirted with Kane. Or men in general.

She flirted with me. And every other girl who came into the club. Even when her girlfriends were around. It was just who she was. "Hey, guys," I said as they neared the bar.

Kane glanced at me then Charlie and back to me again, sending me a curious smile as if to ask what was up with her.

I raised my hands in an I-don't-know motion.

"Oh, hey, Jade," she finally said when she noticed Kane looking at me. "I was just telling Kane about my date for tomorrow night."

"Date?" She'd broken up with her actress girlfriend a few weeks ago when the woman had been outed in a tabloid for kissing another starlet. Charlie had taken it harder than she'd let on, throwing herself into work. But if she had someone new, that might explain her overly affectionate behavior. "What's her name?"

Charlie frowned. "Not a her. A him. And his name's Bax."

"Bax?" Kane and I said at the same time.

"Yeah." Her brows knitted in confusion. "As in Baxter."

We both stared at her wide-eyed.

"What?"

"Ah, nothing." Kane shook his head at me. Not that I was going to say anything. She was free to date anyone she wanted. But in the time I'd known her, she'd never shown interest in the opposite sex. In fact, she'd been rather vocal about her love of women.

I cleared my throat. "Charlie?"

She met my steady gaze. "Yes?"

I wanted so badly to ask her why she'd suddenly changed her tune, but instead I asked, "Where'd you meet him?"

"School. He's in one of my business classes." She walked behind the bar and uncapped a bottle of water.

Kane sat on a stool next to me, watching her as if trying to decide how to respond.

She gulped down a quarter of the water then slapped the bottle on the counter. Meeting his confused gaze, she asked, "What?"

He raised his eyebrows. "It's quite the departure for you, isn't it?"

"So?" Defensiveness streamed off her in waves. "I wouldn't say anything if you wanted to date a man."

"I'd hope you would!" I added. "Considering he's married to me."

Her expression softened as she turned to me. "Right. That wouldn't be cool. I just meant I wouldn't care if he decided to switch teams, that's all."

"Hey," Kane said, holding his hands up. "It doesn't matter to me what team you're on. No judgment here. You just took me by surprise, is all. And honestly, it's none of my business anyway, so forget I said anything."

She put the cap back on her water bottle and stared at the bar. Unease and doubt swirled around her slowly as if the emotions were just starting to form, but then she squared her shoulders and they vanished. "Okay. We'll just forget about it."

Why was she forcing herself to go out with a man? It seemed clear to me that deep down she didn't want to. I lifted my hand to place it on her arm, to reassure her she didn't need to do anything—or anyone for that matter—she wasn't comfortable with. But I lowered my arm, afraid I'd upset her further.

"I'm going to go get lunch before I start rearranging the shift assignments," she said. "Can I get you two anything?"

"No thanks. We've got a lunch meeting soon," I said.

She shoved her hands into her jeans pockets. "All right then." She nodded to Kane. "I'll call and let you know if we need to do anything drastic."

"Thanks. I'll be back this evening to make sure everything is running smoothly, so that probably won't be necessary, but if things change, I'll let you know."

"Sure thing, boss." She waved as she strode to the back of the building, no doubt intending to go next door to see if Pyper needed anything. The pair took care of each other while they were working the same hours.

When we heard the back door click closed, I asked Kane, "What was that all about?"

"The date?"

"Yeah."

"You got me. Charlie has never once even hinted she might be interested in a man before."

"She doesn't want to go. I could feel her apprehension." I walked behind the bar and poured myself a Diet Coke. Some conversations couldn't be held without caffeine.

"Then she shouldn't go. Dammit. I wonder if this has

anything to do with the ex-girlfriend being plastered on every tabloid from here to China."

"It could." Stranger things had happened. "But I don't think so. Charlie isn't the jealous type. More like a love 'em and leave 'em kinda girl."

He held his hands up in surrender. "Then I got nothing."

"Me neither."

"Hey," I said. "Did you check on Pyper?"

He nodded. "Yeah. She's fine. Totally normal. Doesn't know anything about what happened last night."

"Well, that's something at least. Though, we still don't know who or what invaded your dream last night."

Kane shrugged. "True. But if it becomes a problem, we'll figure it out then." He grabbed my hand and stroked my thumb and forefinger while I sipped my drink. The place was quiet, and I didn't want to get on with the day. Life was so much simpler when I only had a house ghost to worry about. My mind fixated on the word "ghost," and I grabbed Kane's hand. "Come on."

He didn't budge. "To where?"

"Upstairs. There's something I need from my apartment."

That pulled a cocky grin from him. "Something you need?"

"Yeah, perv. Now get up and help me."

His smile fell. "Is this going to be heavy?"

"No."

"Good. Then why do you need me?" Kane leaned in and nuzzled my neck.

"I just do." I shivered from the delightful tingle he sent all the way to my toes.

"Hmm, you just *want* me."

"No argument," I said, slightly breathless. "Now get on your feet, or I'm leaving you here to fend for yourself."

He stood, and I couldn't resist teasing him as I ran my hand lightly up his chest.

His eyes smoldered, drinking me in. Then, before I could initiate anything else, he grabbed my hand and pulled me out of the club into the back hall. We took the stairs two at a time, both of us wanting to be alone for just a moment or two. The club wasn't private enough.

When we were on the third flight of stairs, Kane turned and whisked me up into his arms, carrying me the last few steps. We didn't even make it inside before he was tugging my shirt up. But I was no better as I reached for his belt buckle. My time in the shadows had left my body charged with need, and I wanted him badly.

After I got his jeans open, I slid my hand down, nearly matching his groan as my hand glided over his velvet shaft. "I want you inside me. Right now."

That was all he needed. A second later, he reached under my skirt and tore my panties in half right there in the hallway.

"Oh, God," I said as he gripped my bottom, lifting me up. My legs wrapped around him and in one hard thrust, we joined in a frenzy of desperation. He was so long and hot and perfect. My eyes rolled into the back of my head as I joined him stroke for stroke, matching his frantic pace.

"You feel so good," Kane mumbled into my neck, his lips brushing over my too-sensitive skin.

In answer, I tightened myself around him and moaned.

His breathing quickened as he slammed into me harder, his shoulder muscles rippling with effort under my clutching hands.

"Yes," I said. "Yes. More."

My words fueled his already out-of-control lovemaking and his grip tightened on my bare bottom hard enough that I knew he'd leave marks. "I want to feel you shuddering around me, Jade. Now." Then he bit down roughly on the place where my neck met my shoulder.

I cried out as my release came hard and fast, every inch of me trembling with pleasure. Kane held still, shaking with his own need, while I shattered around him. And as I relaxed slightly, my muscles still quivering, he thrust again, and again, and again until he echoed my cry, burying his face in my neck, his breathing ragged.

We stayed locked together against the door, hanging on to each other. The entire scenario felt surreal. The apartment on the other side of the door had been mine for a time, and while I didn't live there anymore, my bed was still in there, along with some other items we'd never moved. Would it have been so hard to just make it through the threshold? I started to giggle.

"What's so funny, pretty witch?" Kane asked, releasing me long enough to gently slip out of me and set me back on my feet.

"Us. There's a bed about five feet away on the other side of the door."

He gave me his sexy half grin as he buttoned up his jeans. "Where's the fun in that? We have a bed at home."

I shook my head, amused and still slightly aroused by the thought that we'd just had sex in a not-so-private place.

"I didn't hear you complaining," he continued as he trailed his fingers along my jawline, staring at my lips.

"No, you didn't." And dammit if the look he was giving me didn't make me want to start all over again. I traced his lower lip with my index finger ever so lightly and then leaned in, catching it gently between my teeth.

His arms came around me as he plastered me to him, his mouth opening and claiming mine. And then—

"Excuse me," a female voice said.

# CHAPTER 8

*K*ane and I broke apart like two teenagers caught making out in the basement.

"Sorry," the tall blonde said, her face turning a dark shade of red. "I heard a noise and thought...oh, never mind. I just wanted to make sure everyone was okay."

I stepped behind Kane and busied myself straightening my clothing.

Kane, on the other hand, stood with a relaxed posture, regarding the woman. "Yes, we're more than okay."

"Kane," I whispered harshly and poked him in the back.

He glanced back at me, his incubus charm oozing from his welcoming eyes. Damn him. "Zoe, right?" he said to the woman as she started to descend the stairs.

She paused on the second step. "Yes. I just moved in a few days ago. Two-B."

"Hi," I said over Kane's shoulder. "I'm Jade. Sorry for, ah... disturbing you." I cut an irritated glance at Kane. "I didn't even know the building had tenants right now." Last I'd heard, the two apartments on the second floor were being remodeled.

And the one on the other side of the door still had a lot of my stuff in it.

Her lips curled into a smile, but she bit down on her lower lip, trying to hide it. "That would explain a lot."

"Sorry, love," Kane said, tugging me out from behind him. "Pyper told me she rented one of the places a few days ago, but with everything going on, I forgot all about it." He walked over to the gorgeous woman and held his hand out. "I'm Kane. It's nice to meet you."

She hesitated, but then clasped her hand around his and shook. "Nice to meet you." They stared at each other for a just a moment longer than was really comfortable. I was about to say something, anything to break whatever weird connection they had going on, when Kane suddenly let go and took a step back.

Zoe stared at her hand and frowned.

"What happened?" I whispered to Kane.

He shook his head and whispered back, "Not now."

Zoe's head snapped up. "What are you?"

He and I exchanged a startled glance.

"Excuse me?" Kane said mildly, although suspicion was flowing from him with enough force to rival the Mississippi river. "What am I?"

"Uh…I meant, who are you? Do you live here?"

"Oh, no," Kane said, his shoulders relaxing. "My wife and I own the building. Technically I'm your landlord, but Pyper usually takes care of everything."

He'd said *my wife and I own the building*. A stupid smile claimed my lips. I didn't know why those words made my insides turn to jelly. I hadn't expected Kane to share any of his assets with me or even think of them that way. He'd owned two houses in addition to this building and the one next door before we'd ever met. Those were his. Well, except for the

Cypress Settlement house he gave me as an engagement gift. He was too much.

Zoe nodded. "I see. Well, thank you for letting me rent such a wonderful apartment. I'm sorry to interrupt. That wasn't my intention."

"Oh, don't worry about it," I said, waving a hand, trying to be casual as I prayed for the floor to open up and swallow me whole. How embarrassing. She obviously knew what we were doing. I was going to kill Kane later. "Nice to meet you," I called after her.

But she was already gone.

"What was that all about?" I asked Kane.

"What? Shaking her hand?"

"Yes." I put my hands on my hips and stared him down.

"There was some sort of weird energy that passed between us. It wasn't magical. I don't know how to explain it, but it was a little uncomfortable."

If it wasn't magical, then there likely wasn't anything to worry about. "She was probably disturbed by our public lewdness."

Kane took one look at my face and started laughing. "You're adorable."

"And you're despicable. I never would've done that here if I'd known a tenant had moved in."

He slipped a key into my old apartment's lock. "I don't think we have anything to be embarrassed about. If it looked anywhere near as hot as it actually was, then we should've sold tickets."

"Shut up." I stifled a laugh as I followed him inside.

He stopped in the middle of the small apartment. It was barely five hundred square feet of space. "Now. What was it you wanted me to help you with?"

I stood just inside the door, staring down at the happy,

tongue-lagging ghost who'd followed me home months ago. He was the sweetest golden retriever ever, and I missed him. "I want to figure out a way to bring Duke to our house."

"The ghost dog?" He raised his eyebrows. "Seriously?"

"Yeah. I hate that he's here all alone. Wouldn't it be better if he stayed at the house?" I smiled down at Duke, who'd flopped on the floor and was gnawing away at the couch leg. Of course, since he was a ghost, he didn't do any damage. He also didn't shed or need to be walked or fed. But he was a good guard dog. So in my eyes, he was perfect.

"Sure. I don't have a problem if you want to bring him home. I just don't know how we can do it."

"Carry a piece of chicken?" I said, only half joking.

"Can he smell anything?"

I chuckled. "I don't know. I'm not an expert on ghost dogs."

"We don't have any chicken, but maybe something else from the cafe." Kane strode back toward me and the door. But instead of leaving, he stopped right in front of me and cupped both my cheeks. Staring into my eyes, he lowered his head and kissed me so thoroughly, I was panting by the time he let go.

"Whoa," I said and almost stumbled from my weakened knees. "What was that for?"

"For being the most amazing, sexiest woman on the planet. What happened out in the hall?" He nodded toward the door.

"Yeah?"

"Fucking hot." He kissed me once more and then said, "I'll be right back."

I watched him leave and when the door shut softly behind him, I stood there transfixed by the magic still buzzing in my veins. The charge we'd built in the hallway was different than it usually was. Since he'd become a demon hunter, we'd always shared power during and after our release. This time we hadn't. The magic consuming me was all mine. Weird. Had the fact that Kane had been suspended from the Brotherhood changed the way he gathered power? Would he be weaker now?

I sank into the hand-me-down chair, suddenly scared for Kane. Incubi gained their power through sexual energy. And the demon hunters through their daggers. Did he have any magic left?

The door swung open and Kane strode back in, holding a small white bag. "I've got just the thing."

I stood. "What?"

He pulled out a bagel sandwich, complete with ham and cheese. "If he has any sense of smell, this will keep him focused."

"True." I grabbed the bagel sandwich and held it out for Duke.

His tail went crazy wagging back and forth as ghostly drool dripped from his jowls.

"Oh, gross." I laughed and moved toward the door, keeping the sandwich at dog level. "Come on, boy. We'll take you to our new home."

He'd followed me here once. Getting him to follow me somewhere else shouldn't be that hard, right? And it wasn't. He had no problem trotting into the hallway and to the top of the stairs.

"Good boy," I coaxed.

Kane closed the apartment door and locked it. His eyes were crinkled in amusement as he watched me lure my ghost dog down the stairs. He'd put up with a lot of crazy crap since I'd blown into his life. I guess this was pretty tame in comparison.

Operation Dog Transfer was going perfect right up until we hit the second floor landing. Then Duke froze, and the hair stood up on the back of his neck as he growled.

"What is it, boy?" I'd only ever seen him growl like that when the evil ghost Roy had been tormenting Pyper and me in my apartment.

Duke lowered his front shoulders and snarled.

"Whoa." I looked up at Kane, but he appeared just as confused as I was. "Let's go, Duke. Nothing's there." And there wasn't. I had my senses wide open, and the only being I felt was Kane. The new tenant, Zoe, was nowhere to be found. And even so, her energy had been normal. I hadn't sensed anything nefarious, and neither had Kane, despite the odd exchange they'd had. Except she was the only one who lived on the second floor, and whatever was bothering Duke was in that corridor.

"Zoe?" I called just in case. No response. I hadn't expected there to be. She clearly wasn't even around right then. Maybe there was some old residual ghost energy he was picking up on. I took a few steps down the stairs. "Come on, Duke. Let's go."

The dog turned his head, studying me with his hackles still raised, but then his eye caught the bagel sandwich. That did it. His concentration was broken and he lunged down the stairs after me.

"That's it." I took off down the stairs, Duke on my heels.

After we left the building, Duke trotted along with me without any issues. And right after we got back to the house Kane and I shared, Duke bounded in and made himself comfortable on an oversized chair.

I laughed and took a bite of the bagel sandwich. The dog stared at me with sad eyes. "I know, buddy. I'd share if I could."

Kane followed me to the back of the house. I grabbed us both a bottle of water and sat with him at the table.

"So," I said, twisting the cap on and off. "Are you doing all right?"

"Sure." He took a long drink of his water.

"Really? Even though there's something about you that's disturbing the shadows and you're being investigated by the Brotherhood?" I hated pointing out the obvious, but if he was going to act like nothing was wrong, I didn't know what else I was supposed to do.

"Well, I'm not thrilled about it, but whatever's happening, I know I don't have control over it. So the only thing I can do is move forward until we have more information." He seemed so reasonable. As if he knew once we had information we'd sort this out.

"You're right." I leaned over and pressed a kiss to his cheek. "Ready to go find some answers?"

He wrapped his hand around the back of my neck and kneaded his fingers into my tense muscles. "In a minute."

I smiled at him. "Take all the time you need."

KANE PULLED his Lexus to a stop in front of Lucien's home in the Bywater neighborhood. The residents were an eclectic group of artists and musicians, as well as interlopers from out of state. When we stepped onto his porch, the door opened seemingly on its own, and I registered the small magical signature as Lucien's. He'd spelled his front door to let certain people in. I guessed we were on the list.

"Neat trick," Kane said.

I smiled. Lucien's house was a single shotgun double, meaning there weren't any hallways and every room was stacked up against the other. We strolled into the living room and passed under an arch into his office.

"Hi, Jade, Kane," he said from his position at his desk. He had three thick reference books open in front of him and a file opened on the computer. Books lined two complete walls, all of the texts pertaining to either art or witchcraft. He claimed the title Art Gallery Manager in his day job. Spinning, he waved to a small couch to his left. "Have a seat."

"Thanks." Kane and I sat, and I immediately went through the events of the last few days, leaving nothing out except the six angels who'd been compromised. I knew there'd be hell to pay if Chessandra found out I'd told him, but he was my second in command. He had knowledge I didn't and if anything happened to me while Kane and I were working on the case, I needed him to have enough tools to be able to step in and help us.

"So, obviously we're at a loss as to what's going on in the shadows and how exactly Kane is connected to that. Any ideas on where to start?" I asked.

Lucien sat back and stretched his legs out as he appeared to process everything I'd just told him.

"I'm going to ask Bea as well. I just haven't had a chance yet."

He nodded and then his head snapped up. Pointing to his large shelf, he stood and walked straight to a nondescript-looking leather-bound book. Nondescript, because most of them looked exactly the same. Brown, old, gold-embossed lettering. There was a mountain of them. He handed it to me. "This is the recounting of one witch's experience with an incubus and if I recall, there was an incident in the shadow world."

"An incident?" I asked, thumbing through it.

"It was a long time ago when I read it, but I seem to recall a reference to an incubus having some control over the fabric of the world? I can't exactly remember. Take a look."

I thumbed through the text, scanning the reference. It involved a specific spell cast by a sex witch and was bound with a blood sacrifice. Nothing Kane had done or would do. I glanced up, frowning. "This doesn't really look applicable to what we're dealing with."

He pursed his lips and scanned the room. "I'm afraid I don't have much material on this because as witches, we don't really deal with the shadows much or incubi." He gave Kane an apologetic look. "The demon hunters and the angels would be a much better resource. Or hell, even the Coven Pointe witches. "

"Hmm," Kane said.

I eyed him. "Explain."

He shrugged. "We know we're not going to get answers from the angels or the hunters."

"I hadn't even considered speaking to the Coven Pointe witches. They do seem to know a lot more than they let on. We just need to get them to talk to us," I said, already dejected. The last thing I wanted to do was go ask Dayla or Fiona for help. Those witches were witches in every sense of the word.

"We could talk to Mati," Kane said.

"Oh. And Vaughn." My gloom lifted. Mati was a sex witch who had gotten trapped in another dimension. And Vaughn, another incubus, was her boyfriend. We'd helped save Mati from the other world not too long ago and had teamed up with Vaughn to take down his black-magic-using stepbrother. "That's a great idea. Even if they don't have any answers, they can get them."

Kane stood and held his hand out to Lucien. "Thanks, man. You've been a great help."

Lucien chuckled. "Not really. But glad I could point you in a direction, at least." He met my gaze. "I'll keep turning things over in my mind and if I come up with anything remotely interesting, I'll call you. In the meantime, you know where I am if you need anything."

I reached over and gave him a quick hug. "Thanks!"

"Lucien!" Kat's voice came from the front room. "Where are you?"

A smile claimed his lips as he stepped to the side to peer through the archway. "In here."

"Omigod!" She came running in from the other room, her arms outstretched. "I got the part! I got it!" She barreled into him.

He caught her and spun her around as she laughed. "Got what?"

"I'm going to be on TV!" she gasped out. "Can you believe it?"

"No. I don't think I can." Lucien's eyes were wide with disbelief as he smiled at her.

"TV?" I asked, overjoyed at her happiness filling the room, but utterly confused. Kat was a silversmith and worked at a shop in the French Quarter. She wasn't an actress and as far as I knew, the only acting she'd ever done was in a couple of high school plays.

"Jade." She pried herself from Lucien's grasp and turned to me, tears of joy sparkling in her hazel eyes. "Can you believe it? I saw a notice for a small part in a new pilot television series, and on a whim I went down and auditioned. They said I had the exact energy and look for it and offered me the part on the spot."

"Wow. That's cool." I moved in to hug her, but she turned back to Lucien. Uh, okay, then.

"I have to cancel tomorrow because I need to get my hair and nails done. And a wax. This thing starts shooting in, like, four days and well, I'm just not going to have time for anything." She slipped past us and seemed to float toward the back of the house.

"Audition?" Lucien asked me. "Did you know about it?"

I shook my head. "No. I had no idea she was even interested in the entertainment business. She's never talked about it before. Not that I can recall anyway." I racked my brain, trying to think of anything that would connect this new development to what I knew of my best friend. Nothing.

Both of us turned and looked at Kane as if he'd have the answers.

He held his hands up and laughed. "Don't look at me."

"Weird," I said, eyeing the door she'd disappeared through. "Cool. But weird."

"What show did she say it was?" Lucien asked.

"She didn't." I put the book down he'd given me. "A new pilot TV show is all she said." I glanced at Kane. "I'll be right back."

He nodded, and I took off to tell Kat congratulations again before we left. I found her in the kitchen holding a bottle of orange soda a few inches from her mouth as she practiced an acceptance speech for her impending Emmy.

"And a special thanks to my friend, Jen, for believing in me when no one else did."

Who the hell was Jen? I cleared my throat. "Hi."

She spun. "Oh, Jade. You scared me."

I bit my lip. "We're taking off. I just wanted to say bye…and tell you congratulations."

She gave me a shy smile as she tucked one of her red curls behind her ear. "It's a dream come true."

"I'd say so." But whose dream? Certainly not hers. But I didn't have it in me to question her about it at that moment. I needed time to process everything that was happening. Instead, I held my arms out, inviting a hug.

Kat smiled, but when she took a step forward, she stumbled on what appeared to be nothing and spilled her orange drink down the front of her dress. "Oh, damn." She glanced back at me. "Sorry, Jade. I need to soak this before it stains."

And before I could say another word, she disappeared into the bathroom. I stared after her, unease eating away at my gut. I could've sworn she'd spilled that drink on purpose. More confused than ever, I slowly made my way back to the office to join Lucien and Kane.

A few minutes later, Kane and I were back at the car. I glanced at him. "To the Pointe?"

He nodded and fired the car to life. "As long as we're not shot at, assaulted, or magically altered in any way like we were last time."

One could only hope.

# CHAPTER 9

*a*s Kane headed to the freeway, I called Mati.

She answered on the second ring. "Jade. Hi." Her tone was hesitant. I couldn't blame her. Our two covens didn't really mix, and we only knew each other because I'd been tasked with saving her from another dimension. My presence didn't exactly evoke pleasant memories.

"Hey, Mati. How are you doing?"

"Good. Still going to school and working with Chessa. How about you?"

"The same. Only no going to school. You know, witch and shadow business." I shifted in my seat so I was facing Kane. "Listen, I know you're probably busy, but would it be okay if Kane and I met up with you today for a little bit? There's a... situation in the shadows and we find ourselves needing to do some research. We thought you and Vaughn might be a good place to start."

"Me and Vaughn?" The shock in her voice made me cringe.

They were both young. Mati was in her early twenties and still in college. Vaughn was a few years older, but he hadn't been part of the Brotherhood for long. Was it stupid to think they'd have any information at all? Mati was Chessandra's sister. Better than going to Dayla's house and being spelled into Goddess knew what. "I was hoping you'd know where we could start looking."

"We can try. When did you want to come by?"

"Is now okay?" I sent Kane a grimace. Nothing like just inviting oneself over.

She laughed at that. "Yeah, okay. Vaughn's on his way, so it's not bad timing."

"Great. Thanks." I hit End and tossed the phone into my bag.

"That wasn't awkward at all," Kane said, making the turn onto the Crescent City Connection Bridge.

"Sometimes you just gotta do what you gotta do."

Ten minutes later, Kane parked in front of Mati's raised basement home. She occupied one of the apartments upstairs. I recognized Vaughn's Indian motorcycle parked in the small driveway. "He's already here."

Kane nodded and led me up the stairs.

"Jade," Mati said when she opened the door. She smiled and spread her arms for a hug.

"Mati, you look fantastic." I wrapped my arms around her, thrilled to feel her vibrant energy swirling around us.

"Thanks. So do you. Come in. Both of you." She waved at Kane, and he nodded. "Have a seat. I'll get Vaughn."

Kane and I sat on her slip-covered couch in the small living room. Her space was full of interesting witch paintings and a few framed handwritten spells. Candles lined the room and on one shelf she had a plentiful supply of herbs and potions. They were prepackaged but judging by the labels, they weren't from Bea's shop in the Quarter. Some place called The Heart of a Witch.

It didn't take long for Vaughn and Mati to return. Vaughn's incubus energy was overwhelming and the second my body tingled in response, I erected my defensive walls. It was disturbing, being physically affected by someone other than Kane. Especially Mati's boyfriend.

"Vaughn." Kane rose and shook the other incubus's hand. "Good to see you."

"You, too. I wish it was under different circumstances," Vaughn said.

"You heard then?" Kane stuffed his hands in his jeans pockets.

"Yeah. We were all briefed. There was no getting around it, really. We all feel the disturbance."

Kane gave him a small nod. "I suppose that's true."

"It's odd though." Vaughn ran a hand through his dark hair. "The intensity of your energy signature shifts each time I slip through the shadows. Sometimes it's strong and other times it's barely noticeable, so faint it's hard to tell who the signature belongs to."

"That's weird," I said absently, rolling his words around in my head. "For me, faint energy signatures have to do with two things. The energy level of the person or their proximity to me."

Vaughn shook his head. "I don't think proximity's the case here. Incubi are connected on a cellular level and when we sense the other, we can tune in as much or as little as we want to in order to find our fellow brethren when he could use assistance. I can't speak to energy level, but if that was the case, the signal has been so faint in some instances, I'd question if Kane was moments from his last breath. And considering he appears to be fine, that doesn't ring true either. But I could be wrong."

I shook my head. "No, that sounds about right. But then, we

can't know, can we? Not unless there's a documented case of the shadows being tainted before."

"You could ask Chessa," Mati said.

I could, but then I'd have to tell her about Kane, and who knew what she'd do if she thought he was involved in what happened to the angels? "No," I said too quickly.

Mati frowned. "Why not?"

Vaughn slipped his arm around her waist. "Because, my love, your sister is an act first, ask questions later kind of angel, and Kane's situation will only get worse if she decides to try to pin any of this on him."

Mati opened her mouth to respond, then closed it. Nodding, she looked Kane in the eye. "He's right. I won't say anything."

"Thanks," Kane said and glanced away. A tiny sliver of shame and frustration streamed from him, brushing against my skin.

I knew he was innocent here, so the shame must be from feeling as if he needed to hide what was happening for fear the angels wouldn't believe he was one of the good guys, just like the demon hunters. Frustration because, well, that was obvious. He was stuck in the middle of something he knew nothing about.

"I can ask Dayla though," Mati said, her eyes sparking with determination. "When we have girls' night and she's drinking, she loves to talk about the good 'ole days. The more booze she has, the looser her lips are. In fact..." She grabbed my arm. "You should come with me tomorrow night. Then you can help me ask questions."

Oh, damn. I wasn't afraid of Dayla exactly. I could probably take her in a magical duel. Okay, probably not, because she had a ton more experience than I did, but I could out-magic her when measuring spell for spell. I was pretty damn strong. "Do we have to do it while she's drinking? Wouldn't it be better to ask to meet her for lunch or something?"

Mati laughed. "Dayla doesn't lunch. Please, she's too busy hiding out in her witch's lair. No, girls' night out is better because she actually leaves her cave. She drinks more and talks more when she's sucking down martinis. Tomorrow night. Meet me here at seven forty-five, and we'll walk over to the Coven Pointe bar. You'll love it. Trust me."

She seemed so sure of herself and excited to have a plan, I just nodded. It couldn't hurt. Right? And if we were in a public place, Dayla was probably less likely to spell me. Though, I had power of my own, so I wasn't too worried about that. "Okay, it's a date. Tomorrow night."

"And I'll see what I can dig up at the Brotherhood," Vaughn volunteered.

Kane stiffened. "That's not necessary. I don't want you to be implicated in whatever this is that's going on."

"It is necessary. You and Jade were there for Mati when I wasn't. I owe you." The conviction in his tone had me nodding before Kane could say anything else.

"Thank you," I said. "Any information you can find is useful at this point. But I agree, please be cautious. We don't want you being benched as well." I slipped my hand into Kane's. "Mati, I'll see you tomorrow night."

"Yes. You will. Dressy-casual."

"Got it."

Kane held his hand out to Vaughn. "Thanks, brother."

Vaughn clasped his hand while clutching his forearm with his other hand. "Thank you." Vaughn cast a protective look in Mati's direction. "We all need a hand every now and then. I'm glad I can return the favor."

AFTER KANE and I got back home, he headed over to Wicked to check on the club before the busy period started, and I walked the four blocks to the Herbal Connection, Bea's new age shop.

The moment I walked through the front door, the fresh-rain-scented air enveloped me and the tension started to drain from my taut muscles. The scent was customized to each customer, a spell that recognized the patron's favorite scent. What better way to make someone feel welcome in a shop.

"Good afternoon, dear," Bea said cheerfully from behind the counter. "How's married life?"

I couldn't help the slow smile from claiming my face. "Even better than I imagined."

Bea's expression turned soft as she scooted out from behind the counter and gestured for me to follow her to one of her displays on the other side of the shop. She stopped in front of her specially blended herbs. "I don't want you to think I'm pressuring you or anything, but now that you're married, I wanted to introduce you to my special line of herbs just in case you're thinking about expanding."

"Expanding?" I imagined my waistline growing as I shoveled in even more cheesecake than usual.

"Yes, dear. Expanding your family." She placed a light hand on my arm and peered at me expectantly.

I picked up the satchel of herbs. Fertility enhancement. "Bea!"

"What?" Her eyes lit with hopeful delight.

"A baby? Now? Are you kidding?"

She shrugged. "Why not?"

I put the herbs back on the shelf and wiped my hand on my skirt as if just touching the satchel would somehow kick my ovaries into overdrive. "Uh, maybe because Kane and I are always chasing after some crisis of the week? Maybe because he's been benched from the Brotherhood and his energy is tainting the shadow world, while we've both been tasked to figure out what the heck is going on? Maybe because we're constantly battling demons and evil magic users?"

"What?" Her grandmotherly playful mood vanished as her shoulders straightened and her eyes hardened with the look of a witch going into battle. Then she grabbed my hand and tugged me into the back room. "Sit. Tell me everything."

And I did. Including the part about the weakened angels. I wasn't supposed to, but I trusted Bea above all others. I needed my mentor's advice.

When I was finished, she asked, "Does Lailah know?"

"Not everything. As far as I know, Chessandra is keeping this under wraps."

"I know," Lailah said, appearing from out of nowhere.

"There you are. I was wondering what happened to you." Bea waved her over.

"You overheard everything I just said?" I asked.

Lailah nodded.

I grimaced. "I wasn't supposed to say anything."

She waved a dismissive hand. "Don't worry about it. I just had a meeting with the angel council and afterward, Chessandra did decide to fill me in on what's going on in my territory." Her irritation was so thick, the static coming off her made her hair frizz. "We've been instructed to cease all operations for the time being."

"Why?" I asked. "If it's just a problem with the shadows—"

"An angel was attacked this morning and taken to the shadows. By the time anyone realized she was missing, it was too late." Lailah's tone was flat, void of emotion. "She's already been drained and has vanished."

Ice cold dread seized me. "Son of a...crap on toast. Who, and why didn't anyone tell me or Kane?"

Lailah gritted her teeth. "Not everything is about you, Jade."

Well, ouch. "Of course not. But we would've done whatever we could've to find her."

"You're not listening," she snapped. It was clear Lailah was taking this hard. She wasn't the bubbliest person I'd ever met, but she did have a kind heart. She wouldn't have been speaking to me in that tone if she wasn't so upset. "No one knew she was missing. The Brotherhood found traces of her and informed Chessandra."

"Traces?" I said absently as I tried to get enough air to calm the panic surging through my veins. An angel had been attacked and taken. What did that mean for Lailah? Were all angels being targeted? Was Lailah in serious danger?

"Her angel pendant was there, along with an echo of her energy signature." Lailah sank down onto a stool, holding the edge of the work station as if her legs were giving out on her. "She's not in the shadows. We fear the worst."

*The worst.* For an angel, that meant Hell. And no one could cross the shadows to go after her. Not any of the angels anyway.

"Will the Brotherhood look for her?"

Lailah shook her head. "They don't go into Hell. Their mission is to keep this world and the shadows demon-free. If they cross the lines into Hell, full-on war will break out."

"Dammit," I muttered as the images of my trip to Hell flashed through my mind. I'd gone in to save my ex, Dan, who'd sacrificed himself for my mother. I hadn't been able to leave him there. But Kane had been with me, and we'd had Lailah and Phillip's help—my last soul guardian. They'd actually come into Hell to get us home. There was no one to help now.

"How did this happen?" Bea asked Lailah quietly, her eyes full of worry. "Is every angel a target? Do we need to cast special protection spells to keep you safe?"

Tears filled Lailah's bright blue eyes as she shook her head. "I don't think so. She was a new angel who was still in training. She was supposed to start at the university this fall."

Bea took her hand in both of hers. "We could try a finding spell just to see." She glanced up at me in question.

"Yes, we can do that."

"Chessa already tried." Lailah sniffed and then disappeared into the employee restroom.

"Damn," I muttered.

Frustration seeped off Bea, and we both sat there, silent. I hated not being able to do anything.

A few minutes later, Lailah returned, her face washed and steel in her spine as she got down to business. "I heard about Kane. Tell me what's going on."

I shrugged. "Not much actually. The shadows are tainted with his energy, only it's not exactly the same. It feels like maybe his energy was taken from him and then manipulated somehow. The first time we went in after it was already tainted, his energy was drained. The second time was after he was stripped of his demon hunter dagger and he was fine. No effects. So other than flying blind trying to research something we know nothing about, I don't have anything else to report… except for the outrageous amount of sexual energy filling Wicked."

Bea frowned.

Lailah raised her eyebrows. "Worse than usual?"

"Way worse. As in people are lined up around the block trying to get in as if they're addicted to the energy."

"Oh, dear," Bea said.

"How long has it been like that?" Lailah asked.

"The last couple of nights. Charlie had to call all the staff in and order extra stock. It's a madhouse."

"The same amount of time the Shadows has been tainted," Bea said, scribbling something in her notebook.

"Yes, but the energy isn't the same. In the club, the allure is Kane's. In the shadows, it's different. Not exactly Kane, but his at the same time. The vibe is darker."

Bea shook her head. "That doesn't matter. It's obvious the disturbance with the shadows and the club is connected."

She was right, and a nagging voice in my head told me I should've taken the club issue more seriously. The seduction of a good-looking spreadsheet had clouded everyone's judgment. If I'd learned anything over the last year, it was that when it came to the supernatural, nothing was random.

"You need to close the club," Lailah said quietly. "If the tension gets out of hand, anything can happen."

A shiver of dread took over. She was right. Anything could happen, from some supernatural disaster to an out-of-control assault. "I have to go," I said and strode toward the door.

"Do you need me to come with you?" Lailah asked.

I paused and glanced back at her. "No. Thanks, but the club is too much of a hot spot right now. It's probably better if you keep your distance."

She bristled at my words, hating to be told what to do as much as I did. But then she sat back on the stool and slumped. "You're right. It's too easy to slip into the shadows there."

I stopped midstep. "Is it easier there than other places for you?"

She nodded. "Yes. Ever since we opened that portal when we battled Roy, the club, and that building in general, has been an easier place to cross worlds. It happens sometimes when portals are unlocked."

Bea nodded her agreement. "A place that has seen that much magic, both black and white, is forever altered."

"I see." It would've been nice if someone had told me then. However, we were kinda busy saving Pyper's life.

"Good luck, Jade," Bea called.

"Yeah, don't let an overzealous tourist get handsy," Lailah added with a hint of a smile.

My lips twitched with humor. "I'm sure Kane will see to that."

# CHAPTER 10

By the time I got back to Wicked, it was nearing six o'clock. Way too early for the nightly rush. But just like the night before, there was a line already formed down the block of people waiting to get in.

The amount of people made me more than a little uncomfortable, and my skin crawled from the pure lust radiating from the massive group. The unfiltered sexual energy was invasive to the point of disturbing. I instantly slid my glass walls into place. And for the first time since I'd learned that trick, I wasn't completely cut off from the emotions around me. The lust was faint, but it was still there, nagging at me.

Our regular bouncer, Jeff, was manning the door. He unhooked a velvet rope and waved for me to pass as soon as he saw me.

"When did that go up?" I asked him, eyeing the red rope.

"Today. Too many people were trying to slip by."

"Good idea then." I waved at him as I braced myself for whatever crazy was going on inside. Taking a deep breath, I walked into the club and stopped mid-step, my mouth hanging open. "Holy crow."

No one was at the bar. No one was sitting in the chairs around the small tables. All of the patrons were crammed around the stage, staring up at the dancer as they chanted, "More. More. More. More."

There was an ebb and sway to their movements as if they were all connected and floating on a massive wave.

And high above them was a tall, sleek blonde who was flying on what had to be an invisible wire. She wore only a thin silk G-string that might as well have covered nothing at all and tall lace-up knee-high boots.

Her hands roamed her perfect breasts while she swung and dipped, taunting the audience, her long hair whipping out behind her.

I was stunned. When had the cable been installed? And was the club insured for that sort of thing? The strippers climbed poles two stories high, but this felt different. More daring. What was she even connected to? She wasn't wearing a harness or anything obvious.

Taking a few steps closer, I stared hard at the woman spinning in place. There wasn't a wire. Not one that I could see. Holy hell. Was she a witch?

Automatically I dropped my guard. Intense longing and frustrated desire wrapped around me, suffocating me with the thick strands of lust. My hands flew to my throat as if I could pry the awful energy from my skin. My nails hit my neck and scraped, leaving a trail of burning marks.

"Jade?"

I jumped, my heart trying to crawl out of my throat. But then I saw her. Pyper.

She reached out and touched my arm lightly.

My energy latched on to her, blocking out the oppressive

sexual energy. I started to relax, but then stiffened when I realized I felt almost nothing from her. No emotions whatsoever. It was so disconcerting, I slammed my walls back in place just so I could focus. I stared down at her, taking in the linen pants, button-down shirt, and her dark hair slicked back into a severe ponytail. She looked like Pyper, but her clothes sure didn't, and her emotional signature was all but gone. I stepped back, putting a bit of distance between us. "What's going on?"

Her brow furrowed in what appeared to be concern. "What do you mean? The dancer?" She glanced up at the entertainer and smiled. "She's an illusionist. Amazing, isn't she? Look at how she's playing the crowd."

An illusionist would explain the lack of wire. I wished I could've tapped into her emotional energy when I'd had my guard down, but I couldn't with so many people around. "She's impressive."

"Yeah. She's new. She just started. Tonight's her first performance. You might want to stick around and check it out." Pyper glanced up at her and then waved as she walked off. "See you later."

What in the world...?

"Pyper!" I called and went after her as she headed to the back. But the crowd swallowed her up, and I lost her. Why hadn't she been affected by the energy like everyone else in the room? And why was she dressed like an office pod person?

I pushed through the crowd, ignoring the sinking feeling in my gut that there was much more to the supposed illusionist flying through the air above us all. I had to get to Kane. *Please let him be here.*

When I finally got to the office door, I barged in, not even bothering to knock.

"Jade?" Kane dropped the pen he'd been clutching and stood. "What is it?"

I pushed the door closed and crossed the room. "Have you seen Pyper?"

"No. Not at all today. Why?"

I waved a hand toward the door. "She was just out there dressed in office wear. It was really weird."

He frowned at me as if I was speaking an entirely different language. "Was she acting strangely?"

I shook my head. "No. I guess not. She just… I dunno, she seemed not quite herself."

"It's a crazy night out there." His lips quirked up into a ghost of a smile.

"Right. About that." I flopped into the chair in front of his desk. "I think you might want to close down for the night. It's getting too dangerous."

His tiny smile vanished. "How so? We have extra security. So far, no one has gotten out of line."

"That's good, but the potential is bubbling just beneath the surface. The sexual tension that's luring them here isn't safe. What if someone goes too far? And have you seen the crowd out there? They're all smashed together transfixed by the new dancer."

"What new dancer?" He was halfway across the office before I caught up to him.

Cutting him off, I placed my hand on his chest. "The illusionist. You didn't know about her?"

"Illusionist? What?" He stared over my shoulder, clearly needing to see for himself what I was talking about.

Pyper used to manage the club, but that was Charlie's job now and Pyper usually just helped out when they were shorthanded. Why did she know about the new dancer and

Kane didn't? Something other than the energy in the club was very off.

"Excuse me." Kane stepped around me and opened the office door.

Immediately the atmosphere shifted. I couldn't see what it was, but even with my guard up I felt it deep in my bones. Magic crackled at my fingertips as I ran after Kane.

He came to an abrupt halt just as he stepped through the threshold.

"Oh my Goddess," I whispered, coming to a stop beside him. All of the patrons had turned and were staring at him as if they were transfixed.

And the illusionist just floated above everyone, waiting.

Everything about the scene gave me the creeps. I stepped in front of Kane, trying to tamp down my magic for fear I'd unleash it on someone unintentionally. But then the illusionist focused on Kane, her facial expression full of unadulterated rage. She flung her arms out in front of her and dove, flying straight for us.

I spread my arms wide as I called, *"Illuminate!"* The pentagram circle sprang to life around me and Kane, locking us in and everyone else out.

The illusionist came to a full stop and hovered in the air near the circle's edge, but didn't try to cross over. It was then I knew for sure she was something other than an entertainer. There was no cable. She was literally flying through the air.

Her lips curved up into an evil smile. "See all my followers? They're kindly feeding my power. One word from me and they'll tear this place apart. Drop the circle, or the club is getting a makeover."

"Don't do it, Jade," Kane said, anger radiating off him in waves.

"Wasn't even considering it." I glanced at the patrons. They were all enthralled, totally under the dancer's spell. She'd said they were feeding her power, but really she was stealing their strength in order to maintain her magic. And she'd trapped them in her web in less than five minutes, the time I'd been in Kane's office.

The evil dancer hissed at us and then lowered herself until she was just above the crowd. Her emerald eyes crinkled with menace. "Hear me, you lovelies," she called, holding her arms out. A wave of their collective lust flew through the air and into the palms of her hands. "Lose your inhibitions and fulfill your heart's desires. Tap into your darkest— Oomph!"

My magic hit her squarely in the chest, cutting off the enchantment she was trying to inflict on the patrons gathered beneath her.

Her gaze snapped back to me. "You'll pay for that."

"You first," I spat. I didn't know what she was, but she'd clearly been spinning the audience into a frenzy in order to use their lust to build her power. Glaring at her, I sent another bolt of magical lightning in her direction.

She dodged, keeping the attention of the patrons below her. They didn't seem to be able to tear their eyes from her.

"Who are you?" Kane asked her, the muscle in his jaw pulsing with tension.

"Not who, incubus, but what." She twirled above us, enjoying the taunt.

"She's a demon," I said to Kane, not entirely sure I was correct, but I was going to work under the assumption she was.

"One that flies?" he asked, raising one eyebrow.

"Why not?"

"I'm not a demon," she snapped.

"No? What are you then? A black magic witch? A rogue angel?"

"I'm your worst nightmare." She bared her teeth to me and dove straight for us again.

Kane stepped forward, trying to shield me.

"Out of the way." I shoved him, my magic already streaming from my fingertips. This bitch wasn't going to stop until she breached the barrier. My only option was to neutralize her. The magic poured from my palms, bolting straight through my already weakened circle. The flash of light hit her in the chest, barely causing her to flinch. A second later, the evil being twirled and vanished right before our eyes. "Dammit!"

"What?" Kane asked glancing around. "She's gone."

"No, she isn't. She's just hiding out." I scanned the confused crowd. Many of them were fleeing toward the front door, but many more sank into chairs to recover from however long they'd been watching the dancer.

"Do you feel her?" Kane pulled me through the club, scanning for any sign of her.

I shook my head. "There are too many people here. We have to shut down. Send them home before someone gets hurt."

Kane gave me a short nod and led us to the front door.

Jeff was standing outside, his feet shoulder width apart, his arms crossed over his chest, taking up as much space as he could to keep the rowdy crowd on their side of the velvet rope.

"We're shutting it down," Kane told Jeff. "Send them home. We'll be inside clearing out the club."

Jeff raised an eyebrow in question. "Seriously? That's some major cash you're throwing away."

"Doesn't matter. Just do what you have to."

"You got it, boss." Jeff spoke into a hand-held walkie talkie, informing the other two bouncers there was a change in plans. "We'll spread the word. Any official line you want us to use?"

"Say there's a plumbing problem." Kane glanced at me. "Do you want to wait out here?"

"Hell no." What was he thinking? "The illusionist could show back up at any moment. The people in there are in danger."

"I know. But I also know how that energy affects you. I just wanted to make sure you were all right." He squeezed my hand. "Come on. Let's go kick some evil ass."

# CHAPTER 11

*T*he moment we stepped back into the club, my head started to buzz with that internal warning. "She's back."

"Where?" Kane took a step, half-blocking me from the crowd.

I cast him an irritated look. "I'm not sure, but I feel her. And so do they." I waved toward the crowd once again pressed up against the stage, staring up at nothing. "She's compelled them, and they're waiting for her."

"We have to do something." Kane's fists curled as he paced in front of me. His left hand reached for his dagger, finding his belt empty. "Dammit," he mumbled, yanking his hand back down.

He was clearly missing the magic he'd become accustomed to.

"Call Lucien," I said. "Tell him to get Rosalee and meet me here ASAP." I was about to have some sort of magical showdown and I needed backup.

Kane whipped out his phone while I took a step forward,

magic already crawling up my wrists. I had to get the crowd to leave, but I couldn't spell them all into submission…or could I? I didn't have enough power to compel them all to do anything. But I could give them a suggestion.

My limbs felt like lead as I forced myself across the room toward the crowd. The obsessive adoration for the dancer streaming from them was so intense, it chipped away at my imaginary glass barrier. My stomach rolled and my head started to pound as if I'd been poisoned.

But I pushed through. If she'd spelled them all by herself, she was extremely powerful, and who knew what she'd do to them? The closer I got, the harder it was to control my magic. It turned unwieldy, trying to spark and sputter, searching for something to connect to.

I paused and reached for the source of my magic just below my heart. Focusing, I pulled on the threads, reeling my magic back until it pulsed just beneath my skin. Confidence replaced the out-of-control feeling, and I glided over to the crowd. I raised my gaze, pretending I was one of them as I searched for the dancer. And then, ever so casually, I brushed my magic-tinged fingertips over an arm, leaving just a suggestion.

*Go home. Relax.*

The woman took a step back and frowned before she backed up toward the door.

Good. My magic was working. I worked my way along the crowd, brushing just enough suggestive magic over hands, arms, and backs. One by one, slowly but surely, people tore themselves from the crowd and migrated toward the exit.

As the crowd thinned, my limbs became lighter and wielding suggestive magic became second nature once more. My headache vanished as my stomach settled. I moved quicker through the crowd, skimming and brushing, barely touching.

But then a hand wrapped around my wrist. Red-hot anger

crawled up my arm, boiling the magic that pulsed there. My knees buckled as I let out a cry of anguish. "Release me!" I demanded in vain.

"Drop the magic, witch," the dancer ordered.

"Let the people go," I countered, sending a bolt of power back at her. The magic burned and sizzled as it collided with hers. But as soon as my magic engulfed hers, she pulled her hand back and hissed.

"You'll pay for that, witch."

"Call me witch one more time and I'll magically gag you." It was a lie. That wasn't something I could do off the top of my head. With a spell or potion, maybe, but I couldn't just will it to happen like I did other bits of magic.

"Go ahead and try it." She reached a hand out, and tendrils of gray smoke emanated from her fingertips.

"Stop that," I said, my tone low and dangerous.

"Make me." She glared and all but snarled.

A burst of magic shot from my palm and collided with the mist. Both trails ignited into a line of fire.

A collective gasp from the remaining crowd rose over the music still filling the club.

Her lips spread into a slow, self-satisfied grin. "That's right, witch. Feed my power. Give me what I need." She shot more mist from her finger toward the crowd.

"No!" I didn't have a clue what her mist would do to our guests, but the energy radiating from it made my skin crawl. Her tainted power could do anything from knocking them over to turning them into zombies. The image sent a bolt of panic straight to my heart. Power welled up and exploded from me, collided with her mist, and created a connection. Our lines of power were locked in a tug of war as the line erupted into flames, dancing between us.

"Kane, get them out of here!" I saw him ushering people out

of the club from the corners of my eyes as she and I circled each other, each trying to gain control over the other. The more I focused on her, the more the flames inched closer toward her. My confidence grew as I realized that whoever or whatever she was, I was the more powerful one.

Pressing forward, I said, "My coven's on the way. It'll be better for you if you give up now."

Her green eyes narrowed with righteous indignation. "Give up? Never!" A burst of gray mist shot from her open mouth and rushed toward me.

"Ahh!" I cried as my eyes burned first, then my skin. "Stop!" Pain radiated from everywhere. My nerves screamed from the burning acid of her mist. I writhed in place, my magic still locked with hers, flames jumping all around me, fueled by her horrifying mist.

My brain had shut down. All I knew was anguish. Raw, unfiltered agony. I couldn't stop her. Couldn't do anything. Her acid was eating me alive.

"Jade!" I heard the faint call of Kane's voice and wept in silence. He was here. He was going to watch me die.

I wanted more than anything to answer him. To tell him I loved him. To tell him he was the best thing that ever happened to me. That I would've loved to grow old with him. To have his children... My throat closed. I gasped for air, unable to breathe. My vision was already gone. I was nothing but darkness. And evil. It was there. Right in front of me. The black shadow of a broken soul. In my mind, I reached for it. Somehow I knew if I gave in, the pain would stop. I'd be free.

"Yessss," the voice hissed. "Relent to me."

The voice was seductive. Smooth. Inviting. "You'll be with me now. The nightmare will end. I'll take care of you."

My magic started to fade as the will to fight slipped away.

"Jade!" Kane's sharp voice penetrated my senses. "Come back to me. Do not give up."

"Kane?" I said weakly.

"He's here, waiting for you," the voice whispered. "Let go, now. Kane's here."

"Jade!" The intensity of Kane's call shot straight to my core, filling me up with unwavering resolve. "Fight this. Do not let the mist take you!"

His words broke through the haze and as I focused on him, my body convulsed with shock as my own magic burst around me, breaking her hold.

The world tilted and swam in my vision as I slammed to the floor, the hold on me broken. Blinking, I stared up at the ceiling.

Familiar magic pulsed in the air. Magic that called to me. My instincts responded and I reached for the magical current surrounding me. Cool relief filled me, numbing my raw nerves.

"Jade?"

I shifted my gaze to Lucien, who had his arm around Kane, holding him up. Kane was pale and holding his gut with one arm. The warning bells went off in my head as reality closed in around me. "What happened?" I croaked, trying to sit up.

A spasm seized my lower back and I sucked in a breath as I stiffened, unable to move.

"You were attacked," Lucien said.

Frustration rose and threatened to choke me. "No kidding." I cut my gaze to them as Lucien lowered Kane to the floor. My strong demon hunter reached out and grabbed my hand.

He was just as emotionally drained as I was. Nothing was radiating from him except relief and weariness.

I squeezed Kane's hand, wishing I had some energy I could share with him. But right then it was all I could do to even stay conscious. "Where's the demon?" My attacker had to be one. She wasn't a witch or an angel. I would've recognized the energy signature. All demons were filled with darkness, just like the illusionist had been.

"Not a demon," Kane said.

I gazed up at him. "No?"

He shook his head. "I can tell. I was stripped of my dagger, but my senses are still intact."

"She's a lesser Goddess. Calling her a demon will likely only anger her more," Rosalee said, coming up from behind Lucien. The pretty witch was wearing tight jeans, a black T-shirt, and boots fit for an ass-kicking. She definitely looked ready to battle.

Crap. A Goddess. I didn't know anything about lesser Goddesses, but the moon Goddess Lailah had summoned for us last year had been scary powerful. I hadn't actually feared her, though. "Is she still here?" I rolled over on my side, peering through the dark club.

"She's been...contained." Lucien glanced at Rosalee, his green eyes gleaming with his considerable power.

The feeling was coming back into my limbs and while my arms and legs were stiff and heavy with fatigue, at least they weren't burning anymore. Curling into a ball, I rolled over on my knees, careful of my back. Of all my injuries, it was the most debilitating. I met Kane's eyes. "Are you all right?"

He nodded. "Just drained."

I caught Lucien's gaze then turned my attention back to Kane. "What happened?"

Lucien cleared his throat. "Rosalee and I had to use some of his energy to reach you."

I stared wide-eyed at Lucien. "You were able to tap Kane's energy?" I was the only empath of the group, and for me it wasn't much effort to manipulate energy. But that wasn't a talent of Lucien's or Rosalee's.

He nodded. "It wasn't easy, but since you two already have a connection, it was the only thing I could think of. We had to tap his aura. He might be a little out of sorts for a while."

*Aura.* I'd never thought of that. I'd never had to, since emotions were easy for me to see and feel…and manipulate if necessary, but manipulation was a last resort. "Yeah, he might." I held out my hand to Kane and we both stood on shaky feet.

He didn't say anything, but his arm came around me as he closed his eyes.

I tightened my grip on his waist, more than grateful he was okay. Then I glanced around the club. The lights had been turned on and shone down on the blue crushed velvet chairs. Everyone had left, including the staff. "That's one way to close the place."

Kane let out an ironic snort of laughter. "Maybe next time we'll just announce last call and close the bar."

I nodded. "Probably a better plan for sure."

Neither Lucien nor Rosalee seemed amused with our jokes.

I took a deep breath. "Okay, tell me about this lesser Goddess. What kind of power are we talking about, and how is she being contained?"

Lucien glanced at Rosalee, who was pacing. "Maybe we should go somewhere else to discuss this."

I raised an eyebrow. "Really? Why?"

Rosalee stopped and stared me in the eye. "Because even though she's gone, she could be back at any moment. Our magic won't hold her for long."

"All right, but if she's a Goddess then why did she attack everyone?"

"Goddesses aren't all good, you know," Rosalee said, her wide dark eyes narrowing. "If they want power, and most do, they'll do whatever it takes to get it. Including trying to drain a white witch."

Foreboding took up residence in my chest. "You're saying she was here for me?"

"No," Lucien said thoughtfully. "She was here for the incubus."

# CHAPTER 12

"Here for Kane?" I exclaimed. "But why?"

"Power, most likely," Lucien said. "This place is so highly charged, any supernatural being who's looking to boost their own powers will be drawn here. It's why we need to go. The fabric of this place is too vulnerable. And so is Kane, considering he's had his dagger stripped from him."

"Is everyone for sure gone?" I asked, glancing around the empty room. Leaving anyone behind wasn't an option.

"We need to do a sweep of the building." Kane let go of me, looking slightly stronger. "We'll do it in pairs. Lucien and I will take the upstairs. Jade, you and Rosalee check the back rooms and next door."

"Got it." As the guys took off toward the back hallway, I called, "Make sure to check on that new tenant, Zoe." Suddenly Duke's reaction to her hallway took on another layer of worry. Something must have been there for him to react that way. What if it had been this Goddess? Or some other supernatural creature waiting for an opportunity? "Tell her the place is being fumigated for termites or something. Send her to a hotel if you have to."

"I'm on it," Kane called back.

Lucien and Kane disappeared into the back hallway, and I cast my gaze on Rosalee. "Where did you two send the Goddess?"

"We didn't send her anywhere. She slipped away into another dimension, I suppose. But there's nothing to keep her there. After we broke the hold she had on you, we were trying to bind her, but she got away. She was sucking your power from you, you know."

My heart sped up as I realized she was correct. She'd said something about feeding herself and she'd meant my magic. "I thought you said she was contained? How did she get away?"

"Lucien was just starting the binding spell when she seemed to slash a hole in the fabric of our world. Orange-red light flowed from it as she dove through the opening. Then when she was gone, Lucien and I sealed the hole, effectively locking her out of the club…for now."

I nodded. If she could tear a hole in our dimension so easily, there was nothing to stop her from doing it again. They were right. She could be back at any moment. "Thanks for that."

Rosalee, one of the more powerful witches in our coven, shrugged. She graduated from college not long ago and was currently managing a Wiccan bookstore. "It wasn't anything you wouldn't have done."

I smiled at her. We didn't say much else as we checked the office, the two storage rooms and then the cafe next door. Empty. Everyone had cleared out. A few minutes later, Lucien and Kane met us back in the club. "All clear?" I asked.

Kane nodded. "Zoe wasn't there. I left a note and my cell number."

"We should call her." Without waiting, I shuffled back into the office and started rummaging through the file cabinets.

My fingers closed over her file just as Kane reappeared. He grabbed my hand and said, "Time to go. Now."

The world shifted into an array of muted colors. Kane's strange energy pressed against my skin, caressing me seductively, invading my senses until I was hot all over with reluctant need. My body responded, but my heart didn't. There wasn't anything inviting about the lust trying to claim me. In fact, it was just the opposite. All my instincts told me to run.

The world righted itself again as my feet slammed back into the ground, sending a bolt of pain through my back. Damn that hurt. A rush of light blinded me and my eyes watered from the shock of it. I blinked rapidly and yanked my hand from Kane's.

"Jade?" he asked.

I took another step, putting more physical distance between us. His clothes rustled as he shifted closer, but I raised one hand. "Please, I need space."

"Sure." I heard the concern in his tone, felt the pang of it in my gut, but I couldn't let him touch me. Not right then. Not after what I'd experienced in the shadows. It was still tainted with his incubus energy. But it also had an evil edge. One that had bile rising in the back of my throat. Kane wasn't evil. I knew that. Knew it deep in my soul. Whatever or whoever had made this happen had used his energy and infected it. But that didn't stop me from having such a visceral reaction to the awful reality that I now associated Kane's energy with evil.

I blinked, finally registering our surroundings. We were standing in the driveway of a small yellow carriage house with vibrant hibiscus plants lining the porch. "That's new," I said, pointing to the security light that had blinded me.

"I had it put in a month or so ago." Bea stood in her yard,

holding a large watering can as she studied us. "There's been a lot more nefarious activity in the last year or so."

The last year was pretty much how long I'd been in town. It wasn't as if Bea hadn't seen her fair share of trouble over the years, but evil seemed to follow me around. I'd been told it was because I was a white witch and those who sought power flocked to those who had it. And I had it in abundance.

"I take it the club closing didn't go well?" Bea said conversationally as if Kane and I popping up out of nowhere was perfectly normal. To her it probably was.

"No. Not well at all." I moved toward her. "Would it be possible to go inside to discuss this?"

"Of course, dear." Bea placed her watering can near the outdoor spigot and waved us onto the porch. "You go inside. I'll be right there."

Kane followed me into the house, but he kept his distance, and for that I was grateful. I was going to have to tell him what I'd felt in the shadows and how it affected me, but not right this moment. Once inside, I headed straight for the kitchen. If there was ever a time for witch's brew, it was now. Bea kept the restorative herbs on hand at all times.

I went to work, staying intently focused on my task.

Kane said nothing as he watched me from the kitchen table in the adjoining room. I could almost feel his gaze boring into me, but I didn't glance up. Not even when I heard the door open and close softly. I knew it had to be Bea, even though I couldn't feel her emotional energy. She was skilled at keeping her emotions to herself in a way most people weren't.

I was so busy grinding the herbs, I didn't notice her take the spot beside me until she placed her hand over mine. I jumped, startled she was so close.

"Have a seat, Jade. You know it's safe here."

Of course it was, and that was probably the reason Kane

had shadow walked us here. Bea had layers and layers of guards that kept other supernaturals away. Her property was protected from everything one could think of. Even demons. The only time demons had ever been on her property was when they were summoned. There probably wasn't a safer place in New Orleans than Bea's small house.

"Sure. Right." I put the pestle down and sat across the table from Kane. Immediately I regretted my choice when his steady gaze met mine, full of questions. *Jeez, Jade. Snap out of it. This is Kane. It's not his fault his energy is tainted in the shadows.*

"Good call bringing us here," I said to him.

"I didn't want anything following us." His voice was measured, as if he wasn't sure what to say to me just then.

Damn. That wasn't what I wanted. I cleared my throat. "What happened? Was something coming? You took us out of there pretty fast."

He nodded. "Lucien felt a disturbance. He and Rosalee should be here shortly. They're driving. But since we seemed to be the targets, I thought it was best we take a shorter route."

"Yeah. I agree." Though I wondered why I hadn't felt the disturbance. Was I too drained? My body was still a mess after the magical duel I'd had with the Goddess. I let out a tired sigh and rested my head in my hands.

Kane's instinct to comfort me caressed my bruised psyche, and I was instantly soothed. That was the energy I was used to. Relief crashed through me. His energy was normal. No taint in sight. I reached a hand across the table, taking his in mine.

His eyes searched mine for just a minute, and whatever he saw there had him relaxing into his chair as he stroked his thumb over the back of my hand.

Bea joined us, placing a fresh cup of witch's brew in front of each of us. She nodded to my cup. "I spiked it with healing herbs."

"Thanks."

"Now then, do you want to start, or wait for Lucien and Rosalee?"

I took a sip of the sweetened tea. The restorative properties hit my system, instantly perking me up. "We can start." I nodded to Kane to continue, since I'd spent a good deal of time locked in my own personal hell while I'd battled the Goddess.

Kane put his cup down and turned in Bea's direction. "We hired a new dancer. Or Pyper hired a new dancer and didn't tell me about it."

"An illusionist," I said.

"Right," Kane agreed. "But she wasn't one. Turns out she was a lesser Goddess and according to Lucien and Rosalee, she targeted my club because of my incubus energy." He went on to describe how everyone was enthralled and how I'd battled her until Lucien had used his magic to free me.

"That's highly unusual," Bea said when he was done. "Lesser Goddesses don't make themselves known very often. In fact, I've only met a handful of Goddesses in my lifetime and that was when they'd been summoned."

"This one was definitely full of darkness," I added. "She tried to burn me alive with some sort of acid energy."

Bea's penetrating gaze assessed me. "Are you all right? Any lasting effects?"

"I'm okay. Tired. Could use an energy boost, but other than that, I think I'll survive. Your herbs will help," I said.

She focused on Kane. "And you?"

"I'm fine." Kane let go of my hand and crossed his arms over his chest. He wasn't fine. Maybe physically he was all right. But mentally? He was struggling with the accusations against him and the fact that he was at the heart of the issues in his club and the shadows.

"We need to figure out what's happening in the shadows. That's when all this started, is it not?" Bea asked.

I nodded. "Vaughn's working on some research on his end, and I have plans to meet up with the Coven Pointe witches tomorrow night to find out what they know. But other than that, we're not sure where to start."

"Where is this Goddess?" Bea asked.

I shrugged. "She slipped into another dimension, and then Lucien sealed the opening to break her hold on me."

"I see." Bea strummed her fingers on the table. "We could summon her in the circle."

I nodded. "That seems like the best plan." I pulled my phone out of my pocket and hit Lucien's number.

He answered on the second ring. "Jade. Hey, have you heard from Kat?"

"No. Not since she told us about the TV show thing she's doing. Why? Can't find her?"

"She's not answering her phone. I told her I'd call as soon as I knew everything was all right. It's not like her to go silent on me when coven stuff is going down. Usually she's calling me a million times before I can even get a chance to talk with her."

I stifled a chuckle. Kat really did hate to be left out. "Maybe she's in the shower. Or taking a nap. I'm sure she'll call soon. Where was she when you came to the club?"

"She was on her way to work on her lines with another one of the actresses."

"Depending on where they met up, it might just be too loud to hear her phone," I guessed.

"Maybe."

"Hey, where are you two?"

"Pulling into Bea's driveway." Just as he said the words, I heard the hum of a car engine.

"Okay. See you in a minute." I turned to Bea. "They're here."

She gave me a patient smile, and I realized she probably already knew that. Her place was loaded with all kinds of wards and triggers. I was certain nothing happened on her grounds that she didn't know about.

A sharp knock came at the door.

Bea flicked her wrist, and the door swung open.

"Show-off," I said with a smile.

She winked at me while Lucien and Rosalee filed in. "Welcome," Bea said warmly. She'd been the coven leader before she'd transferred the power to me, although I was still uncertain why she'd done it. I knew it was because I had power, but I was still such a newbie that I always ended up running to her for help when we were in a crisis. She said she'd wanted to retire, but that hadn't happened. Not really anyway. She should've just kept the title and the power.

"We're going to summon the Goddess to the coven circle," Bea said without any preamble. "It's the only way we'll find her without using anyone as bait."

Bait. Guh. I hadn't even considered that. If the summoning didn't work, would we resort to offering up a sacrificial lamb? I hated the idea. And if we did, who would we offer? Me? Kane? One of our friends? Pyper? Or Kat? Lucien's words of wondering where Kat was triggered another worry in my mind. Where had Pyper gone after the attack? And where had Charlie been all night?

I pulled my phone out one more time and hit Pyper's number. While it rang, I asked Kane, "Where was Charlie tonight?"

He shrugged. "She said she had something important to do. At first I was frustrated, considering how busy we've been, but she works so hard and does such a fantastic job I didn't feel right about saying so. In retrospect, I'm glad she wasn't there.

She didn't need to get caught up in the good versus evil Goddess B.S."

"Yeah. That's true." The call to Pyper went to voicemail. I frowned. When her message ended and I heard the beep, I said, "Hey, Pyper. Listen, I hate to do this in a phone message, but the club's been compromised. It's not safe to be there or the café or your apartment. So far everything's all right, but to be safe, Kane's shutting down both buildings. If you need a place to stay, please just come to our house. You have the key." I hit End and glanced at Kane. "Did you let Charlie know she's off the hook until further notice?"

"I did."

"Okay, then." I gestured to Lucien and Rosalee. "I think the next thing to do is summon us a Goddess. Are you in?"

"Hell yes," Rosalee said. "It's been a while since we've had a good calling."

I was grateful for her enthusiasm, but also disturbed. We never called on anyone unless it was of major importance. The intrusion was too great. Of course, I couldn't care less about the Goddess's private affairs. No one tried to mess with Kane and got away with it. Not on my watch.

"Ready?" Bea asked.

I stood. "Do we need the rest of the coven? Or do you think the five of us can handle it?" Technically, Kane wouldn't be of much use. He had magic because of his incubus status, but without his dagger, his power was only good for seducing unsuspecting females. It wasn't the flashiest of powers, but it had its uses. Especially when we needed information out of someone.

"We've got this," Lucien said.

Bea nodded to confirm.

"Okay then. Let's go."

We left the small house and made our way to the two

parked cars, Lucien's Jeep and Bea's Prius. Just as I was about to slide into Bea's Prius, my phone went off. The number wasn't one I recognized. Normally I wouldn't even answer, but too many strange things were happening. Anyone could be calling.

Jade?" Lailah said, her voice strained after I answered.

"Yeah. What's up? You okay?" I asked.

"No." There was crackling over the connection, followed by a sniffle.

Lailah crying? The world was ending.

"Where are you?" I asked.

"At home. Look, Jade, I got a new printout of whose souls are in danger."

That ominous feeling in my gut came flooding back. "And?"

"There are three new names on the list."

"Three! Ones you know?"

"Ones we both know." Lailah sucked in a breath. "And I've been ordered to stand down because of the shadows. I can't do anything. Do you understand? Nothing. I need you to keep them safe."

"Of course, Lailah. Anything. Who are the three in danger?"

She paused and sniffled again. Then she shot the names off in rapid fire. "Pyper, Kat, and Charlie."

# CHAPTER 13

*A*fter Lailah's phone call, we headed back in the house to regroup. We were brainstorming a plan of action when Lailah showed up on Bea's doorstep. Her long blond hair was tied up in a messy haphazard bun, stray strands fallen around her blotchy face. She wiped at her red swollen eyes as she flopped down on the sunflower couch. "I don't know what to do. I can't just not go looking for them. This is my job. What I was trained for. And they're all my friends." She clutched her hands into a ball in her lap and fought back another onslaught of tears.

Ever since her phone call, I'd been alternating my time from calling each of them, to writing down a plan of action. I sat next to her, pen poised over a piece of paper. "We'll work on this together."

She nodded but didn't look up at me.

I locked eyes with Kane. Fear coiled around him tightly. Besides me, Pyper was his only real family. They weren't related, but were as close as brother and sister. His parents were off somewhere in Europe, pretending to be socialites. His grandmother, who'd raised him, had passed away a couple of years ago. I sent him a reassuring smile, but I was pretty sure it came off as more of a grimace.

Lucien was outside pacing. He'd been ready to leave to look for Kat the moment I'd relayed the news, but he had no idea where she was. She'd just said she was meeting up with a new acquaintance.

Kat had been my best friend since forever, and I loved both Charlie and Pyper, too. My heart ached, knowing they were in danger. I'd gladly trade places if I could. "I'll do everything in my power to keep them safe," I said to Lailah. "Just tell me what I need to do."

"What *we* need to do," Kane corrected.

This time when I looked up at him, my smile was genuine.

Lailah took a deep breath. "You need to make them aware they are vulnerable. But that means you have to find them first. The fact that none of them are reachable tells me they've already been compromised."

A sharp pain darted through my heart. *No.* The word reverberated through my mind. *This isn't happening.*

"Okay, so we summon them first." I wrote the directive down, as if I'd forget. *Right.*

"If you do that, you risk pulling in whatever it is that went after their souls."

A stone-cold determination settled over me. "Good." The word came out hoarse, full of emotion. I felt Lailah turn to stare at me. Without looking up from my paper, I said, "If anyone has harmed or is planning harm to our friends, nothing is going to stop me from ending them." I glanced up then and met Bea's hardened eyes. "Nothing."

She gave me a short nod.

It was all I needed. I stood and faced Lailah. "We're heading to the coven circle now. We'll call you as soon as we know anything."

Bea grabbed a supply bag full of candles and herbs. She paused as she walked past Lailah. "Stay here. It's the safest place for you."

Lailah nodded mutely. She was so utterly gutted it startled me. The angel I'd come to know was strong and proud. She wasn't willing to walk away from anything. Not when a soul was on the line.

"Let's go." Bea strode out the front door, her shoulders stiff. A cloud of determination clung to her and brushed against my skin. But there was also a hint of frustration mixed with fear that surrounded her, and that unsettled me. It was rare for me to feel her emotions. It meant she was just as unnerved as Lailah, but she did a good job of hiding it from everyone else. Her head was held high and she had a false air of confidence about her.

I straightened my own shoulders and willed myself to calm down.

Three people had come up on Lailah's list of endangered souls, and all of them had gone missing within a few hours. The implications were unnerving. That meant the being responsible for the abduction was powerful. We'd need to bring our A game.

I took Kane's hand and just because I could, I forced some of my energy into him. He shivered from the intrusion but said nothing. He squeezed my fingers in acknowledgment.

The five of us piled into Lucien's Jeep. In just five short minutes, we were parked and headed through the thicket of trees to our coven circle.

Bea took the lead, and I was all too happy to let her. Summoning spells were tricky at best. The stakes were too high for me to mess it up. There were two ways to do this as far as I knew. We could summon them using a specific distance, like within a two-hundred-mile radius. That was easier and more accurate. The other way was a general summoning, although the only time I'd done that was when I'd been calling my father. DNA had been used from my blood as a connection. I didn't think blood would work for people we weren't related to.

"What type of summoning are we going to do?" I asked, placing votives along the edge of the coven circle.

"A general one." Bea stood back and eyed the moon. "If Pyper, Charlie, and Kat have really been abducted, they could be anywhere by now. What we really need is to talk to them. So we'll summon their spirits. The connection Kane has with Pyper and the one Lucien has with Kat are deep enough that we should be able to reach at least one of them. But hopefully we'll find Charlie as well, and see if any one of the three has a clue where they are. Then we'll go from there."

I'd actually summoned a couple of angels straight into the circle before. Transported them through space. I wished with all my heart I could do that now, but I wasn't even sure how I did it. It had been an accident. "Blood sacrifice?" I asked.

"Yes." Bea pulled a couple of ceremonial knives from her stash and handed them to me and Kane.

Lucien and Rosalee already had theirs. Damn. That made me feel like a neglectful witch. Mine was at home in my witch stash.

"That will work?" I asked.

"To summon their spirit, yes. But we won't be able to transport them."

That was what I was afraid of.

"Take your spots on the circle," Bea ordered.

I hesitated, not knowing if I should take the northern most point, the leader's spot. Bea was the better choice, but she handed me a bag of herbs and gestured for me to take over.

"Here you go, dear."

With the small pouch in one hand and the knife in the other, I waited for Lucien to take his spot opposite me and for Bea and Rosalee to fill in the east and west spots.

"Kane," Bea said, "stand next to Jade. You're needed for this."

He did as he was told, his elbow brushing up against me. His solid presence fortified me in a way I couldn't explain. Magic pulsed through me, and my head cleared. There was only one thing on my mind—finding Kat, Pyper, and Charlie.

Bea stretched her arms out to both sides. "This is going to be a little different than the summoning in the past. I have a hunch that whatever is happening, is happening to all three of them at once. Which means their energy will be connected. So actually summoning them at the same time will be more useful than summoning each one individually."

"Okay," I said. "Do we each need to think of a different person so that they're all captured in the spell?"

"Yes," Bea said. "Kane should concentrate on Pyper. Lucien on Kat. And both Rosalee and I will focus on Charlie, since neither of us have a strong personal connection to her."

"I have a connection with Charlie," I said. We'd worked together quite a bit in the last year and were good friends.

"But you'll be leading the spell. You need to focus on each of them at different times, but we'll do the heavy lifting." She glanced around at us. "When Jade says the word 'sacrifice', each of you needs to slice your hand or finger and feed the earth with a drop of your blood. Make sure to concentrate on your person."

Everyone voiced their agreement and when Bea stared at me pointedly, I raised my hands high in the air. "From north to south to east to west, heed my call. We, the New Orleans coven, seek the presence of our loved ones."

All the candles on the circle lit with a surge of power. Lucien's eyes met mine, and magic filtered from me to Bea and Rosalee and on to Lucien. The current ebbed and flowed, mixing our magic and strength until the light illuminated the circle with our combined energy.

I tilted my head back and called, "From north to south to east to west, we offer a blood sacrifice in exchange for knowledge. To speak to those we seek."

From the corner of my eye I saw Kane slice open his palm. The surge of energy in the coven's collective told me the others had done the same. I raised my arms higher and focused on Kane and Pyper. Then Bea and Charlie. Lucien and Kat. And finally Rosalee and Charlie again. With determination and will, I imagined the three of them standing in our circle.

The wind picked up, and the ominous sound of magic crackling through the air made my hair stand on end. One glance told me everyone else was affected the same way. If someone were to plug us in, we could've probably powered the entire city.

"Now, Jade," Bea demanded over the rushing of air.

"Come forth. Show yourselves. Reveal the ones we seek."

The air stilled suddenly, and all I heard was the pop of magic sparking in the air. I glanced around, seeing nothing but the illuminated circle and my fellow witches. Then the wind picked up once more, and all the candles blew out. The magic died, and the five of us stood there in the pale glow of the moonlight.

"What happened?" Rosalee asked, confusion clear in her tone.

"Nothing. It doesn't appear—" Another loud snap of magic cut Lucien off, followed by a thundering boom.

I kept my arms raised in the air, magic pulsing at my fingertips. But then I saw it. The vague outline of a person, followed by another shadow.

"There she is," Lucien said, his voice full of emotion.

I followed his gaze and made out the outline of Kat. She was standing upright, her hands clutching a railing. Her face was full of exuberance as she talked and talked and talked. Only we couldn't hear her, and I had the impression she was giving some sort of monologue.

To her left was Pyper. She was sitting at a desk, typing faster than a demon on speed. Her fingers were flying so fast, I could barely see movement.

"Where's Charlie?" I whispered to Kane.

He pointed toward Rosalee. Right at her feet was an outline of someone huddled into herself. She was rocking back and forth as if in a tragic trance.

I glanced at Bea. "Why can't we talk to them?"

Her face morphed from confusion to utter rage as her lips turned down and her eyes clouded with hatred. "Show yourself!" she demanded.

A tinkle of laughter reverberated through the circle.

Someone else was there. The magic pulsing in my chest intensified as I focused on the laughter. Another high-pitched giggle sounded from near Bea. I narrowed my eyes, palmed a ball of power, and said, "The leader of this coven respectfully requests the honor of your presence. Please show us who lies behind the veil. Reveal yourself."

The tall, blond Goddess from the club solidified in front of Bea. She had her hand held out, her fingers crooked as if she was trying to coax something from Bea.

"Step away," Bea demanded.

And to my surprise, the Goddess did as she was told. "I was only studying your impressive magic." Her tone was light and airy, her smile pleasant. A shimmer coated her body, and it was then I realized she hadn't solidified at all. We had trapped her essence in the circle but not her physical body. That meant there was nothing we could do to fight her, but we could keep her there.

"You're not fooling anyone, you…spirit stealer," I shouted. I wasn't sure how she'd done it, but the only way she could've ended up in our circle was if she had control of our friends' spirits.

"Oh, you've figured it out then." She tossed her hair to the side. "They aren't really who I was after, but they'll do in a pinch." The Goddess sauntered over toward Kane and me. She stopped right in front of him and reached a finger out as if to run it down his chest. Only, the circle's barrier stopped her and a bolt of magic shocked her. She yanked her hand back and scowled at me. "I was going to offer to make a trade, but now I think I won't."

"Trade for what?" I asked, ignoring her blatant taunt.

"Your incubus, of course. He's so…" She smacked her lips together. "Delicious. Too bad you showed up in his dream last night. I had plans."

That bitch. She'd been impersonating Pyper to get to Kane.

"Release them," Kane ordered. "They don't have anything you want."

Her eyes danced with amusement as she regarded him. "Now that's where you're wrong, handsome. They might not be you and they won't help me with my ultimate goal, but they do have value."

"What's the trade?" His tone was cold, full of impatience.

She took two steps back and waved at them. "The trade was the three of them for you." She glanced at me and shook her head. "But I can see you two are far too connected. The witch has tainted your incubus magic. Pity."

"I'll do it," Kane said.

"No, he won't!" I clasped my hand around his wrist as if that would stop him.

"Jade," he warned.

"You can't do this." It wasn't that I was scared for him, though I was. But the bigger problem was we didn't have any idea what this being was capable of or why she wanted him. Kane's energy was somehow tied to the shadow world. Weird, unnatural energy that wasn't all his. Trading him for our friends could and likely would be an even larger disaster.

"Enough." Bea lowered her arms and peered at the Goddess. "Who are you, and what exactly are you after?"

She laughed and flittered away toward Rosalee. Studying the small witch, she tilted her head to the side and winked. "You're adorable."

"And you're crazy." Power pulsed around Rosalee. She wasn't going to put up with any shit from the Goddess. Good for her.

"I know who she is," Lucien said, his voice full of hatred.

The Goddess moved to the center of the circle and sat down cross-legged, waiting for him to continue. "Oh, this should be really interesting."

"You're Genesis, the younger sister of the Goddess of Spirit. You're everything she isn't."

All the humor left the Goddess's expression and she stood, her hands on her hips. "How did you know that?"

Lucien narrowed his eyes and glared.

"Tell me, witch. Or I'll take her spirit now." She pointed toward Kat, apparently knowing exactly how much Kat meant to him.

Hatred radiated off Lucien in the form of a red smoke cloud. "Mythology is one of my hobbies. You look just like your sister. Only, she's kind and watches over people. Helps them grow and better themselves. You're the opposite. You feed off spirits in order to stay young."

The Goddess flew into the air, twirling in a fit of rage.

But she had nowhere to go. Our circle had her trapped. The five of us stood strong, unwilling to waver. She flipped and dove, shot back up, and came hurtling back down.

"Way to have a complete fit," Rosalee mumbled.

I cast my coven mate a warning glance. The last thing we needed was to piss her off any more.

"Let me go," Genesis demanded.

"Free our friends, and we'll consider it," I said calmly, realizing that as long as she was in a snit, we weren't going to accomplish anything.

"No!" She stalked over to me, her finger pointed in my direction. "I'm in charge here."

I glanced around at my fellow witches. "I'm not so sure about that."

"No? I am." She waved a hand in Pyper's direction, forcing her to type even faster. "Free me, or I'll work them all to death."

"Don't do it, Jade," Bea warned. "She's not strong enough to do that."

I caught my mentor's eyes, searching for the truth. Bea was much more experienced than I was and I didn't have a reason to doubt her, but already our friends were suffering.

Genesis glared at Bea. "You're a trouble maker."

Bea sent her a smile, and I knew right then Bea was right. Genesis was mostly talk. I wasn't letting her out of this circle without striking a bargain.

"Free our friends, and you can go," I said again.

Genesis growled. Actually bared her teeth and growled at me as she stalked over to where Charlie was curled into a ball. "I'll give up this one. The other two are mine."

My heart skipped a beat. Progress. "All three of them. You don't need them for anything. They aren't magical."

"I do. They have spirit." Her eyes went wide and her lips twisted into a maniacal smile. "They're rich with it." She waved at Charlie. "Take the deal, or I'll suck her dry right here."

"What—"

The Goddess reached both hands out toward Charlie. A force shifted in the air, and energy flowed from Charlie to the Goddess. Genesis's complexion brightened and a glow started to outline her body.

"Stop!" I cried. "Stop it. It's a deal. You can go free if you release Charlie."

Lucien gasped, and Bea sucked in a harsh breath. But that was too bad. I wasn't going to stand there and let her kill Charlie before my eyes. And I couldn't stop her. Not with her there only in spirit.

The Goddess lowered her hands and moved back to stand in front of me. "How can I know you're telling the truth?"

"You're just going to have to trust me."

"I don't think so." Genesis moved over to where Kat was still silently speaking into the void. "I'll release the one you call Charlie, but if you don't free me and cease this calling immediately afterward, I'll drain this one."

Lucien's rage filtered over me from the other side of the circle. I couldn't deal with him just then. Nothing on this planet would stop me from keeping Kat safe. "Fine. Let Charlie go."

The Goddess walked back over to Charlie, leaned down, and blew into her face.

Sparks of light flittered over Charlie's skin as a silver cloud, in the shape of a short woman, radiated from her and evaporated in the air. After a moment, she uncurled and glanced around at all of us. "Jade? Kane?" she said, her eyes full of fear and confusion.

"Charlie. Are you all right?" I asked.

She wrapped her arms around herself and glanced around again. "Yes. I think so."

I reached into the circle, my hand breaking the barrier. "Grab hold."

Charlie slowly reached out, and I nearly cried when our hands united. She was solid. The Goddess had released her and in doing so, she'd left her in my circle.

"Hold on tight, okay? No matter what happens."

Charlie nodded, threading her fingers through mine.

"Release us, witch," Genesis demanded. "Now."

The way she was eyeing Kat, I had no doubt in my mind she'd drain her. If she sucked Kat's spirit out, there was nothing any of us could do. My heart ached at the realization of what I had to do, and a choked sob got caught in my throat. I wasn't going to be able to save all three of them. Not in that moment. And if I tried, I'd lose my best friend.

A sharp pain stabbed me in the chest as my resolve solidified. There wasn't any other choice. I had to do this now. With tears streaming down my face, I threw my free arm up in the air and shouted, "*Libero!*"

Genesis smiled as her body started to fade into the night. And a second later, there was a flash of magic as the Goddess vanished, taking Pyper and Kat with her.

# CHAPTER 14

*E*veryone was silent as we stared at the empty circle. I clutched my chest, trying to keep my heart from shattering into a million pieces. My two best friends were gone again, taken by a spirit-eating Goddess. And Lucien, my second in command, was glaring at me in judgment.

"Charlie," Kane said as he wrapped her into a hug.

She clung to him and buried her face into his shoulder, trembling with shock. "I don't know what happened."

He shook his head. "Neither do I, but you're safe now."

"But Pyper…and Kat." Their names were barely audible as the reality of whatever she'd went through hit her hard. "They need help."

"I know," Kane soothed. "We're working on it."

Lucien stalked over to me. "Are we? Working on it? How could you let her go and take them with her?"

I pressed my fingers to my tired eyes. "What was I supposed to do, Lucien? The Goddess was going to kill someone. I did what I could. Now we have to figure out where to go from here."

"But Kat—"

"Stop!" I said. "Don't make this harder than it already is. I love her, too, you know."

Lucien clamped his mouth shut, either too fed up to argue with me or too disgusted. I didn't care. I just needed time to think.

Bea came up beside me and touched my hand.

I met her worried gaze. "Are you going to judge me, too?"

She shook her head sadly. "No, Jade. You did what you thought you had to do."

I nodded. "Yes. I did. You have to know I'd never—"

"I know." Her voice was full of pity, which pissed me off. It shouldn't have, but it did. I closed my eyes and took a deep breath.

"Jade?" Kane put his hand on the small of my back.

I looked up into his worried eyes.

"I want to bring Charlie back to the house with us tonight. Is that all right?"

I nearly cried at the tenderness in his tone. "Yes. Please. I want to be sure she's safe, and it would be nice if we could talk to her about what she's been through."

He nodded and wrapped his arm around my waist. "Then let's get out of here. She really needs a quiet place to pull herself together."

I spotted Charlie standing off to the side away from Bea, Lucien, and Rosalee. She was pale and appeared as if she might pass out at any moment. Raw anger and helplessness warred in my chest for what she'd been through. Charlie worked for Kane and knew about some of our supernatural adventures, but she rarely witnessed them, and she'd never been in the line of fire before. Why had Genesis targeted her? Had she just been there for the taking?

"Let's go." I took off in Charlie's direction and slipped my hand into hers. "Hey, you. Let's get you home."

Her head snapped up and she stared at me with wide, panicked eyes. "Kane said he wanted me to go to your house."

I nodded slowly, desperate to force some calming energy into her, only there was nothing calm about my state of mind and I had nothing to give her. "Is that okay?"

The panic fled and the tension in her shoulders eased. "Yeah. I don't really want…" She stared off into the trees and shrugged.

"Understood." I tugged on her hand, and the three of us made our way back to Lucien's Jeep. Bea, Rosalee, and Lucien followed shortly. We now had six people instead of five, so I sat on Kane's lap and no one said a word on the way back to Bea's.

Lucien pulled to a stop in front of her house but didn't kill the engine. "I'm going home to do some research."

"Okay. Thank you," I said.

He gave me a curt nod and as soon as we piled out, he took off with Rosalee in the passenger seat.

"I'll call a cab," Kane said.

"Come inside while you wait," Bea said.

Charlie and I followed her while Kane made the phone call.

"It's okay. It's safe here," I said to Charlie and led her into the house.

Lailah jumped off the couch as soon as the door opened. "What happened?" Then she spotted Charlie and ran full force, catching her in a hug. "Thank goodness. Where were you?"

Charlie stared at me over Lailah's shoulder and shook her head.

"Lailah," I said gently and tugged her away from Charlie. "Let's all sit at the table, huh? Bea?"

My mentor glanced over at us.

"Do you have more tea and something Charlie could snack on?"

"Of course."

I guided Charlie over to the table. She sat and stared straight ahead.

"What happened?" Lailah asked calmly, her normal professional demeanor sliding back into place.

I went through the summoning and when I got to the part about Genesis, she held her hand up.

"You mean a lesser Goddess is targeting them?"

I nodded. "Yep. Lucien knew who she was and she didn't deny it." I lowered my voice and leaned in. "She feeds on a person's spirit in order to stay young and beautiful."

"Son of a…" Lailah jumped up and started pacing. "Not even a demon. But how does this tie in to the shadows?"

I shrugged. "No idea. But right now, with Pyper and Kat in danger, obviously battling her takes top priority."

"Agreed." She tapped her fingers on the table. "Let me do some research, and I'll call you in the morning."

"Lucien is researching, too."

"Good." Lailah placed a light hand on Charlie's arm. "I won't let this happen again."

Charlie gave her head a little shake and then focused on Lailah. "Why would you worry about me?"

Lailah leaned in. "Because I'm your soul guardian."

"What?" Charlie stood so fast her chair clattered to the floor.

The angel gave her a patient smile. "Maybe we should have a chat?"

Charlie's body went rigid as she looked from Lailah to me.

I smiled. "She's my soul guardian, too."

"Really?"

"Really. And she's good at it."

Charlie let out a slow breath. Then she nodded and joined Lailah in the living room.

Bea sat down beside me. She slid a cup of her witch's brew my way, and the pair of us sat there not saying a word. And for that, I was grateful. There wasn't anything to say. I'd made a decision and now I had to live with it.

Lailah and Charlie spoke quietly until Kane walked back in. "The cab is here," he said.

As I rose, Bea placed her hand over mine. I stared at the connection and then raised my gaze to hers.

"You did the only thing you could." Her words were gentle but there was a fierceness in her expression.

I swallowed the lump in my throat. "Thanks."

CHARLIE WAS quiet on the way back to our house. So was I. Kane tried a few times to engage us, but neither of us were very responsive and he gave up.

Once we were back home, I led Charlie to our guest room. "You'll be in here."

She stood in the doorway, hesitating.

"What's wrong?"

She shook her head. "Nothing. I just... This is all a little overwhelming."

"Yeah. It is." I moved into the room and sat in the chair in the corner. "But here's the thing. We—Kane, Pyper, and I—we won't ever let you go through any of this alone. It's not fair and it sucks. But we've got your back."

She didn't say anything at first. She just watched me. Then her eyes crinkled as she smiled. "I guess hanging with Kane and his gorgeous wife isn't so terrible."

I laughed and shook my head, more than relieved she sounded like her old self. "Don't ever change."

"Not on your life."

Then, as reality set in, we both sobered.

Charlie sat on the end of the bed, her hands clasped together. "We have to save Pyper and Kat from that evil bitch."

"We will." There was conviction in my tone. I only wished there wasn't the nagging doubt eating away at my heart.

"We will," Charlie echoed.

"Hey," Kane said from the doorway.

"Boss man," Charlie said. "Thanks for letting me stay here tonight."

He shook his head, one of his dark locks falling over his eyes. "You didn't have a choice. After today, we weren't letting you out of our sight."

"Well, thanks."

"I'm ordering food. Any special requests?" He held out a menu to the neighborhood po'boy shop.

"Oyster," I said.

"Shrimp," Charlie added.

"I'm on it." Kane retreated, and a second later we heard the front door click closed.

I rose and moved toward the door, but then stopped dead in my tracks. "Charlie?"

"Yeah?"

"Did you really go out on a date with a man?"

She stilled and bit down on her bottom lip as she grimaced.

"You did, didn't you?"

She groaned and nodded.

I sat back down. "Can I ask why?"

She groaned again and flopped back onto the bed.

"Sorry. I… Well, I guess I'm a little confused. You know I don't care who you date. It just seems so unlike you, and with the crazy stuff going on, I wanted to check with you to make sure there isn't anything…off."

She let out a burst of laughter and then sat up. "Off. I think that's the operative word."

I leaned forward. "And?"

She shook her head. "I don't really know what happened. One day I was slinging drinks at the bar, and the next I was flirting with one of the regulars. And when he asked me out, I said yes."

My eyebrows rose in curious surprise. "But why?"

She shook her head. "I don't know. It was awful. I mean, I don't date guys. You're not wrong about that. I'm not attracted to them. So the odd part about this is not that the guy was awful. He's been to the club often enough that I kinda know him and like him well enough. The awful part was I had these strange, really overpowering conflicting feelings about the whole thing."

"That's new right?" Something told me this was all related to the Goddess and the club's energy. I just didn't know how.

She ran a hand through her short red hair. "I felt like I had a split personality. I didn't want to be there at all. In fact, when he tried to kiss me, I physically felt ill. But then there was this whole other part of me that was excited to be out on that date." She averted her eyes and lowered her voice. "I actually wanted him to touch me. You know, hold my hand."

I sat there, not sure what to say. Then I cleared my throat. "Charlie, there's nothing wrong with dating to see who you're attracted to."

"That's the thing. I wasn't attracted to him." She stood again and grabbed one of the pillows. "All the desire to be there with that guy, it was foreign, as if it wasn't coming from inside me."

"Hmm, that's odd. When did the feelings start?"

"A few days ago."

A tingle of suspicion tickled my mind. "Before or after the club became supercharged?"

"After. The first night, actually. That was the night he asked me out and before I could charm him with my sass as I turned him down, I was saying yes. And felt happy about it all while my mind was whirling with a big dose of 'what the fuck?'"

I laughed at her expression. "Sorry. I couldn't help it because I can totally picture that and to be honest, it freaks me out a little."

"Freaks you out? I'm losing my mind. I've known I was a lesbian since I was eight years old!"

"Well, I don't know if this will freak you out more or less, but I don't think you were suddenly having a sexual identity crisis."

"No? What else would you call it?" She eyed me with suspicion.

"I'd call it an invasion. Or spell. Or some other supernatural phenomenon. Think about it. That all started the night the club went haywire. The weird energy in the club got to you and turned you into someone you're not."

She leaned against the closed door and regarded me. Then her eyes narrowed. "What if it wasn't the club? What if I'm broken? Or having some sort of crisis?"

I gave her a look. "How are you feeling about men right now?"

She wrinkled her nose.

"Not feeling it?"

"No. Not at all."

"Not even for the boss man?"

"Oh, Jesus on a cracker. You did not just say that."

I grinned. "Is that a yes, then?"

"No. Dammit. Don't even go there."

"Well, then. If you're not interested in the sexiest man alive, I think that settles it. You're not into dudes."

Her eyes sparkled as she laughed at me. "Thank God for that."

# CHAPTER 15

*A*fter dinner, Charlie excused herself and retreated to the guest room. Kane and I sat at the table, sharing a Guinness. Kane took a long swig of the beer and then passed it to me. "I'm going to dreamwalk Pyper tonight," he said.

"Do you think you can?" I tilted the bottle to my lips.

"I can try." There was a deadly serious determination about him that I rarely saw. Kane was confident and an excellent demon hunter, but this was personal. The Goddess had taken Pyper, and he'd stop at nothing to find her.

"I'm going with you."

Kane studied me for a long moment.

"I'll be there in your dream. You can't stop me." For months now every night when we fell asleep, I slipped right into Kane's dreamwalks. While I wasn't a dreamwalker, we shared a deep connection, and I doubted he could keep me out even if he tried.

"Good." Kane slipped his hand over mine. "We're going to find them."

"We better."

~

KANE and I lay in our bed. My heart rose up and clogged my throat. The decision to let Genesis take Kat and Pyper weighed heavily on my soul. I let out a long sigh and pressed my cheek against his chest.

His arms tightened around me as he kissed the top of my head. "I'll be waiting."

Images of Pyper and Kat played in my mind and a tear slipped silently down my temple.

Kane stroked his fingers through my hair, saying nothing. He didn't have to. The only thing I needed was for him to hold me.

Before long, his chest rose in a steady pattern, and I knew he was already asleep. I wished with everything I had I could let go of all the turmoil running through me long enough to relax, to slip into the dream state that would allow me to accompany Kane to find our friends. Dreamwalking was our only hope at the moment.

Settling myself, I focused on Kane's breathing. In. Out. In. Out. Soon enough, my body started to relax and I felt myself drifting into oblivion. Darkness closed in followed by the beginnings of weak light. An uneasy tightness formed in my gut when I didn't see Kane right away as I usually did.

I was standing in a hazy mist of an alternate reality. Or was I? "Kane?"

"I'm here." He appeared out of nowhere and slipped his hand into mine. "Come on. I've found them."

The next thing I knew, our surroundings shifted and we were standing in the middle of Kane's club. I blinked, trying to focus. Everything was distorted, as if we were seeing the room through a filter. "You've seen them?"

He shook his head. "No. I hear them. Listen."

We stood on the stage, silent.

Then I heard it. Kat's voice. And she was reciting passages of Shakespeare. A Midsummer's Night Dream. "It's Kat," I said.

"Pyper's there, too. I can hear her having some sort of conversation."

We were silent for another moment and although I couldn't quite tell if I could hear Pyper or not, I had something better. I felt her. And Kat, too. "They're this way."

Clutching Kane's hand, I tugged him into the back of the club. With each step, my friends' energies intensified.

"I already checked back here. I didn't see anyone."

"They're not down here." I pointed toward the stairs. "They're that way."

Kane tilted his head to listen.

"Trust me."

He paused when we got to the stairs leading to the second floor.

"What's wrong?"

He shook his head. "I don't know. The energy is…"

"Creepy?" I supplied.

"Yeah. Everything just feels wrong."

"You can say that again. We *are* dealing with a spirit-eating Goddess."

"Right." Squaring his shoulders, he took off up the stairs two at a time.

Well, damn. I didn't mean for him to be that focused. Steeling myself, I headed upstairs, prepared for the worst.

Kane stopped at the top of the second floor landing, holding his arm out to keep me from going ahead of him. "She's here. The Goddess."

I peered over his shoulder into the darkness and let my guard down. A chill crawled over my limbs in the form of desperation, but it wasn't from the Goddess. I shook my head. "It's someone else. We need to get in there."

"Who?"

"No idea. But whoever is in there is in trouble."

That was all Kane needed to hear. He strode to the apartment door and without knocking, he tried the handle. Locked. But this was a dream. Kane could transport us to wherever he wanted. He clasped his hand over mine and in the next second we were standing in the middle of the sparsely furnished apartment.

I let out a loud gasp. A large pentagram was drawn on the far wall. Zoe, our new tenant, was suspended right in the middle of it, her wrists and ankles tied to large spikes. Her eyes were wild with fear and she was clearly screaming, but I couldn't hear her at all. It was as if her voice had been silenced.

"Zoe!" I ran to her. But when I got a foot from her, I smacked into an invisible barrier and jerked back, crying out in pain. No wonder I couldn't hear her. She was trapped behind an invisible force. My skin burned everywhere I'd touched the barrier. "Son of a bitch!" I held my arms out, inspecting the burns. We were in a dream, and even though I knew when I woke up I wouldn't see the marks, the pain would still be there until I healed.

"What happened?" Kane asked.

"Electrified, I think." I stepped back and tugged on my magic. I was spitting mad and my magic sprang forth with very little effort on my part. Aiming just to the left of Zoe, I unleashed a torrent of raw magic. It collided with the barrier, both sparking, and then my magic jolted through and crashed into the wall about a foot away from Zoe.

Her mouth dropped open in a silent cry and the wall crumbled.

"Damn it all… It wasn't enough." The barrier was still intact with a near perfect hole where my magic had penetrated it.

Kane reached for his dagger. He scowled and swore under his breath when he came up empty.

"I've got this," I said and let loose another round of magic just to the right of Zoe. My magic blasted through, creating a similar hole on the opposite side. More plaster from the wall clattered to the ground.

Kane glanced at me. "Now what?"

The barrier hadn't budged. I walked up to it, positioned both hands near the edge of the holes, and released much smaller blasts of magic, using my mind to nudge it toward the center. Tiny cracks formed and ran in chaotic lines until the barrier caved and shattered at our feet.

Zoe stared at us, her expression pinched with pain as her mouth moved but was unable to form speech.

"What's happened to her? Why can't she talk?" I asked Kane.

But before he could answer, a rumble sounded from above, followed by a thunderous boom.

I jumped back, grabbing Kane's arm. And then right before our eyes, the bindings vanished from Zoe's limbs. She rose above us and her skin started to ripple and her form stretched and shifted from the captured woman to the Goddess Genesis.

"You!" She pointed at me, her eyes wild with rage. "How dare you invade my sanctuary?"

Her words just pissed me off. "You do know Kane owns this building, right? It's you who's invading our space."

"So naïve." She rose up above us and widened her arms. "Nothing belongs to you when you're dealing with the otherworlds." With a grand sweeping gesture, she lowered her arms, and the room shifted from a small apartment to a vast stone cave, complete with live-fire torches on the walls. "This is my home. And these—" her lips curled into something sinister, "—are my pets." An invisible veil lifted, revealing Pyper and Kat.

A guttural cry erupted from me as I ran forward, desperate to free them from the chains binding them to the stone floor.

"Jade!" Kane grabbed my arm. "Wait."

He stopped me just before I reached them. "What?"

"Look."

I glanced down at my two friends. There was a sheen of magic covering them. The same that had been protecting Zoe. Frustration overwhelmed me as I realized there was no blasting through it this time. Not unless I wanted to hurt Pyper or Kat. "Let them go!" I demanded, whirling on the Goddess.

Genesis floated to the ground, her face serene. "Why? They're perfectly happy in their alternate realities, living the lives they always dreamed of." She snapped her fingers and a large screen appeared, showing Pyper in a high rise office running some sort of important meeting. She wore a sexy business suit and had her hair piled high on her head as she used a laser pointer to highlight critical points of her presentation.

The picture on the screen shifted. Kat was there in a TV production, reading lines with an ensemble cast. She held a script and while she looked exactly the same, she seemed more polished. Her hair and makeup had been professionally done and she wore high heels with her jeans and blouse.

"That's not what either of them dreamed of," I said, as if that even mattered. They were chained to the floor.

She laughed. "Trust me. They're content."

Her smug smile caused rage to ball in my gut. My fists were clenched and if Kane hadn't had a hand on my wrist, I was certain I would've already rushed the Goddess, fists flailing.

She let out a soft laugh and elevated back up so she was staring down at us. "You can't win. Not against me, a Goddess."

"What do you want?" Kane asked, dead calm in his tone.

She tilted her head and regarded him. "I already have what I want. Youth and power. And thanks to your club, now I have adoration. And a long line of willing participants to...feed my needs."

"Why my club?" Kane asked.

I was too busy trying to rack my brain on how to save Kat and Pyper to care about why she was doing any of the things she was doing. It didn't matter. I'd just as soon destroy her than worry about what she needed.

Closing my eyes, I homed in on Kat's energy. Her vibrant, easygoing nature was barely there, replaced by someone else who was full of determination, need, and a drive for success that Kat had never had before. Kat was a jewelry designer. A free spirit who worked for herself. She was good at it, loved it even, but career driven was not a term I'd have ever used to describe her. And that was what I was getting off her in spades right at that moment.

Then I felt it. The distinct energy signature of someone who wasn't Kat. Only hers was there, too. Son of a...

I shifted my focus to Pyper. Anger mixed with satisfaction hit me full force, but I bypassed those emotions and quickly zeroed in on her signature. Her sassy, confident energy barely pulsed within her, pushed out by something darker and more intense. There were again two signatures.

My thoughts shifted back to Charlie and how she'd had feelings she didn't recognize, that had felt foreign to her, and suddenly I knew what had happened.

"Kane!" I spun and focused on him.

He was staring hard at Genesis as she said something about how the club's location was perfect for her needs. That since

Kane's energy had filled the area with powerful sex magic, she had found her ideal spot.

"I know what's going on," I said slowly as I stalked toward Genesis.

"Really?" She laughed. "I highly doubt that."

I glared at her. After a second, I fused my mental energy to Kat's as if I was keeping her safe and then pushed with everything I had on the foreign soul that had invaded her body. Almost immediately I felt the invading soul release her.

"What are you...? No!" The Goddess flew to Kat's side and grabbed her, shaking her listless body. "How are you doing this?"

The Goddess's complexion turned ashen as small wrinkles formed around her eyes. Her body morphed from toned and perfectly shaped to slightly pudgy. She was aging right before our eyes.

The magic that had been coating Kat evaporated and she sat up. Her eyes went wide as she took in the manacles holding her down. "Let me go!" She cried and flailed wildly. Then her gaze landed on me and she clamped her mouth shut as she glanced around.

"I'm not leaving without you or Pyper," I said to her. "Count on it."

Kane ran to her side and tested the chains. If he'd had his dagger, he could've freed her right then. But he didn't. Instead, he grabbed hold of the chains and pulled. A loud creaking noise filled the space.

"Don't touch that!" Genesis flew toward Kane, but she was wobbly from the effort and before she got to him, I shot a bolt of magic at her. The Goddess's body hovered in the air and twitched from the electric current running through her. Then she fell and crashed into the ground.

"Get them free," I called to Kane as I reached for Pyper's

emotional signature. Her infectious spirit was there just beneath the high-powered determination of the foreign spirit. I grabbed hold and tugged. But before I could separate Pyper from the other spirit, Genesis's body vanished in a cloud of gray smoke and reappeared just above Kat. Her appearance was once again Zoe's, only disheveled and at least a decade older.

Ropes of slithering gray mist wound their way around Kat's arms and legs and then wrapped around her neck.

Kat coughed and sputtered, clawing at the mystical ropes.

"Let the dark one go," Genesis ordered. "Or this one dies."

Without even a second thought, I unleashed my magic at the Goddess.

"Dammit!" I scowled as my limbs grew instantly heavy. Instead of my attack taking her down, she sucked the stream of power in, growing stronger with each blast that hit her. She was literally filling up on my magic. No, my soul.

"Jade!" Kane jumped in front of me and my magic, his body going rigid upon impact.

"Kane!" I leaped forward and placed my trembling hands on his still body.

"He's mine now, white witch." The Goddess snarled and kicked me out of the way. She whirled and with one hand clutching Kane's wrist and the other on one of Pyper's chains, the three of them disappeared.

The room shifted again, leaving me and Kat in the sparse apartment. She was lying sprawled on the floor. I scrambled to her side and when I touched her, a silver shadow in the form of a young woman rose from her body and vanished into thin air. Just as it had done with Charlie back at the coven circle.

"Oh my God. Kat?" A sob got caught in my throat as I stared down at her through my thickening tears.

"Jade?"

"You're okay. You're okay," I said over and over again, trying to reassure both of us.

She blinked up at me, confusion swimming in her hazel eyes. "Is she gone?"

"Yes," I choked out, trying my best to hold it together. To not think about Kane being gone. Even though we'd dreamwalked Kat and Pyper, somehow I knew dealing with the Goddess had changed the rules. We were no longer in a dream. Kat and I were wide awake in the apartment above Wicked. "The Goddess is gone."

"Goddess?"

"Yeah. The one who kidnapped you." Maybe she didn't know who Genesis was.

Kat slowly shook her head. "No. She didn't take me. The lost soul did."

"Lost soul?" What was she talking about?

"The one that escaped Hell."

# CHAPTER 16

"*C*ome on." I helped Kat to her feet. "We need to get you home." I wasn't sure if she was giving me important information or if she was just confused after her ordeal.

She glanced around, her brows pinched. "What am I doing here?"

I was torn, half of me desperate to look for Kane and Pyper while the other half knew I had to get Kat somewhere safe. If Genesis showed back up, it would be too easy for her to grab Kat in her weakened state.

"Jade?" Kat clutched at my arm.

I wrapped my arms around her and hugged her hard. "I'm so glad you're okay."

She hugged me back, her body trembling.

"You're safe now. I'll take care of you."

She nodded and let me guide her out of the apartment. We walked in silence down the stairs. But instead of leaving through the side door, I ran into the club just to make sure neither Kane nor Pyper were there.

They weren't. My heart dropped and tears stung my eyes.

"Jade?" Kat said again. "Tell me what's going on." Her voice was stronger now.

I glanced at her and saw the conviction in her expression. "Let's go outside." Kane's incubus energy was crawling all over me, and I couldn't focus on anything else. The familiarity made me want to stay in the club, searching even though I knew he wasn't there. Only his energy was, just as it had been the last few days.

She followed me and the minute we stepped out into the humid night air, she clutched my arm again. "I need to know what happened."

"I'm not entirely sure," I hedged.

Exasperation streamed off her in waves.

"I'm serious." I glanced at her to let her see my sincere expression. "You said a lost soul took you, but I don't know anything about that. All I know is a lesser Goddess had you trapped in another dimension as she used you to feed her power. She had Charlie as well, but she's safe at my house now."

Kat was silent for a moment. "And Pyper? This lesser Goddess has her, too, doesn't she?"

"Yes." The word came out strained. "And now Kane, as well."

A small gasp slipped from her lips. "We need to find them!"

Sadness weighed on me, and I blinked back tears. "Right now, I need to get you somewhere out of harm's way. Then I'll go back for them." I quickened my pace and rounded the corner to the home I shared with Kane. Hope sprung forth, almost overwhelming me. Was he there? We'd been dreamwalking. I'd been kicked out of the dream, along with Kat. But he was the dreamwalker. He could still be in our bed.

"Hurry," I said to Kat as I broke out into a run. He had to be there.

We burst through the front door, startling Charlie. She jumped out of the oversized chair, her fists raised.

"Charlie," I called, running past her. "Is Kane here?" I didn't stop to wait for an answer. I rounded the corner into the hall and pulled the door open to our bedroom.

"No," Charlie said from behind me as my eyes focused on the empty bed.

"Fuck!" I spun and rushed to the phone. I knew it was a long shot. Hadn't really expected him to be there, but that damn hope had taken up residence in my heart.

I grabbed the phone and hit Lucien's name as I watched Charlie and Kat hang on to each other in a tight hug.

"Jade?" Lucien said when he answered. "What's happened?"

"Kat is here. You need to come now."

There was a rustling on the other end of the line, followed by the slam of a door. "Kat's with you? Is she okay? What happened?"

I sat at the kitchen table and held my forehead with one hand as I relayed the night's events.

"But Kat's okay?" he asked again when I finished.

"Yes. She appears to be all right. Hold on." I held the phone out to Kat. "It's Lucien."

She grabbed the phone and hurried into the other room, while Charlie sat beside me.

"I can't believe this is happening," she said.

I met her defeated gaze then averted my eyes. "I'll get them back." My tone was strong, full of conviction, my words a declaration. "You can count on it."

The door burst open, and I heard Kat let out a gasp, followed by Lucien's voice. "Thank the Gods you're all right."

"Stay here with Lucien," I told Charlie. "I'm going to get Pyper and Kane."

"But Jade—"

I held up a hand, determination swirling inside me. "I can't do this right now."

She gave me a small nod and slumped back in her chair.

On my way to the living room, I grabbed a bag of herbs from the pantry. I didn't have time to make any special potions, but the basics would be better than nothing.

"Jade?" Lucien said over Kat's shoulder as I hurried into the living room.

"Lucien." I gave him a nod and kept going.

"Hold on. I have information."

"It'll have to wait. I have to find Kane and Pyper." Clutching the door handle, I closed my eyes as a wave of emotion threatened to overwhelm me.

"It's about the Goddess. I found her in one of my research manuals."

When I opened my eyes, he'd let go of Kat and was standing right in front of me.

"You want this information for when we battle her." His eyes were focused, business-like.

"When *I* battle her," I said. "You're staying here to keep them safe."

His already anxious energy bristled against my skin. "You can't go alone."

"And you can't go with me. I'm going into the shadows. I couldn't take you even if I wanted to."

"Shit." He grabbed a book from the entryway stand that hadn't been there before. "You need to see this before you go." He flipped the book open to a marked section. "This is a book on the history of Gods and Goddesses. Remember when I said I studied them? Well, I found Genesis." He held the book out to me. And as I took it, he continued. "It says in there that as a young Goddess, Genesis was known to be extremely vain. For her, youth and beauty was everything, especially since she was in the shadow of her much-revered sister the Goddess of Spirit. When Genesis turned twenty-five, she sought out a powerful demon. One who was known to be a favorite of the devil himself. He told her he had the power to give her eternal youth, but there was a price."

"Of course there was," I said dryly.

"Yeah, that price was souls. He granted her the power to stay young, but it only lasted one hundred years. The payment for each one hundred years after that was three souls and an angel. The spirit of her victims would keep her young for another one hundred years, but she had to deliver the souls and the angel to the demon as payment."

Three souls and one angel. She'd had the three souls. Four actually, if we included Zoe. Did she have the angel as well? The one who had gone missing? I glanced at the passage Lucien had pointed out and noticed a note in the margin. *Happens every year on the summer solstice.*

"That's in two days," I said.

He nodded. "That's when the sacrifice is made."

"So she's been collecting her offering? Kat, Pyper, and Charlie?"

"Yes. And she's been using enslaved souls to control them." He clenched his teeth together in irritation. "It's why Kat was so obsessed about the acting. That wasn't her. It was another soul."

I glanced at Kat. She'd said a soul had taken her. Genesis had soul minions doing her dirty work. I'd seen it leave after Kat had been released from Genesis's clutches. Just like I had with Charlie.

Whoa. That was why Charlie had wanted to date a man. It wasn't her. It was some other soul.

"This case just took a left turn," I said. "That all makes sense with what we've seen so far, but what does Kane have to do with any of it? And do you think the tainted power in the shadows is related?"

Lucien shrugged and took the book from me. "I don't know the answer to either question. Maybe Genesis wants him instead. Because he's an incubus, his spirit is a lot more enticing, I'm sure."

"Ugh." I swallowed the bile trying to rise up in the back of my throat. "I have to go. I can't stay here waiting." I yanked the door open.

"Are you headed back to the club?" Lucien asked.

"Yes. It's the center of everything."

"I want to come with you."

"No!" I spun, frantic. "You have to watch over Kat and Charlie. With you here, they'll be safe. I can't be worrying about them, too."

Resignation settled over his features as he took a step back toward Kat. With his hand snaking around her waist, he said, "I'm calling the rest of the coven. They need to know what's happening."

"Yeah." I sucked in a breath, trying to calm myself. "It's better they know." And without waiting for an answer, I bolted out of the door. The club was only a few blocks, but I ran the entire way there and when I stopped in front of the entrance, I was winded.

"Get it together, Jade," I told myself.

I reached for the door handle and hesitated, only then realizing I hadn't thought to bring the keys. "Damn." My palm warmed with magic and, focusing on the lock, I heard a small click. Then I ran my hand along the upper section of the door until the unmistakable thunk of a dead bolt turning filled my senses.

Being a witch came in handy sometimes, even if it did sort of turn me into a criminal. Kane owned the building, so technically I wasn't breaking and entering, but if anyone was watching it would look like I was.

The door swung open and with a surge of determination, I entered the building. It was exactly as I'd left it only a half hour before: empty, full of Kane's incubus signature, and tainted with something evil.

I stood just off to the right of the stage and took a step into the shadows. The energy hit me hard, nearly knocking me off my feet. And this time, even though it still felt faintly like Kane's energy, it was much more sinister. Unease crawled up my spine as I felt the fabric of the dimension pulse with fear and despair. The desire to curl into a ball just as Charlie had earlier nearly did me in.

But Kane's face flashed in my mind, and a ripple of strength materialized from deep inside me. I would not let the Goddess keep Kane or Pyper. Wherever they were. I knew it was too easy to think I could enter the shadows and they'd be right here waiting. Genesis could be holding them anywhere.

I had to find her, then I'd find them.

The only thing I knew to do was to search for their energy. Except the only emotions I felt were hopelessness and desire, coming from beyond the shadows. There was no way I was going to be able to connect with either Kane's or Pyper's energy signatures. I had to try something else.

Frantic to be out of the shadows of doom, I rummaged through my bag of herbs and came up with dandelion leaf. It was worth a shot. Dandelion was used as a summoning agent for spirits. I could call on those of the shadows for help to find Kane and Pyper.

I hastily formed a circle with the crushed dandelion leaves and stepped into the middle, reaching for my power. Electric magic shot through me and not only did the circle light up, but so did I. Light shimmered over my skin.

Whoa. That wasn't the plan. Immediately a handful of spirits appeared, hovering around my circle. Two were so old and decayed, I could barely make out the shape of their half-formed faces. Another bounced back and forth, appearing to be mesmerized by the light. But the fourth stood tall, regarding me with interest. Her eyes were wrinkled with age and shone with wisdom. She'd passed on later in life, most likely from natural causes, judging by the shimmering cloud of peace clinging to her.

"Hello," I said.

"It's not safe in the shadows," she said, her tone wispy as it faded into the night.

"That's why I'm here. I need your help."

She shook her head. "This is not your place. It's nobody's place now." Her gaze shifted from me to a dark space just beyond my circle. "The longer she's here, the further his wrath reaches."

"Who? The Goddess? I'm here to defeat her."

The spirit floated to me, her eyes full of pity. "No one defeats the wicked."

"I do," I said with conviction. "She has my loved ones and I won't leave until they're found."

She froze. Then her eyes turned wild. "He's coming."

"Who?" I asked, quickly scanning the area. I saw nothing but the club in a crumbling form.

Her body started to fade and right before she disappeared, she whispered, "The evil one."

# CHAPTER 17

"*D*on't listen to her," a masculine voice said from behind me.

I spun, expecting to see the evil one himself. Except he didn't feel evil and he certainly didn't look it. The spirit was a young man who wore board shorts, a T-shirt, flip-flops, and had some sort of metal leaf pendant dangling from a cord around his neck. "The evil one isn't coming?"

He shrugged. "It's possible, but she's been saying that for days. It hasn't happened yet."

"You don't feel anything?"

"I'm dead. What's there to feel?" His grin was lopsided, and I couldn't help the smile that claimed my lips, despite the seriousness of the situation. "Ah, finally someone who isn't obsessed with death and power."

I raised my eyebrows. "What are you talking about? Who else has been here lately?"

He gave me an impatient look. "Who hasn't? The demon hunters are here all the time. And then lately the spirit sucker."

"Genesis? You've seen her?"

He nodded.

My heart raced. If I could find her, I could find Kane and Pyper. "Where?"

His easygoing nature vanished as he backed up and scowled at me. "She truly is evil. A spirit eater. The worst kind of deity."

The way he said the words made me think he'd suffered a loss at her hands. "Does she consume the spirits of the shadows?" Lucien had said she needed spirits to stay young. Did she come here to feed?

He shook his head. "She needs fresh offerings."

*Fresh offerings.* Spirits that came from live beings was what he meant. "Right. That's what I thought and also what I'm trying to prevent. If you have any idea of how I can find her, the information would be most helpful."

His eyes darkened and then flashed with fiery rage. "No one can stop her. The demon makes sure of that."

A bolt of fire came out of nowhere, consuming the surfer-boy spirit. The flames sputtered and sparked and just as quickly vanished, leaving nothing behind.

"Shoot!" I scowled, frustrated and worried the spirit had been taken somewhere horrible...like Hell.

Clapping sounded from beyond my field of vision, followed by a familiar tinkling laugh.

"Genesis!" I cried. "Show yourself."

The Goddess strolled up to my circle. Her skin still sagged with the passage of time, though she appeared thinner, more toned that she had when I'd seen her last. "Are you here to surrender yourself, white witch?"

"Hardly." I reached into my herb bag and clasped my fingers around a smile vial. "I'm here for Kane and Pyper."

She stared at me, her expression incredulous. "You think I'm going to just hand them over to you? Those two delicious beings? I'd heard you were naïve, but I hadn't expected you to be stupid."

I stared at her blankly. "You're the naïve one if you think I'm going to let you take either of them."

"Take?" Her laugh filled the air, making my ears ring. "I already have them." She snapped her fingers and light illuminated the area around her, revealing Pyper and Kane locked together in another shimmering cage.

Pyper clung to Kane, her head buried in his shoulder. But Kane was staring straight at me, his eyes boring into me as if he was trying to talk to me telepathically. I shook my head, indicating I couldn't pick up on whatever it was he wanted to tell me.

"No?" the Goddess mocked, misinterpreting my communication with Kane as a denial of her statement. "They belong to me, and you'll never get them."

Kane's gaze shifted from me to Genesis and back to me again. Then he mouthed, *Take her.*

It was all I needed. If he wanted me to fight her, then I would. Still clutching the small vial, I let the circle of light fade away, leaving no barrier between me and the Goddess.

Her eyes went wide with lust and opportunity. "You're mine now!" She flew at me full force, but before she could reach me, I flung my arm out, releasing the contents of the vial.

Liquid Lily of the Valley splattered over her as I cried, *"Pello pepulli pulsum!"*

She threw her hands up in defense and hissed, smoke coiling from her skin as if I'd drenched her in acid. Screaming, she reached out, trying to grab for me, but it was useless. Her body was being propelled backward away from me in rapid speed.

*Jade!* I heard in my mind and startled when I realized it was Kane calling to me. I turned and met his determined gaze. He pressed his hands to the shimmering barrier, barely wincing at the shock it must've given him. Then he pointed from the barrier to me and back again.

*Break it,* he mouthed.

The magic rushed through me as if he'd commanded it. An electric current of power burst from my fingers. But before it hit the shimmering box, I held my hand out, halting it. Then with my mind, I imagined the magic pooling into itself until it was a large, flat surface. Instead of one powerful thin bolt, it was now a large circumference designed to crush instead of pierce.

Putting all my energy back into the magic, I let loose and it crashed into the shimmering box just as Kane wrapped himself around Pyper, shielding her from the shattered shards of magic.

The ground rumbled under my feet and a roar of energy filled my ears, but all I saw was the angry gashes covering Kane's skin.

"Kane!" My heart nearly pounded out of my chest as I ran forward. He lay limp over Pyper's body as she struggled beneath him.

"Jade?" Pyper called back. "Help."

"I'm coming." I fell to my knees, blocking out the ever-growing ominous sensation that something was seriously wrong. Something worse than Kane being injured. I didn't care. All I could focus on was Kane.

I pulled him off Pyper just enough so she was able to roll out from underneath him. She immediately scrambled to her knees, helping me position Kane on his stomach. I needed to attend to his multitude of wounds.

"Oh my God," I whispered and ran my hands over his back, forcing bits of my magic into him. I couldn't heal his wounds. All I could do was transfer enough energy into him to wake him so we could get out of there.

"He's going to be okay. He has to be." Pyper's voice rose in a high-pitched panic.

"Yes, he will if I have anything to say about it," I agreed with confidence, hoping my insistence would calm her. Unfortunately, other than the fact that Kane was still breathing, he hadn't responded.

Pressure built around us as if the walls were closing in on us. I had to focus. Had to do anything to awaken Kane.

"Jade," Pyper whispered, her voice hoarse.

"What?" I pushed Kane over on his back, wincing at the thought of all those wounds hitting the dirty ground.

"We need to go. Now."

I glanced up and barely held back a cry of horror. The fabric of the shadows was ripping right before our eyes. Long red-leather claws poked out of the tear and slid down, slicing a long gash. One black eye peered at me, followed by an ominous laugh so evil it seemed to touch me deep in my soul.

My body recoiled, pain clutching at my gut, but I couldn't tear my attention away. The demon trying to crawl right into the shadows felt...familiar. I focused on Kane and placed my hand over his heart. His energy rushed into me, mixing with the demon's, and suddenly I knew why the demon's energy was familiar.

The awful, gut-wrenching evil that streamed from the demon also had a tiny hint of Kane's incubus energy. An undeniable allure that was probably used to seduce souls into Hell. My stomach rolled with the association.

"Kane, wake up," I pleaded and forced my magic straight into his heart.

He woke with a gasp, his eyes wide with shock.

"We need to go," I said to him, trying to tug him to his feet.

Pyper grabbed his other arm and the two of us got him upright.

"Hang on," I said to Pyper then looked Kane in the eye. "We need to do this together. We're going home."

He seemed to understand and when I nodded, we both took a step.

The three of us tilted and a second later, we landed in a tangle of limbs in the middle of the club, not home. Good enough. At least we were out of the shadows. I scrambled to my knees, quickly taking inventory. Pyper was sitting up, holding her head, and Kane was lying on his back, staring up at the ceiling.

Hot tears welled in my eyes at the sight of them. I hadn't truly believed I'd find them in the shadows. Or that I'd be able to get them out by myself.

"You did well," I heard Bea say from somewhere nearby.

I jumped up and spun.

My mentor stood next to Rosalee and two of the younger witches of the coven. They were holding tapered candles and the scent of sage filled the air. They'd come to the club to do some sort of cleanse. "Lucien called you."

Bea handed her candle to Rosalee and nodded as she walked over to me. "We wanted to be here in case there was anything we could do to help." She glanced down at Kane and frowned. "He's hurt."

"It was me," I forced out. "To free them I had to..." I couldn't get the rest of the words out. Emotion choked me.

Bea patted my arm sympathetically. "We all do whatever it is we have to do. Let's get you three home and we'll work on mending everyone's wounds."

"Thank you," I said, grateful she was here and taking charge.

I SAT NEXT to the bed, holding Kane's hand, while Bea doctored Kane's wounds with an herbal cream. Rosalee and the other coven witches had gone home, while Bea had escorted the three of us to our house. Now she was on a mission to put Kane back together.

"These will heal in no time, Jade," she said, swiping healing balm over one of Kane's cuts.

"It looks awful," I said, eyeing one of the ugly gashes.

"Only the first bit when she applies the cream," Kane said, opening his eyes to meet my gaze. "After that, the area goes numb."

"Well, that's something at least."

"How's Pyper?" he asked and flinched again.

"She's resting in the other room with Charlie." I clutched the bottle of water I was holding.

His penetrating gaze bored into me. "That's not what I asked."

I grimaced. "Not that great. She's nauseated and has a headache. I can't get Ian on the phone, though she doesn't seem to care that much."

Kane scowled. He'd never been a fan of Ian's, especially since I'd gone out with him once before Kane and I had gotten together. But he'd been trying, since Pyper was dating him. "Where is he? Chasing ghosts again? While his girl is fighting off crazy Goddesses and demons?"

"He was asked to work on that traveling ghost reality show. He's been gone for a week."

"He should be here."

"Why? So he could set up his equipment and study the supernatural?" I sat back in my chair. "That's not what she needs right now."

All the conviction drained from Kane's face as he closed his eyes. "No. It isn't."

Bea finished her administrations and signaled for me to join her in the other room.

"I'll be back," I told Kane. "I have to talk to Bea and then I'll check on Pyper."

"About?" He rolled to his side and glanced at Bea.

She didn't look up as she gathered her herbal remedies.

"Witch stuff, I'm sure." I smiled at him. "I'll check on Pyper afterward."

He didn't look happy we were going to talk in another room, but he nodded anyway. No doubt he could use a moment to collect himself.

I squeezed his hand before I let go and then followed Bea out of the room.

Lailah was sitting at the kitchen table, both hands wrapped around a cup of tea. Bea sat next to her as I rummaged around in the cupboards until I found a fresh bag of sugar cookies. Tearing the bag open, I joined them at the table and then gobbled down two cookies before passing them around.

Bea shook her head as Lailah joined me in my cookie scarf-a-thon.

"We have a situation," Bea said.

"Would it involve the fact that we left a demon in the shadows and that a lesser Goddess is trying to eat peoples' spirits?" I bit into another cookie.

"Yes…and no." Bea poured herself a cup of tea but made no move to drink it.

I glanced at Lailah. She was studying her cookie like it was the last speck of food on the planet. "What's going on?"

"It's Pyper," Lailah said quietly.

"What about her?" I put my cup down and swallowed hard. "Is she hurt?"

Lailah shook her head. "No. Not physically. At least, not yet." She frowned. "Lucien filled us in on the Goddess and what she's doing here."

"Okay." My blood rushed to my head as my patience started to wane. "Just tell me what's going on."

Lailah pushed back from the table and blew out a long breath. "Charlie and Kat came back to us without any hold from Genesis. Pyper didn't."

My gut clenched as I realized what they were trying to tell me. "Pyper's still compromised by an extra soul, isn't she?" I hadn't seen the soul leave. I hadn't broken the hold Genesis had on her. I'd only kicked the Goddess's ass and brought Pyper and Kane home.

Lailah nodded. "And that means Genesis can control Pyper no matter where she is. We can't protect her."

A chill crawled over my body. "At all?"

The angel shook her head slowly. "We can try, but all it takes is Genesis calling the soul back to her. And if that happens, Pyper could disappear right before our eyes."

# CHAPTER 18

*J*umped out of my chair. "Then I'll just expel the extra soul. I did it with Kat. I can do it with Pyper, too."

Lailah shook her head sadly. "I wish it was that easy. The soul occupying Pyper is magical. Whoever it belonged to before was likely a witch. It's started to fuse with hers."

I sank back down onto the chair, my gut feeling as if the wind had just been knocked out of me. "Dammit! We need protection wards or something. Anything until we can defeat the Goddess.

"We will," Bea said mildly. "But all that takes too long. Complex wards take time to cure. It's going to take some time."

"So what? We just sit here and wait for Genesis to take her?" I couldn't believe how calm they were being about the situation. If this had been one of the coven witches, I was sure they'd be springing into action. "I can't—"

"Jade." Bea put her hand up to stop the onslaught of my rant. "Lailah has a plan. We just need to get it cleared first."

I took a deep breath, trying to calm myself. "By who?"

"The high angel."

"Chessandra?" I asked incredulously. "She doesn't care about regular people. She only cares about souls."

"Exactly," Lailah said. "If this foreign soul stays with Pyper, eventually they'll either completely merge or one of them will take over. Since the foreign soul is tainted with energy from Hell, it's likely it'll cause damage to Pyper's pure one. The only thing we can do at this point is ask Chessandra to take her to the angel realm, where they can keep an eye on her to make sure she isn't harmed in any way."

"Is that the only option?" Kane asked from behind me.

I startled and twisted to look up at him. "Dang it. I had no idea you were there."

He put his hand on my shoulder and straightened me out. "Will they take care of her?" Clearly he'd heard most of the conversation.

"I think so." Lailah fingered another cookie but didn't eat it. "At least until we can deal with the lesser Goddess."

"Then we'll request a meeting with Chessandra." Kane glanced down at me. "Are you okay with that?"

"I…" I closed my eyes and gave a little shake of my head. "I don't know. We need to ask Pyper."

"I really don't think she has a choice," Lailah said, all her sympathetic nervousness gone. Now that she had Kane on board, it appeared she was confident her plan was the way to go.

"Let's talk to her first." I stood and glared at all of them. I knew they had Pyper's best interest at heart, but I couldn't just send her to the angels without clearing it with her first. While they weren't evil, they didn't exactly care about individuals either. If something happened to Pyper's soul, there was no telling what they'd do.

"Of course we'll talk to her first," Kane said and placed his hand on the small of my back. "We'll check on her now."

Lailah sent him a relieved smile as we left the room.

"I don't like it," I said, standing outside the guest room door.

"I don't either, but I can't let that evil thing get her hands on Pyper again. She has no way to defend herself. As long as she's in the angel realm, the Goddess can't get to her."

He had a point. No one could cross the borders of the angel realm except angels and those they invited. Their magic couldn't either. Physically, Pyper would be safe…as long as we forced Chessandra to give her word they'd protect Pyper *and* her soul.

"Ready?" Kane asked, gesturing to the door.

"Ready."

He knocked once.

A faint "Come in" sounded from inside the guestroom.

We found Kat and Charlie inside with Pyper. The three of them were sitting cross-legged on the bed with a bag of red licorice in the middle of them.

"Hey," I said softly.

They all waved and gave us tired smiles.

"You guys having a party without us?" Kane teased.

"Yeah, one with Red Vines and wine." Kat held up her glass of Cabernet.

I laughed. "Sounds like the best kind of party."

Charlie got up. "Here, have a seat. I'm going in search of something with a little more substance." She winked at me as she passed us.

"Me, too," Kat said as she stood and wobbled a little. She giggled. "Oops. Guess that wine went to my head."

"I'm pretty sure there's some leftover pasta in the fridge," I said watching her stumble after Charlie.

"Lightweight," Pyper called after her.

Kat raised her middle finger and flipped her off without looking back.

Pyper just laughed, her face lighting up.

It brought tears to my eyes. I didn't want to ship her off to the angel realm.

"Well, take a seat and tell me whatever it is you have to say," she ordered and patted the bed.

Kane chuckled and sat at the end of the bed, while I grabbed a Red Vine and leaned against the headboard.

"Did anyone fill you in on what happened?" Kane asked.

Pyper nodded. "Lailah and Kat did."

"Do you still have a strange desire to work a corporate job?" I asked and made a face.

Pyper let out a long sigh and nodded. "It's really weird."

"There's a reason for that." I met Kane's gaze and nodded for him to continue.

But before he could say anything, Pyper said, "I'm still carrying an extra soul, aren't I?"

Kane nodded. "Yes. And Lailah says you're in danger if you stay here. The lesser Goddess has complete control over that soul. She thinks you should go to the angel realm until we can deal with the Goddess."

Pyper took in a sharp breath.

"Lailah says it's the only place you'll be safe," I added, trying to keep my tone neutral. I didn't want her to go. The entire idea made me uncomfortable. But I didn't have a better plan.

She pulled her hair out of its neatly tied ponytail and went to work on redoing it. A sure sign she was nervous. I couldn't blame her. Then her blue eyes flashed as she met Kane's gaze. "I'll do it, but you have to promise to take that bitch down."

He moved and sat next to her, pulling her to him. "That you can count on."

I slipped off the bed, preparing to give them a few minutes alone together, but Pyper reached out and clasped my wrist. "Wait."

"What is it?" I asked.

"I just wanted—" Her eyes widened and her face paled as she stared past me near the door.

"Pyper?" Kane asked, his voice a mix of panic and concern.

I glanced from her to the place near the door. Nothing was there. Nothing I could see, anyway. But awe and wonder, mixed with shock, burst from Pyper. Her energy took on a lightness that I usually associated with joy.

"Pyper?" Kane nudged her slightly to get her attention.

"What do you see?" I asked her quietly.

"Not what. Who." She turned to me, tears standing in her bright eyes. Then her other hand wrapped around Kane's as she started to tremble.

"Who is it, Pyps?" Kane whispered.

"It's Mom." She let go of both of us and crawled off the bed, her hand outstretched.

Kane shot me a worried glance. "Do you feel anything out of the ordinary? Any evil or dark magic or anything?"

I shook my head, transfixed by the joy on Pyper's face. "No. Not at all. Has her mom passed?" I asked in a hushed tone.

He bent his head to mine. "Yes."

"I think she's here."

We watched tears stream down Pyper's face as she choked out, "Where have you been all this time? How come I haven't seen you before?" Her hand squeezed as if she was holding hands with someone. Raw emotion shone in her wet eyes and then her lips curled into a small smile. She met Kane's eyes. "Mom says she has been here the whole time, but I couldn't see her. It appears my time spent sharing my body with a spirit has awakened my seer senses."

"That's wonderful," Kane said, happiness for her radiating off him.

"Yeah." Pyper nodded and then she laughed. "Mom also says she's been watching you, Kane."

Kane let out a startled groan. "Seriously? Tell her I'm profoundly sorry about anything she's seen."

Pyper laughed and shook her head, still appearing to be listening to her mother. "She can hear you just fine and she says she's proud of you, that she's thankful you've—" she choked back a small sob, "—been watching over me all these years." She sniffed and nodded.

"It's the least I can do after she created such a generous and supportive daughter," Kane said as he rose from the bed and went to stand next to Pyper.

My heart sang with joy that Pyper was getting a moment with her mother, but I felt like an intruder. Pyper loved me and I loved her, but Kane was her family. Her best friend. And that wasn't a relationship I wanted to get in the middle of. I pressed against the headboard and clasped my hands together, trying to fade into the background.

"Mom's laughing at you," Pyper said and ran a palm down her cheek. Then she sobered and straightened as she appeared to be taking something in. After a few moments she nodded and clutched Kane's arm, leaning into him. "Oh my God."

"Is she gone?" Kane guessed.

"Yeah...she told me to go with the angels. That they'd take care of me no matter what happens." She glanced back at me. "And that my soul is important. They won't want to mess with it."

I raised a curious eyebrow. "Really? I wonder what that means."

Pyper shook her head. "I have no idea. But she seemed pretty adamant about it."

"Well, all souls are important to the angels. We already know that. We just need to make sure they don't go trying to take it from you." The physical memory of my soul being ripped from me was still enough to bring me to my knees if I let it.

Fear rippled from Pyper, and I wanted to kick myself for scaring her.

"I'm sorry," I said. "I'm told what happened to me was highly unusual. I'm sure it's not anything to worry about."

"No. Don't be sorry. It's important to remember they aren't completely trustworthy." She wrapped her arms around herself and shivered. "I feel weird."

Kane chuckled and then pulled her into a sympathetic hug. "Don't we all?"

She hiccupped through a small sob as she buried her face in his chest. "Stop trying to make me laugh."

"I wasn't. Not really." He kissed the top of her head and met my gaze.

It was time.

# CHAPTER 19

*K*ane, Pyper, and I stood together in the living room as Lailah raised her arms and called the light.

A second later, Chessandra and my father, Drake, appeared.

"Jade," my father said. "It's good to see you're well."

"Well" was relative. And I didn't especially want to see him. I recently found out he was my father, and I barely knew him. He'd left my mom before I was even born for his mate, Chessandra. Every angel had one. It was only a matter of time before they found each other. It was a connection humans didn't share. I forced a tight smile. "Hello."

"What information do you have?" Chessandra asked. She never was one for niceties.

"We haven't seen your missing angel. But we think we're getting closer to what's going on with the shadows."

"And?"

"Nothing definitive yet," I hedged. I hadn't told anyone what I'd felt when the demon had been trying to rip through the fabric of the shadows. I needed to talk to Kane about it first. And possibly Maximus, even though going back to the Brotherhood was just about the last thing I wanted to do.

Chessandra narrowed her eyes, suspicion staring back at me.

I stifled a sigh and went for what we did know. I told her everything we'd learned about Genesis. "She eats spirits in order to maintain youth. So it's possible she's the one draining the angels. According to Lucien's research, she also has to bring one angel to the demon she made her fountain of youth deal with…and as much as I don't want to even think about it, it's likely she has your missing angel."

Chessandra's fists clenched. "We need to know what's going on with the shadows."

"You'll know when we know," I said calmly.

"We've lost an angel." Her tone was cold and full of judgment.

The reality of what she'd said hit me hard, gutted me even. None of us were so self-centered that we'd just leave an innocent with the Goddess— Holy shit. We had. Zoe. I had no idea who she was really, or even where she could be. But I'd taken Pyper and Kane home from the shadows without even giving her a second thought.

"We'll find her," I promised. Kane shifted beside me, but I didn't dare look at him. I didn't want to know if he disapproved.

The anger fell from Chessandra's expression and she seemed to lean into Drake. He wrapped an arm around her in support. I couldn't keep from staring at them. I'd never seen Chessandra show weakness before. Not even when her sister, Mati, had been stuck in the void not too long ago. The stress of not knowing how to keep her people safe must've been wearing on her.

"We have a request," I said.

Chessandra looked from me to Kane and back again. "Yes?"

I placed my hands on Pyper's shoulders and glanced at Lailah. She nodded her encouragement, and I forced the words out. "The Goddess infected Pyper with another soul. One she controls. We're under the impression that should the Goddess call the other soul to her, Pyper will be at her mercy. We're respectfully requesting that Pyper be given sanctuary in the angel realm until we're able to resolve this situation with the lesser Goddess."

Chessandra stared at me, her expression blank. Drake studied Pyper, his green eyes seeming to pierce her with his gaze.

"Is it true?" Chessandra asked Drake.

He nodded. "Yes, she's a vessel for two souls."

I vaguely wondered why Chessandra hadn't been able to sense the souls for herself, but I didn't have time to ask.

"Your request is granted." Chessandra raised her hand, and the bright white light shone once again in our living room.

Drake held his hand out to Pyper.

She glanced back at us, fear crawling all over her.

"It'll be fine," Kane soothed. "You'll be safe there. And we'll come for you before you know it." He stepped forward and kissed the top of her head. "See you soon."

Pyper stared up at him and then the light vanished, taking her, Drake, and Chessandra with it.

A pang of loss hit me hard. I hated to see her go. At the same time, a weight lifted from my bruised heart. She would be safe for now.

"Jade." Kane slipped his hand over the back of my neck.

"Yeah?" I glanced up to see his eyes just as weary as mine felt.

"Maybe we should get some rest."

I nodded. "That sounds good."

We found Lailah and Bea in the kitchen with Kat and Lucien. "Where's Charlie?" I asked.

"The guest room. She's trying to get some sleep," Kat said.

I yawned and my eyes watered.

Bea stood abruptly. "We should go."

"You don't have to," Kane said. "We're going to try to get some sleep, but if you four are brainstorming or trying to work anything out, there's no need to go."

"No. It's the middle of the night. It's time."

I glanced at the clock, noting the sun would rise in a couple of hours. "Actually, it's the morning."

"All the more reason." Bea caught Lailah's eye. "I'll give you a lift."

The angel rose, her mascara smudged under her eyes. "Thank you."

The pair of them took off, making us promise to call with any new developments. Kat and Lucien followed.

"Take care of her," I said, giving Lucien a hug.

"Count on it." He shook Kane's hand, and a moment later Kane and I were finally alone again.

He didn't say anything as he took my hand and led me back to our room. But instead of stopping at the bed, he steered me into the bathroom and turned the shower on. I was entirely too exhausted to do anything other than let him undress me and place me under the warm stream of water.

The shower door clicked closed, and then Kane stepped up behind me, slipping his hands around my waist as we stood there, letting the water wash away the horror of the last twenty-four hours.

"Let's not do that again, okay?" I said.

"Which part? The dreamwalking? Battling an evil Goddess? Or..."

"The part where we were dreamwalking and then we weren't. That's not right."

He chuckled and nuzzled my neck. "Agreed."

Kane took his time gently washing me. I reveled in his soft touch, blocking out all the events of the last few days. When he was done, he dried me off and carried me back to bed. And this time when we fell asleep in each other's arms, there was only sweet oblivion.

WE SLEPT most of the day away and woke up early afternoon. Charlie was already in the living room, watching reruns of *The Walking Dead*.

"Seriously?" I gave her my you've-got-to-be-kidding look. "Zombies? After all that's been going on?"

She took a sip from an oversized coffee mug. "Don't judge me. It helps take my mind off things."

"If you say so." I headed to the kitchen and busied myself by baking a batch of chocolate cream cheese cupcakes. The over-the-top treats were my number one go-to comfort food. Unless cheesecake was available, but cupcakes were easier to make.

Kane appeared fresh from another shower. His hair was damp and he smelled faintly of his fresh rain soap. "Cupcakes?"

I smiled when I caught his amused look. "Yes. I know I should be researching or brainstorming or something, but none of that is going to happen until I go to my happy place. And these cupcakes are the only thing that will help."

One of his dark brows rose in question. "The only thing?" The heat in his eyes nearly had me abandoning the rich chocolate batter.

"Maybe not the only thing." I grabbed the front of his white button down shirt and pulled him close. Smiling up at him, I lowered my lashes and said, "Show me what you've got."

He bent his head and brushed his lips over mine, his tongue lapping at mine as he let out a satisfied moan. When he pulled away, he stared at my mouth hungrily. "You taste really, really good. I think in light of my sampling, you should keep baking the cupcakes."

"What?" I asked, breathless, not caring a damn about the baking.

He laughed and touched a finger to the corner of my lips, then pressed it against my mouth.

Rich, sweet chocolate melted on my tongue.

"You've been sampling as you go, and damn if tasting you just now didn't make my mouth water."

"Oooh." Heat claimed my cheeks as I thought of all the alternate ways we could use the cupcake batter. Smacking my lips, I let my gaze travel the length of his body.

Kane dipped his finger into the batter and then brought his hand up to my neck. Pressing the tip of his finger against my pulse, he smeared the chocolate over my skin.

Eyes smoldering, he bent his head and his lips closed over the area, gently sucking.

I let out a little gasp and melted into him.

"Oh, jeez," Charlie said and then cleared her throat.

I jumped backward, but Kane just straightened and smiled down at me.

"Pardon me," she said, moving past us to the fridge. "Looks like you two didn't quite spend enough time in bed today." She smirked and grabbed a glass for her soda.

"Uh—"

"Jade needed cupcakes," Kane said, laughing.

Charlie's lips twitched. "I can see that."

"For Pete's sake." I swatted Kane's shoulder. "Y'all just give me a break or I won't share when they're done."

"In that case..." Charlie quickly poured her drink and then scooted toward the dining room. "We can't have that." With a wink, she disappeared.

Kane just stared at me, his eyes dancing.

"What are you thinking about?"

He tucked a lock of hair behind my ear and gave me the most tender look. I thought I might cry right there.

"What?" I asked softly.

"I was just thinking about how full my life has been since you came into it."

I frowned. "But we're always off fighting demons or ghosts, or black magic. You can't tell me you don't long for a little peace."

He chuckled, but then shook his head. "Peace wasn't part of the deal, and I knew that when I signed on with you." Trailing his fingers lightly down the side of my face, he added, "I think you know what I long for."

I stared at his lips, my mouth suddenly desperate for his. "Chocolate?"

"Yeah, chocolate. The melted kind. All over your naked—"

The stove timer buzzed, cutting him off.

"Oops!" I pushed him back and grinned. "Cupcakes are calling."

"Damn." Kane gave me a mournful look, grabbed another cup of coffee, and took off to talk with Charlie.

I replaced the tray in the oven with a fresh one and then, too impatient to wait, I pulled one of the cupcakes out of the tray and cut into it. Hot cream cheese and melted chocolate chips oozed from the center of the little cakes.

Perfection.

I closed my eyes, bit into the cupcake, and pretended for just a moment that the decadent little cake was enough to make everything better.

# CHAPTER 20

wo hours later, with Kane off supplying Maximus with an update, I stood in front of Mati's house teetering on four-inch silver heels. They were higher than what I normally wore. Much higher, but she'd said dressy casual for girls' night, and the shoes were doing the bulk of the work. Smoothing my black gauzy blouse, I braved her uneven sidewalk and then climbed the stairs. By the time I got to the top, my baby toe on my right foot was screaming in protest.

"Crap," I muttered and slipped my foot out of the death contraption. I wasn't going to make it through the next few hours if that kept up.

"Why don't you just numb it?" Mati asked from her doorway. Her sleek, dark hair was piled effortlessly on her head and she wore a simple, short sheath dress that showed a lot of leg. A long silver necklace adorned with a tree of life pendant completed her outfit.

"With what?" I asked, wiggling my toes.

"Uh, magic?" She stepped back into her house, holding the door open. "Come in for a second before we go."

I hobbled inside and said, "I'm not a healer. I'm better at giving boosts of energy. You know, something to wake someone up, or refresh them. Not numb anything."

"I see." She pursed her lips. "I'm not a healer either, but I can manipulate body parts." Her lips formed a seductive smile.

Of course she could. She was a sex witch.

"Take a seat. Let me see what I can do." Mati gestured to her pristine white couch.

I did as she said and placed my foot on her coffee table.

Crouching down, she brushed her fingers down the side of my foot and my little toe. Magic tingled over my skin, grew warm and then cool until I could no longer feel half of my foot.

"Hey." I grinned. "It worked."

"Good. I'll be right back." She disappeared into her bedroom and after a few minutes she reappeared, wearing heels with laces that crisscrossed halfway up her calves. Her sexiness was off the charts. Even if she hadn't been a sex witch, she'd have no problem finding suitors. "Ready?"

"Sure." I stuffed my foot back into my silver shoe and stood, wobbling as my numb foot tried to balance me. I grabbed the back of her couch before I toppled over. "Yikes."

"What is it? Did the spell go wrong or something?"

I shook my head. "No. Just me being uncoordinated. I'll be fine."

"If you say so." She sent me a dubious look as she grabbed her small clutch bag.

"Honestly. It's all good." I followed her outside and teetered all the way down the stairs, clutching the railing. *Holy cow bells.* When had I become utterly ridiculous?

Mati laughed. "You're not going to make it."

"Sure I am. The car's right there." I pointed to Kane's Lexus I'd parked in front of her house.

"We were going to walk."

I groaned. I wasn't the most coordinated person on the planet on a good day, but with my foot half numb and the sidewalks of the neighborhood just as uneven as the streets, I was likely to kill myself. "Is there parking near this place?"

"Yes. But do you think driving is going to be any better?" She glanced down at my foot. My right foot.

I let out a long sigh. "No. Let's go. I'll just limp."

She wrinkled her nose in sympathy. "Sorry about that. I was just trying to help."

"No worries. Lead on. I'm ready for girls' night."

Mati led the way down six blocks and over two, and when she stopped she pointed. "See, you made it."

I glanced up, noting the rustic open-air bar with the music patio. "It's cool."

"Just wait."

"Huh?" I took another step and promptly tripped, falling forward into a planter that was partially blocking the sidewalk.

"Holy shit, Jade. Are you okay?" Mati took my hand, steadying me as I got my feet underneath myself.

I glanced down at my white pants and grimaced. "Damn!" My right pant leg was streaked with dirt. "Classy."

"Oh, Jade." Mati put a hand over her mouth to keep from laughing. "I'm sorry. This sucks."

I sucked in a breath. "So much for dressy casual. It's not like the place is real fancy anyway." It was just an open-air bar. Once I was seated, no one would even notice.

She grimaced. "It doesn't look like much from here, but when we get inside…well, you'll see."

Frustrated beyond belief, I sulked behind Mati into the Coven Pointe bar. My eyes widened once we got inside. It wasn't a bar at all. We were in a private entrance that was closed off from the rest of the establishment. The walls were lined with high-end Wiccan art, and there was a hostess at a podium waiting to take us to our table.

She smiled at Mati. "Hello, Matisse. You're looking especially lovely tonight."

"Thanks, Dara. This is my friend, Jade. She's joining us tonight."

Dara studied me, and her smile vanished as she took in my disheveled appearance. Heat crawled up my face and my body temperature seemed to raise at least ten degrees. Gritting my teeth, I averted my gaze.

"We had a bit of an accident just before we got here," Mati said, slipping her arm through mine.

"I see. Well." Dara tucked a couple of menus under her arm and turned around. "Follow me. Your party is waiting."

She led us through two rooms, each of them richly decorated with a witch theme. One was potions, the other astrological. The third room was full of lit candles and a collection of what had to be handcrafted pentagrams. In the middle was a large round table where Dayla, Fiona, and two other women sat, staring at me.

I was grateful for the soft candlelight, though I was certain my white pants weren't hiding anything.

"Matisse," Dayla rose and hugged her niece. "You look lovely as always."

Mati smiled. "So do you, Auntie."

Dayla wore a gauzy white blouse with cutouts in the shoulders to show off her toned arms, and sleek black trousers. Her light hair was done up in a complicated updo and there was a pentagram pendant fastened to the front of her choker necklace. She screamed elegance and money. All the other ladies were put together just as nicely, and it made me want to slip into the shadows just to escape their judgmental stares.

I chose to act as if I didn't look like the drunk who'd

embarrassed herself on the red carpet and held my hand out to the leader of the Coven Pointe witches. "It's good to see you, Dayla. Thanks for including me in such a lovely evening."

"Ms. Calhoun," she said with an air of formality as she scanned the length of my body. "It appears you could use some help."

I shook my head. "No, I—"

She reached out and took my hand in hers. Foreign magic pricked my palm and then danced along my skin until I glowed with red-tinged light. The magic dug in, pinching at my skin, and I cried out, belatedly reaching for my own power. But before I could even think to defend myself, Dayla's magic left my body and concentrated on the fabric of my clothes.

"What's...?" I watched as the magic rippled and then burst into tiny fireworks of magic.

"There. All better." Dayla smiled serenely and sat back in her chair.

I glanced down. My mouth dropped as I realized she'd changed the color of my clothes and magically cleaned them. My dirty white pants were now black, and my favorite white shirt was now sunshine yellow. I hated yellow. It made my strawberry blond hair look orange.

Dayla cast me a look, daring me to challenge her. I had the feeling she was making sure I knew who had the power here. Message received.

I did my best to keep the scowl off my face, but only because I wanted information from these witches. It was considered very bad form to use magic on someone without asking. The last time Dayla had done something like that, she'd spelled Kane into an incubus. My wardrobe was a minor infraction compared to that, but it still pissed me off.

"Have a seat, Jade," Mati said, eyeing me carefully.

"Sure." I sat between Mati and Fiona, Mati's cousin.

Dayla rose again and glanced at me. "Jade, these ladies are all part of the Coven Pointe Coven. You know Fiona. This lady to my right is Maven. She's Matisse's mother."

I nodded to the witch with kind blue eyes.

She smiled at me. "It's nice to meet you finally, Ms. Calhoun. Thank you for your help this last spring when Mati was trapped in another world."

"No thanks is necessary. I'm just happy Mati is home safe."

"And this is Jocelyn." Dayla waved at a pixie of a witch who had rings on every finger. She wore one large emerald on a silver chain that hit her just below her breasts. Her right ear was lined with multiple earrings and she had small studs embedded in her cheeks right where her dimples would be. I got the impression she was more likely to be wearing leggings and combat boots than the silk halter top dress. She smoothed her long, jet-black hair and smiled knowingly. She didn't really want to be here either, and the knowledge made me like her instantly.

"Hi, Jocelyn."

"Jade." She nodded in my direction.

Dayla sat back down and took a sip from her martini glass. "Why don't we just get down to business, shall we?"

The other witches nodded and they all swiveled their heads in my direction as if on cue.

My palms started to sweat. All I'd wanted to do was ask Dayla about the shadows and what they might know about it containing Kane's energy, but I wasn't sure I wanted to share that with all of them.

"Well…" I took a sip of water. "I think—"

"Wait, Jade needs a drink first." Mati picked up a padded menu and held it in front of me. "Which one?"

"The Cabernet," I said automatically. I really wanted a beer, but it didn't feel like a beer-appropriate occasion. And a cocktail seemed too dangerous.

"You got it." Mati slid her finger over my choice, and a wine glass materialized out of thin air, along with a bottle of my favorite brand of wine. I reached for it, but the bottle upended and poured me a glass all on its own.

"Wow," I said, staring at the glass now sitting in front of me.

"It's part of the charm." Mati put the menu back. "Okay, now you can tell us your secret."

I nearly choked on a sip of wine. "Secret?"

"Yeah. That's the price into girls' night. Every month we get together and share something we can't tell the rest of the world. You know, witch stuff."

"Oh, uh, give me some time to think of something," I hedged and set the glass down. I wasn't telling them anything until one of them went first. What if they were setting me up? Dayla and Fiona hadn't exactly proved themselves trustworthy the last time I'd dealt with them.

"We want incubus details," Jocelyn said as she leaned in, her eyes alive with mischief.

Mati rolled her eyes. "You always want incubus details."

"I'm living vicariously, all right? Give a witch a break." Jocelyn's gaze landed on me. "Well?"

Son of a… They seemed serious. I hadn't been prepared for this to be a real girls' night. Like one I had with Pyper and Kat. I wasn't exactly turning cartwheels to share even the most mundane details of my life with these witches. I barely knew them.

"I'll go," Mati said suddenly.

I sent her a grateful smile.

"A few nights ago I was in a club with Vaughn and we were dancing. You know how things heat up with a sex witch and an incubus." She waggled her eyebrows for effect.

"Yeah, baby," Jocelyn said.

The three older witches just smiled knowingly.

"Well, there was this other couple who came on to us. You know, Vaughn and I don't really share these days. So when they wouldn't take no for an answer, we really turned on the charm, and well, by the time we were done with them, they were practically having sex right there in the middle of the club."

"Mati." Maven shook her head in disapproval. "That wasn't nice."

"Was it nice when the guy grabbed my ass and told me he wanted to fuck me up against the wall?" Her eyes flashed with impatience.

"Well, no, but—"

"Don't even tell me I have a responsibility here. I was only into Vaughn, trying to have a nice night out. I wouldn't have done anything if he'd backed off when I told him to."

"And what about her?" Dayla asked thoughtfully.

"She stuck her tongue in Vaughn's ear and tried to put her hand down his pants. It wasn't pretty."

Dayla laughed. "Then they got what they deserved."

"So what happened after they lost control on the dance floor?" I asked, fascinated. Kane and I didn't have that problem. Well, not much anyway. But then, I wasn't a sex witch.

"They were caught on the dance monitor and their images went out on a live feed. I heard they both had significant others...who might have happened to find the link in their email boxes. Oops."

"That's boring," Jocelyn said and took a long swig of her drink. "I thought you were going to say they started an orgy or something."

"They almost did, but management threw them out."

"Still boring."

"Well, what's your thing?" Mati asked Jocelyn.

"I turned a rabbit into a man." Her eyes gleamed. "It was the best night of sex I've ever had."

"Holy fuck," I said.

"You can say that again." Jocelyn raised her glass to me.

"You're lying," Mati said, laughing. The other witches chimed in their agreement.

"Ha. You'll never know, now will you."

I peered at her and caught a hint of indignation. She wasn't lying. The image of rabbit-man humping her in rapid motion made me almost spit out my drink.

"Jade? You all right?" Mati asked.

"Fine. Yeah, just fine." I clutched my napkin to my chin, wiping away any residual wine.

"Your turn. What odd thing happened lately?"

If I wanted to stick around and get them to trust me, I had to give them something. But it wasn't going to be sex related. That was going too far. "Let's see...Kane pulled me into a dreamwalk last night, but instead of waking up in our bed, we were separated. He was kept in the shadow world, and I woke up in his club."

Everyone sobered as they stared at me.

"Uh...wrong kind of share?" I made a face. "Sorry, I—"

"It's fine, Jade. We're all just a little wound up about the shadows. Chessandra's told us to stay away," Mati said.

Dayla watched me with her hawkish gaze. Finally she put her glass down. "You're clearly not here for girls' night. You're more uncomfortable than a pig in Spanx. Why don't you just tell us what it is you want?"

The tension drained from my shoulders. That was all I'd wanted to do in the first place. "Here's the deal. The shadows are tainted with poisonous energy. But the energy in that world feels like Kane's...almost, but not quite. Because of that,

Maximus took his dagger away while the Brotherhood investigates."

"And what do you want from us?" Dayla narrowed her eyes at me.

"Nothing. Just information. If you know anything more about incubi or how their energy can be stolen without their knowledge."

"Stolen without their knowledge?" Mati asked. "Is that even possible?"

Dayla shook her head. "No. Incubi can be manipulated to do things they don't want to do, though."

"Kane didn't do this," I said with conviction. "I can tell."

"Empath," Maven mumbled.

Mati nodded. "Yep. She'd know."

"If it truly wasn't him," Dayla said, "then it's someone or something related to him."

I frowned and fingered the napkin. "None of his relatives live nearby."

"They don't have to be living. For that matter, they don't even need to be in this world." She went very still as if she were listening to a far away voice, and then her tone dropped a register as she stared right at me, her eyes deep black pools. "Research his family tree. Once you find out where he comes from, you'll find your answer."

# CHAPTER 21

*I* wasn't sure if Dayla had gone into a trance when she'd told me to research Kane's family history, but afterward everyone got really quiet and refused to talk about it. Dayla herself had seemed drained all of a sudden, and girls' night ended roughly twenty minutes later.

Mati kept mostly to herself on the walk back to her place. I trailed behind her, opting to go barefoot because after the zap of magic from Dayla, the numbness had worn off. My toes were killing me.

We stopped next to Kane's car.

Mati touched my arm. "Take care, all right?"

"I'll try." I forced a smile.

She nodded and then pulled me into a hug, whispering, "Vaughn's trying to help. Just know Kane has a friend in him if he needs him."

I pulled back, somewhat stunned. "Really?"

She nodded. "He's not super crazy about the Brotherhood's method of doing things."

That I could understand. "Thanks…" I paused. "Is Dayla a seer?"

Mati stiffened.

"Hey, if it's a secret, forget I asked. My aunt's one and she never talks about it."

Mati let out an exaggerated sigh. "It's not exactly a secret. We just don't talk about it much because she's uncomfortable with the ability. So yes, she is a seer, but she keeps her visions to herself because of an incident that happened years ago. Every time one comes on, she holes up for months. It's why the mood shifted so suddenly."

"I see." And I really did. I knew Gwen had never suffered through a tragic incident due to her visions. Something like that would've killed her. She wasn't a witch, but if she was and had used her power to help someone and it had backfired, she would've never gotten over it. "I hope Dayla's back to herself sooner rather than later," I said as I climbed into the car.

"Thanks, Jade. I'm sure she'll be fine. Let me know if there's anything we can do to help."

"I will. Thanks. " I sped off down the street as the gorgeous sex witch climbed the stairs to her apartment.

On the drive back to my side of the city, I called Kane.

"Hey, gorgeous," he said on the first ring.

"Hey, yourself. Any luck?"

"No. They were all out, supposedly hunting demons," he said bitterly. "What about you? Any leads?"

"I think so. Meet me at Bea's house?"

"Sure, but I'll have to catch a cab."

I clutched his steering wheel tighter. "Right. I have your car."

He laughed. "No problem. See you soon."

The line went dead, and the uneasiness that had been forming in my gut started to fade. Dayla's words while she'd been in a trance had resonated with me. I had a hunch, but I needed to run it by Bea and Lucien first.

I STOOD in Bea's kitchen, leaning against the counter and was stuffing my face with a turkey sandwich, when Lucien joined me. I'd called him to meet us as soon as I'd pulled into Bea's driveway. If my theory was correct, we were going to need his input.

"Ready?" he asked.

I nodded and grabbed a cup of coffee. Bea and Kane were already waiting for us at the table.

Kane pulled the chair out for me, but I shook my head. "I'd rather stand if you don't mind."

He gave me a noncommittal shrug and pushed the chair back in.

I put my mug down and walked a few paces. "Tonight was interesting." I paused and met Bea's gaze. "This information is not to go any further than this room, but it appears Dayla is a seer."

Bea nodded. "Yes, I was aware of that."

Of course she was. "Okay, so tonight she went into a trance while we were talking about Kane's energy tainting the shadows. She said to look up where he comes from. To search his family ties. And a few days ago, Gwen called with a message telling me to research the history. So clearly there's a pattern here."

The three of them nodded.

Then Kane said, "Are they saying someone I'm related to did this to the shadows?"

"Yes. I think so. But I don't think we're looking for an

immediate relative. More like a distant one who shares your type of energy."

Bea frowned. "Another incubus? Or a witch?"

The only way Kane could've become an incubus was if he'd had a sex witch in his family line. Incubi were born from sex witches when demons enslaved them. So her question was a reasonable one. "Something like that, but I don't think we're talking about a witch here."

"Then what? Another incubus?" Kane asked.

I shook my head. "A demon."

"You think a demon did this?" Kane got up and moved to lean against the counter. "But how? Ever since I've become a demon hunter, the area near and around the club has been monitored for demons. If any enter within a certain area, the alarms go off. It's only happened once, and we were there to take him down within minutes."

"Because he hasn't entered the shadows yet. Although one tried yesterday before we managed to get away." I grabbed my coffee mug and took a sip. "He's using his Goddess to do the work for him."

"Okay," Lucien said. "Let me see if I'm following this. There's a demon who may be the patriarch of Kane's line who poisoned the shadows to suck the life from angels, and he used his Goddess slave to do his dirty work?"

"Yes, that's my working theory. I saw him yesterday and more than that, I felt him. The energy was horrifically awful, but underneath it all, there was a hint of something that reminds me of Kane. Either way, I feel like if we take this demon down, we solve at least one problem. The Goddess will lose her power. And if he's the one who tainted the shadows, then that would be solved, too."

"It would explain a lot," Bea said, finally joining the conversation. "If he shares blood with Kane and he felt

Kane's presence at some point, he could've latched on and basically stolen some of Kane's incubus energy, in effect connecting them. Only those most intimately familiar with Kane would realize the energy signature in the shadows wasn't his."

"So, I'm not crazy?" I asked glancing around. "We may have found an answer?"

"It's possible," Bea said.

"Assuming everything Jade just said is true, what would we do then?" Lucien asked.

"Then we'd summon the demon and end him." Bea's eyes were hard with determination.

Kane raised his gaze to mine. "I want to run this by the Brotherhood first. See if it's even plausible."

I felt my blood pressure rise with frustration. Now that I had a solid hunch, I wanted to see it through. Was ready to call up the demon and end this disaster as soon as possible.

"Jade, please. If we're going to summon a demon, it makes sense to have the hunters there."

I couldn't argue with that logic. "All right. But we're doing this no matter what Maximus says."

"I never thought any differently." Kane pulled out his phone and dialed. A few minutes later, he tossed his phone on the table with too much force and swore.

"What is it?" I asked.

"They're not taking my calls. They aren't at the house. It's like they up and disappeared."

Man, I hated power-hungry leaders. I vowed to never become that person.

"Call Vaughn," I suggested. "He said he'd do what he could for you. Maybe he can get a message to them."

Kane took a deep breath, visibly calming himself. Then he picked the phone back up and walked outside.

"We're going to do this, right? Summon the demon?" I asked Bea and Lucien.

They shared a look. Then Lucien raised his hands as if to say, *What else are we going to do?*

"I know I don't have to tell you how dangerous this is," Bea said as she clutched one of her spell books.

"But?"

"A demon who makes deals with Goddesses and can suck energy from a world he isn't even in means he's more powerful than any demon you can imagine. This is a major battle, and we have to prepare for it."

Her warning sobered me. "Okay. How do we prepare?"

She stood and waved me over to her kitchen. "Potions. Powerful ones." Handing me the pestle and mortar, she put me to work grinding fresh herbs.

"What are we making?" I asked.

"Everything."

IT WAS JUST after dark the next day when Bea, Lucien, Kane, and the rest of my coven members met at the coven circle. Kane had never heard back from the Brotherhood, though he had spoken with Vaughn. The younger demon hunter hadn't said what they'd been doing, but he'd promised to relay the message.

Bea, Lucien, and I had spent half the night and most of the morning and early afternoon brewing protection spells, healing spells, and a powerful summoning spell.

The air was thick with humidity, and fog covered our sacred circle. Everything was still in the silence. What should've been a peaceful evening instead was ominous and as eerie as if we'd been standing in the city of the dead.

I put those thoughts out of my mind and placed candles around the edge of the circle. My coven members stood off to the side as Lucien filled them in on the plan. None of them were happy about the summoning and two flat out refused.

I joined Lucien and the other coven members and said, "I know this is scary. No one wants to summon a demon...ever. And this one is particularly dangerous, as he's been sucking the life out of people and collecting souls. It seems wrong to summon a demon out of Hell, as that's where we'd like them to stay, but this evil bastard is hurting people without even being here. If we don't do something, we're going to lose more souls. We may already have. An angel and a woman have gone missing. It's my job to see that it doesn't happen again."

Scanning their faces, I focused on Joel, a young college-aged witch who wasn't always the most stable. "You don't have to do this. It isn't your job, nor is it what you signed up for when you decided to be a part of this coven. So if you want to leave, you can. No one will think less of you."

Joel straightened his shoulders and frowned. "I'm not going anywhere."

I smiled at him. "I'm glad to hear it."

A murmur of agreement filtered through the witches and in the end, they all decided to stay, even though at least half of them were so scared their residual energy was physically making me ill.

"Bea?" I called.

"Yes."

"Did we bring any calming herbs?"

She checked her list. "Yes."

"Can you start handing them out to the coven members? I need them to stay on point."

She nodded. "I'm on it."

"Ready for this?" I asked Kane.

He shook his head. "No. Are you?"

"No." Trepidation welled in my chest and all I wanted to do was bury my face in his shoulder. "Why haven't the demon hunters responded?"

He shrugged. "I can't say. But you've done this before and won. I know you can do it again. You're stronger now."

I stared up at him, awe and appreciation overwhelming me. "I hope you're right."

He kissed me tenderly and when he pulled away, he said, "I know I am."

With love filling my heart, I said, "Okay team, let's kick some demon ass."

# CHAPTER 22

*M*agic rippled through the air like static electricity. I stood cloaked in my velvet witch's robe at the northern most point of our circle, a white pillar candle in my left hand. Kane stood beside me, a ceremonial knife in his fist.

"Ready, Jade?" Bea called from across the circle.

I glanced around at the nervous faces of my coven. My stomach rolled with nausea. I'd asked them to take their lives in their hands to summon the worst of the worst, and they'd agreed. The sheer level of trust they'd put in me and Bea was awe inspiring, and the weight of responsibility bearing down on me was crushing. If anything happened to any of them, I knew I wouldn't recover.

"You can do this," Kane whispered to me.

I gave him a tiny nod. We didn't have much of a choice. Kane was our connection to the demon. It was the only way we could summon him. And neutralizing the demon meant weakening the Goddess and cleaning up the shadows. I clutched the protection potion and scanned the witches on the circle. "Please raise your candles."

Everyone clutched a white candle and held it out. The collective magic flared to life. The connection filled me up and strengthened my will. They were all with me one hundred percent. And I'd do anything to keep them safe.

"Before we start, I have a protection spell I'd like to invoke. The way it works is I swallow this potion and then share my power with each of you. It'll keep us connected and create a stronger bond."

Bea smiled her encouragement, and the rest of the coven made murmurs of agreement.

I lifted the vial to my lips, gulped down the cinnamon-flavored potion, and said, "From one to three to three to one, I share my power, thy will be done."

Magic bubbled up from the depths of my being, building pressure in my chest. Then I blew out a breath. Mist expelled from my lips and wound its way through the circle. The moment each of the eight witches was affected, I felt them as if they were a part of me and our magic flowed as one. And then, just as I was ready to start the summoning, Kane's energy rushed into me, binding us even tighter.

I glanced at him. "The protection spell affected you, too?"

He nodded.

"Interesting." I hadn't expected that to happen, since he wasn't part of the coven. "Okay, cool." I glanced around the circle. "Remember, our function here is to lend our magic to the blood sacrifice. Once Kane feeds the earth, everyone will use the candles as an offering. Understood?"

Our connection made it possible for me to feel their agreement before they even vocalized it.

"Good. Then we're ready," I said.

We'd done a number of summonings in the past, and this

one would largely be the same. The only differences were we'd made up a special potion and we were counting on the fact that Kane's blood could call up a demon. If there *was* a DNA connection, this would work. If our hunch was wrong, this might all be for nothing.

I wasn't sure what I hoped for more.

Raising my arms skyward, I held my candle high with both hands. "Magic of the circle, hear my call. The coven of New Orleans holds the key to the power you seek."

A thread of magic spun like a web from me and moved around the circle, mixing with each of the witches. As the threads wound through them, they lifted their candles in offering.

"We're bound together, all united in one goal—to call the one who lives for harm," I called.

The magic intensified around us, churning with anger and disgust. The spell was working. It made my head ache from the evil seeping into our circle.

"From the shadows to Hell and everywhere in between, we summon the evil one." My voice cracked from the raw, fiery power that rumbled from deep in my core. It heated and boiled and ate away at everything I held dear in my heart. Frustrated rage took over as power consumed me. I vibrated with it, longed to lash out, to take something, anything down. I was lost on the wave of righteous indignation, calling up every last bit of power.

The candle slipped from my raised hands, but it didn't fall. It hovered in front of me, the unlit wick taunting me. I spun in Kane's direction, barely seeing him, and yelled, "Now!"

"Take the blood offering!" he shouted as he sliced his palm, dropped the knife then poured the summoning potion over the wound.

The earth rumbled beneath our feet. A few cries of shock reached my ears, but I ignored them.

"Feed off the blood of your descendant. Take it in. Become one," I commanded.

Lightning rippled around the circle. And when Kane's blood hit the spelled earth, my body went rigid, filling up on the spell. The power was intoxicating and instantly pushed back the power that had almost consumed me. I straightened my body, steady and full of pure clean magic. I could do anything. Call anyone. The world was mine to command. "Ignite!" I cried.

The candle in front of me flared to life, the flame scarlet red in the moonlight.

"Ignite!" the rest of the coven echoed.

Magic filled the circle in a thick fog and crackled with intensity.

"Show yourself!" Intense, terrifying magic poured from my fingers. There was a tiny voice inside my head that whispered, *Too much. Let this go. The magic is destroying you.*

But I was too far gone. I couldn't stop even if I wanted to. My body was a slave to the white-hot magic claiming me.

"Offer your sacrifice," an ominous voice called, barely reaching me.

It was the demon. He'd heard our call. "You've been fed the blood of your descendant. Come rejoin him."

A loud boom rumbled through the circle followed by another demand, "Offer your sacrifice!"

I longed to throw the rest of my power into the circle, but something deep inside me stopped me. I was intimately connected to the entire coven. If I lost control, I'd weaken them all. Instead, I turned to Kane. "More blood."

He shook his head. "That isn't what he wants."

"Then what?"

Kane dropped the ceremonial knife and with one last glance at me, he stepped into the circle.

Dark clouds gathered over the circle as currents of magic sparked all around Kane. His skin lit up with the same crimson red flame that blazed on my candle.

"Kane!" I took a step forward.

"No!" He held his hand out, stopping me. "Stay where you are. He's coming."

The rest of the coven members chanted the words of my spell. "From the shadows to Hell and everywhere in between, we summon the evil one."

My vision cleared of the overwhelming magic, and I stood there, holding my candle as I watched the red flames dance over Kane's skin. He didn't appear to be in any pain, but the effect was more than unnerving. In fact, his energy told me he was strong, ready for battle.

"Jade, focus!" Bea ordered from across the circle.

Her voice shook me out of my Kane-induced trance. I opened my senses, let the coven's chant mix with the magic flowing from them to me. And then I bent and unleashed the torrent of energy right into the ground.

The earth rumbled with complaint, nearly knocking me on my ass.

"Hold steady," I heard Lucien call.

I straightened and focused on the disturbance right in the middle of the circle. Magic shot from me, Lucien, Bea, and Rosalee in an arcing stream, and that same red fire jumped from Kane and erupted right where our magic joined.

The blaze grew into an inferno so hot that heat broke out over my entire body. "Whoa."

Kane took a step toward me, his clothes charred, but thankfully his body was unmarred. Our eyes met and in that moment a torrent of relief, mixed with determination, shot from him to me. An overwhelming urge to join him within the circle seized me. I didn't want him to do this alone. Didn't want him in that circle at all. It was too dangerous.

But just as I was about to take a step, the magic that was consuming me vanished, leaving me empty, gutted, and the red fire died to a slow burn right before it winked out. I glanced around, my thoughts jumbled. What had happened?

"Holy crow," one of the younger members muttered.

The air was perfectly still, the night cloaked in near darkness now.

"Did it not work?" one of the female witches asked.

No one answered her. A soft whistle blew in on a light breeze, and I shivered with unease. If we hadn't just been unleashing massive amounts of magic into the atmosphere, I'd think a tornado was coming. The night was thick with humidity as the wind picked up within the circle, swirling around, pushing against us. All of our witch's robes flared out behind each of us.

"He's coming," I said softly.

"No." Kane raised his hand in a stop motion. "He's here."

A loud boom filled the night, followed by a flash of bright red flames once again in the middle of the circle.

We all stared open-mouthed as the flames suddenly quenched, leaving behind a ten-foot demon with red leather skin and unending solid black eyes.

"Oh my God," one of the younger witches said. Another gasped.

Kane took another step in my direction, but the demon swiveled and pointed a finger right at him.

"You! How dare you summon me from my place beside the king?" He took two steps forward and crooked his finger.

Kane doubled over in pain and his body propelled forward as if the demon had him on a hook.

"No!" I threw both hands out in front of me and unleashed the tiny bit of magic still pulsing beneath my heart. The white stream bounced off the demon, fizzled, and then faded away into the night air. Fear surged through me as I acknowledged for the first time that the demon might be more powerful than we'd anticipated. If we couldn't take him down with our collective magic, we were in deep trouble.

The demon scowled in my direction and then gave me a dismissive glance. Focusing on Kane, he flexed his fingers once more. Kane stumbled forward, now only about a foot from the demon. "Who are you?"

"No one," Kane answered on a cough.

"You're a hunter," the demon said thoughtfully. Then his chapped lips curved up into a frightening smile. "But your power's been stripped." Laughter rumbled from deep within the demon. Shaking with sick humor, he turned his evil eyes on me. "Is he an offering?"

"No," I said defiantly.

"No?" The demon tilted his too-large head and eyed the rest of the coven. "Shall I take them all instead?"

Holy shit. Our magic was barely an annoyance to him. He was no doubt the most powerful and oldest demon we'd ever come in contact with. There was no way we were going to be able to eliminate him.

"If there is anyone to be taken, it'll be me," Kane said and squared his shoulders. "I'm the one who offered a blood sacrifice to summon you here."

"Interesting," the demon hissed. "We're of the same mold." His gaze roamed over Kane as he assessed him. "We could be a very powerful team, you and I."

My stomach rolled at the thought of Kane in Hell, working with such a vile creature.

"We could," Kane agreed. He straightened his shoulders and cast cold, empty eyes on the demon. "If I didn't have a soul."

"That can be arranged." The demon narrowed his large black eyes, assessing Kane.

"And why would I give up my soul? So you could feed my spirit to Genesis? Where is your minion, anyway?" Kane asked, clearly fishing for information.

Magic tingled from either side of me, barely brushing my skin. My coven was rekindling the connection we'd lost when the demon arrived. I met Bea's gaze from across the circle. She cut her eyes to the demon and then back to me as power filtered around the circle in an arc.

My body hummed with the combined magic again.

"She's collecting my payment," the demon said conversationally as if he wasn't towering over Kane, looking like he could rip my husband's head off with one swipe of his giant claw.

"You want me?" Kane asked, staring up at the demon with hate in his eyes. "The only way that's going to happen is if we work a trade. Me for the lesser Goddess."

A trade? What was he talking about? That wasn't the plan. Shit! He knew we'd never be able to defeat the demon and he was changing the game. Dammit! There was no effing way I was letting him go anywhere with the demon.

"Genesis?" The demon rubbed at his chin. Then his eyes narrowed. "Why would I trade her? She's been a good servant the last millennia."

"Those are the terms. Me for her. You hand the Goddess off to the coven, and I'll rule with you in Hell."

Seriously, what in the world was Kane doing, offering himself up to the demon? Making a deal with a demon was permanent. He had to know that. He was a hunter.

The demon licked his lips, showing blackened teeth that

were sharpened into points. Good Goddess, he was hideous. For some reason, his interest in Kane was piqued.

"Why?" I called suddenly.

Kane twisted and glanced over his shoulder at me, giving me a small hard shake of his head.

"Why what?" the demon asked, focusing on me for the first time. "Oh, you are delicious, aren't you?" His tongue snaked out as he tasted the air. "Hmmm, and you're strumming with incubus power."

"She's off limits," Kane said, a muscle in his jaw twitching.

"But she's yours, is she not?" The demon held out a hand to me. "So powerful and fresh. It's been forever since I've had a white witch."

The way he was looking at me made me want to gag.

Kane's fists clenched as he glared at the demon from behind. "The deal is me for the Goddess."

He rotated slowly in Kane's direction, fire erupting over his skin. "I'm the one who's in charge here, incubus. Don't you forget it."

"Hey, demon," I called, desperate to get his attention off Kane. "Your Goddess already had her souls. Why was she trading them for Kane?" I asked, recalling Genesis's obsession with him.

"I have plenty of regular souls. It was time for a new payment. Someone with power, someone with my blood." The demon reached out and grabbed Kane by the neck. "Submit or die by my hand."

Kane opened his mouth to speak, but when he couldn't get the words out, he glared and mouthed "no."

Oh my god. The demon had ordered Genesis to bring Kane to him. My heart slammed against my ribs as I frantically tried to think of something I could bargain with for Kane's life. Nothing. I had nothing to give but myself. I was just about to plead my case when the demon let out a loud roar.

"Fool! No one denies me." The flames transferred from the demon's hand to my husband's skin, erupting as if Kane had been doused in gasoline.

Kane howled and writhed, trying to get away from the demon's grasp.

I shot a powerful stream of magic right at the demon's face, hitting him directly in the left eye. The demon let go of Kane and stumbled backward, appearing more stunned than hurt.

"We were having a conversation here," I spat at the demon, wishing I could blast him apart with the coven's magic.

The demon shook his head and then he snarled and leaped for me. I didn't even flinch. He was in the circle and couldn't get to me unless I crossed the barrier.

He stood directly in front of me. "You'll pay for that."

"Maybe, but we were in the middle of negotiating a deal, were we not?" I did my best to not show any fear. I'd never get what I was after if he didn't think I had value.

"You'll do as I say, or I'll end him." He pointed at Kane again and then curled his hand as if he was crushing Kane's throat. Kane sputtered and his face flushed red.

'Stop!' I cried. "We'll make a deal. All I ask is that you bring the Goddess to the circle first. We have unfinished business." I wanted to offer myself in exchange for Kane, but I knew if I did that, the demon would likely take us both. I had to make sure Pyper was going to be safe before I could go down that route.

"No." He tightened his grip, and Kane's eyes started to bulge out of his head.

There was no more reasoning with the demon. He'd gone over the edge into beast mode. There was only one thing left to do. "Release!" Magic exploded from me as all the power my coven had been sending my way blasted him.

Bea, Lucien, and Rosalee followed suit, and our wrath poured into the demon at an alarming rate.

"Release!" I commanded again and focused on the demon's hand clutching Kane's neck. Slowly, one by one, each of his fingers lifted until Kane fell to his knees, holding his throat, gasping for air.

The demon stood in the center of the circle, vibrating with our magic, but then he stilled, seeming to gather his senses. He scowled and spun around in a circle, creating a small vortex around himself, shielding him from our raw stream of power.

"Focus," I ordered the coven and guided every last bit of power into the magical current, but all it did was bounce off him.

"Stop," Bea called from across the circle. Then she started to chant something I didn't recognize. Latin or Greek maybe. I wasn't sure, but a cloud of mist rose up around her, hung in the air, and then shot at the demon. His vortex shattered and he froze, breathing heavily as he eyed us all.

"You'll all end up in Hell," he warned. "I'll come back for each and every one of you before your days on this earth end." Then he lunged for Kane.

Kane rolled over on the grass, pulling something from his boot, and when the demon landed on him, Kane jabbed the small dagger into the demon's neck. The demon bucked and howled, thrashing, but Kane held on and twisted.

I stood still, unsure what to do. I knew the small dagger wouldn't do anything other than irritate the demon. Although that didn't stop the demon's blood from running down his face and pooling onto the earth. I wanted to help, to unleash more magic, but we'd thrown everything at him already, and he'd flicked us away as if we were fruit flies. Our magic was nothing to this demon. He'd just been toying with us, and now I knew we'd be lucky to get out of this alive.

Frustration took over, filling my chest. I wanted to scream and shout, to attack and end the demon with my bare hands. But I couldn't. And if we didn't do something soon, we'd lose Kane.

I met Bea's worried gaze from across the circle. Her expression was just as dejected as mine must have been. We weren't going to be able to defeat the demon. The best we could do was release him back into Hell. Our summoning would be for nothing.

We had no other choice. It was time. We couldn't keep the demon here.

I raised my hands skyward once more and shouted, "From the earth to the shadows, the coven no longer seeks—"

Smoke shot up from a pool of the demon's blood at the exact same time the air shifted, and demon hunters spilled from the shadows. Six of them circled us, their daggers raised.

"Release the circle," Maximus ordered.

I was so relieved to see him, I did as I was told, no questions asked. Dropping my arms, I let all the magic go and yelled, "Let them through."

Each of my witches took a step back, and the barrier vanished.

The demon hunters surrounded Kane and the demon.

Daggers flew, and I clasped my hand over my mouth, terrified for Kane. He was in the middle of them, unarmed except for the small knife still clutched in his hand.

Bea rushed to my side and grabbed my hand. "He'll be okay."

I shook my head, unable to speak. I could no longer sense Kane. The moment the demon had attacked him, his connection to the protection spell had shattered.

The demon erupted from the center of the hunters, and with fists flying, he roared and lunged. His large jaws closed over the shoulder of one of the demon hunters. The hunter stiffened and his dagger fell to the ground. Then a second later, his skin started to melt right before our eyes.

Horror filled me as I took a step back. The demon was poisonous.

Everything seemed to stop for a split second as the hunters registered what was happening.

A gasp came from behind us, and I felt my coven close in around me.

The demon let the hunter go and stalked toward the five remaining warriors. His eyes had turned red and his razor-thin claws were extended, ready for more battle.

The hunters seemed to steel themselves and then as if on cue, they all threw their daggers at the demon directly where his heart would be. Each dagger hit one right after the other in perfect succession.

The demon stumbled backward and fell to one knee when the last dagger pierced his chest. Blood still dripped from his maw, but the red glow of his eyes had faded.

Their magical daggers had weakened him.

The hunters spread out, forming a small circle around him and Kane. It was my first glimpse of Kane since the hunters had shown up, and he was lying flat on the ground, his eyes closed.

"Oh my God. Is he alive?" I whispered to Bea, my heart pounding so hard I feared it would jump right out of my chest.

"Of course he is, dear," she said reassuringly and slipped her warm hand into mine.

Maximus strode up to the demon and stared down at him. "Victor, favorite of the damned, I hereby condemn you to final death." Maximus whipped another dagger out of a side holder and plunged it into the demon's right eye. He held on as the demon writhed in pain beneath his attack. And when the demon stilled, a blast of magic shot from Maximus's hand into the hilt, and then the demon lit up with brilliant white light.

Maximus stepped back and a second later, the demon evaporated into a puff of white smoke.

# CHAPTER 23

"Kane!" I sprinted to his lifeless body and fell to his side. Placing one hand over his heart and the other on his neck, I quickly found his pulse. Still beating. A sigh of relief escaped my lips as I pulled the healing potion Bea and I had made out of my pocket.

"Here," Bea said. "I'll do it."

I glanced up to find my mentor standing over us, along with the five remaining demon hunters. The sixth one, the one the demon had poisoned, was lying with Bea's witch's robes covering him. With a shaking hand, I surrendered the potion to Bea. She was much more skilled at healing than I'd ever be. "Thank you."

Bea lowered herself to her knees on the other side of Kane. "I'm going to need you to give me some room, Jade," she said gently.

I pulled my hands away but didn't leave his side. Instead, I slipped my hand in his and waited.

Bea swiped a dab of the potion over Kane's forehead and then moved her hands to his bruising neck. The skin was already turning purple where the demon had tried to crush his throat.

I squeezed my fingers over his and barely noticed the tears on my cheeks. Kane was hurt. The implications of just how serious his condition was hit me hard. My insides were gutted.

"Give him a jolt of your magic, Jade," Bea said. "You carry a piece of him with you. All you need to do is share some of yourself with him and he'll awaken."

Right. I carried his incubus magic with me now, just as he did my witch magic. Power sparked from just below my chest. The magic tingled through my veins and collected at my fingertips. "Wake up, Kane," I whispered, caressing his palm.

Warmth grew between our hands, and as the magic filtered into him, his complexion took on a healthy glow.

"That's it. A little more," Bea coaxed as she tipped the potion to his lips.

Magic strained to pour into him, but I held it back, only giving a small dose at a time.

"Again," Bea said, frowning.

Panic started to take over and my magic surged.

Kane's body jerked and jumped a foot off the ground. As he landed back onto the hard earth, he sucked in a large breath, his eyes wide.

"Oh my God. Kane. I'm so sorry." I clutched his hand and held it to my chest.

He blinked and focused on me. Licking his lips, he frowned. "What happened?"

"The demon tried to suffocate you. Bea healed your wounds."

"But Jade brought you back," Bea said. "The demon sucked enough of your energy that you'd slipped into a coma." She got to her feet. "I'll talk to the rest of the coven and give you two a moment."

Kane glanced around at the demon hunters. He cleared his throat. "You made it."

Maximus stared down at him. Then after a moment, he held his hand out.

No one said a word as Kane stared at Maximus. His expression gave nothing away, and even I wasn't sure what he was going to do.

"I should've never taken your dagger," Maximus said. "Trust is the foundation of the Brotherhood. I forgot that. It's my fault we lost a brother today. I don't want to lose another."

A low murmur filtered through the remaining hunters as their surprise bubbled up and burst around them in a display of tiny sparks only I could see. Maximus must not admit when he was wrong very often.

Kane cut his gaze to Maximus's hand, then sat up and clasped it.

Maximus pulled him to his feet. Kane stood tall and strong before the leader, the bruises on his neck already faded from Bea's superior magic. The two shook hands, and then before Kane could let go, Maximus pulled him into a manly hug, clapping him on the back twice before releasing him.

The Brotherhood leader stretched both arms out in front of himself, hands palms up. He met Kane's gaze and held it as he bowed. "For my fellow brethren, may your power be strong and sure. May your mind be sharp and your heart be true. And may your brothers be wise enough to always remember who is loyal." Bright white magic sparked in his hand in the shape of the Brotherhood's dagger.

We all stood in awe, watching the dagger solidify, the symbol on the hilt shining with a brilliant glow of light.

The power radiating off it was stronger than the one Kane had been given the first time around. I could feel it pulsing deep in my bones.

As Kane studied the weapon, an intense longing filtered from him to me. It was as if he craved it.

"It's yours," Maximus said, his voice full of conviction.

Kane finally reached for the dagger. When his fingers closed around the hilt, a burst of its power flashed and then sank into Kane's skin. The fatigue around his eyes vanished and energy pulsed around him. It was clear he was ready for anything. A ghost of a smile claimed his lips, and he stepped back, giving Maximus a small nod.

Pride swelled in my heart as I watched the display. Kane was being treated as an equal. From now on he would be one of them. Trust had been earned.

The air between the pair shimmered slightly, leaving behind a feeling of respect. Maximus's attitude toward Kane had just shifted, and I got the impression they'd have a more balanced working relationship from now on.

Too bad someone had to die in order for Maximus to get there. Anger rushed through my veins at the thought. But I gritted my teeth and said nothing. The remorse clinging to Maximus and the other demon hunters was thick and heart wrenching. They were suffering a massive blow and all of them felt it deeply.

"We'll take him back to the mansion," Maximus said, staring at the fallen hunter.

"I won't be coming." Kane slipped his hand into mine.

Maximus nodded, his dark eyes full of regret. "Take all the time you need."

One of the hunters bent and lifted the fallen hunter over his shoulder. A second later, the five of them took a step forward and disappeared into the shadows.

"We should all get home," I said to the coven members.

There was a few mumbles of agreement, but everyone was

still too shocked to say much else. For most of them, it was no doubt the first time they'd witnessed the loss of life.

"Thank you…" I paused and then shook my head, knowing there was nothing else left to say. "Just thank you."

Lucien waved the coven members over to him and talked to them in hushed tones. I sent him a grateful smile and stuck to Kane's side. "Are you all right?" I whispered.

He shifted closer to me and wrapped an arm around my waist as he kissed the top of my head. "Yes. I'll be even better after we find the Goddess and release her hold on Pyper."

I closed my eyes, battling against the helplessness threatening to claim me. "I don't know how to find her."

"I don't either, but we will…one way or another."

KANE and I stood outside the back door of Wicked. "Are you sure you want to do this?" I asked.

"Yes. I have to know." He slipped his key into the lock, but before he could open the door, I put my hand over his, stopping him.

"I'm worried you're not one hundred percent." We'd just come from the coven circle and were on our way home to regroup when he'd pulled into his parking spot behind the club.

His hand slid up my spine and cupped the back of my head. "Don't worry about me, Jade." He tapped the dagger now safely tucked back into his belt. "I've got what I need."

"If you say so."

"I do." He seemed so solid, so sure of himself, my unease faded into the background.

The door creaked open, and silence greeted us. None of the hall lights were lit, and the place was darker than I'd ever seen it. It even felt dark. Ominous. But not from Kane's energy this time. It was deserted. Empty.

All the lingering lust and excitement that usually filled the club was gone. None of the residual emotions that never failed to turn my stomach were present. There was just nothing. "Does anything feel differently to you?"

Kane paused. "No. But it does to you. What is it?"

I shook my head. "Nothing. That's the thing. I can't feel any residual energy at all."

"That's good, right?"

I squinted through the darkness. "I don't know yet."

He took two steps and then stopped again. "You don't feel my incubus energy?"

"That I feel." Sort of. I was aware of his energy, but it wasn't overwhelming me like it usually did. Not at the moment anyway. "But the taint is gone."

"Completely?" There was a faint trace of relieved hope in his tone.

"Yes. At least in the club anyway. When you reopen, you probably won't have people lined up down the block like you did before. The allure just isn't here."

"Good."

I chuckled. "That's the first time I've heard you say anything positive about the club not having customers."

He laughed with me. "You're right. And it'll probably be the last."

As we neared the office, Kane flipped the switch that illuminated the lights on the walls. Sure enough, no one was there. But the place looked like a hurricane had hit it. The chairs were toppled over, empty booze bottles were strewn over the stage, and something had clawed at the blue-velvet walls.

"Holy shit," I whispered. "What happened here?"

Kane walked slowly around the room, taking in the destruction. Red-tinged anger swarmed around him. His jaw worked, but he said nothing as he kicked his way through the debris.

I had no idea who could've done such a thing. The back door hadn't been tampered with. I was willing to bet the front door hadn't been either. There just wasn't any residual energy in the club at all. And it was very strange. An attack like this one would invariably leave something behind.

"Kane?"

He jerked his head up. "Yes?"

"We need to search the building. I can't feel anything at all. I don't know what's going on, if the place has been cloaked in order to hide energy from me, or if it's been cleansed or what. But since everything about this is off, we need to do a sweep and make sure no one else is here."

"Yeah. You're right." Together we walked the perimeter of the club, finding nothing but debris. Then we checked the office. Interestingly, nothing was out of place there except the door had been broken off the hinges.

"This is beyond weird," I said.

Kane nodded, but tugged me into the hallway and upstairs. Nothing was out of place in any of the apartments except for Zoe's. There were marks on the wall from where she'd been tied up, along with the large spikes. But she was nowhere to be found and all her things appeared to be accounted for, including her purse, which housed her wallet and her keys.

"Do you think Genesis still has her?" I asked, clutching my throat.

"She has to." We both stood staring at the wall where we'd last seen her in Kane's dreamwalk.

"We have to find her," I said.

Kane nodded and before I could say anything else, he ushered me toward the door.

"Where are we headed?" I asked.

"To the shadows."

My internal alarm went off. "We can't do that. Not without notifying someone."

"Then call Lucien. Or Bea. Or Lailah. We cannot leave here unless we check for her. And since that's the last place she was seen, we don't have a choice."

I had to run to catch up with him as he flew down the stairs, and a few moments later we were standing in his office.

"Hold on." I pulled my phone out of my pocket and grimaced when I saw the red light indicating the battery was almost dead. There was only time for one text. I sent a group message to Lucien, Lailah, and Bea.

*Kane and I are checking the shadows for Zoe. If you don't hear back from us within the hour, send reinforcements.* I nodded in satisfaction at the Sent notification. "Done," I said.

"Are you ready?" he asked me.

"Ready."

Our fingers slipped together and the world shifted.

I blinked through the grayness and instantly knew that the energy in the shadows had been restored. "It's not tainted," I said to Kane, relief flooding through me.

But he didn't answer. He was staring off to the right, righteous indignation building from deep inside him. "Let her go," he commanded and took a step away from me.

I peered past him, still unable to see what he did. "Kane?" But he didn't seem to hear me, and the farther he walked away from me, the harder it became to read his emotions.

"Kane?" I said again and tried to catch up, but as I took another step, suddenly a strange ripple reverberated through the fabric of the shadows, distorting my view.

I rubbed at my eyes and squinted.

"Keep moving, Jade," I heard Kane call from a far-off place. "Just take two more steps."

I felt as if I was frozen in place, unable to move forward or backward. I saw nothing but blurry lines of gray. Where was I? What had happened?

"Jade!" Kane gripped my wrist and the next thing I knew I was being yanked through the distorted magic.

My bare arms and face stung from the contact. I blinked rapidly, rubbing at my watery eyes as the cool air brushed over my stinging, sensitive skin. "What was that?" I asked, still unable to see.

"A magical barrier to keep us out," Kane said, his tone rough and dangerous.

"Keep us out of—" My vision cleared, and what I saw made my stomach turn.

Zoe was laid out in the shadows, her arms and legs shackled together, an IV jabbed in her arm. Leaning over her was a hunchbacked old woman with wrinkles lining her face. The woman glared up at us and snarled. Her long white hair shifted, and that was when I saw it. The syringe.

The old woman was extracting blood from Zoe's chest just over her heart.

"Stop!" I sprang forward.

But I was too late. The woman ripped the syringe from Zoe and jabbed it into her own neck.

Flashes of dark magic blossomed over the old woman as her body seized. Rising a few feet in the air, her arms spread out and the black magic consumed her.

I took a step back, unable to control the powerful magic strumming through me, brought on by just the hint of dark forces. I'd fought against black magic before and won. I could do it again. But whatever was happening to her in that moment, she'd done to herself, and I wasn't quite sure what I'd be fighting just yet.

"What the hell?" Kane said and gripped my arm, pulling me to his side.

My eyes widened with disbelief. The woman's skin rippled as her body straightened. Then out of nowhere, a billowing burst of black smoke consumed her. And when it cleared, I stared straight into the eyes of the Lesser Goddess, Genesis.

# CHAPTER 24

"*G*enesis," Kane barked. "What have you done?"

She laughed, that high-pitched giggle of hers grating on my nerves. "Only what I should've done years ago."

"Steal the life force from an innocent woman?" My voice shook with anger and magic clung to my fingertips, ready to be unleashed.

"Innocent?" Genesis raised her eyebrows and gave us an incredulous look. "There's not much of anything innocent about that girl. Not anymore. Not after what she's done for me the last few weeks."

I glance at Zoe, wondering what that meant, but then quickly discarded anything the Goddess had to say. If Zoe had been forced into anything, it didn't matter what she'd done. Genesis was the one using black magic to make herself appear young again by stealing Zoe's essence. I hadn't felt anything sinister from Zoe before. Whatever Genesis was referring to didn't make her evil.

"You're lying," Kane said and flashed his dagger.

Genesis hissed. "You can't hurt me with that blade, incubus. I know the rules."

She was right. The dagger given to Kane was to be used only when fighting demons…or in self defense when he was magically attacked. "You're mistaken," I lied, taunting her. "Black magic is fair game. One flick of his wrist and you'll be history."

It was a gamble. Kane wouldn't use his dagger unless she attacked him first. But as a white witch, I didn't live by such rules. As soon as she stepped away from Zoe, I'd take her down.

Fear flashed through Genesis's eyes. But she blinked it away and raised her arms, the black tendrils of magic curling from her fingers and around her wrists. "Prove it."

The dark energy shot from her hands straight at Kane. The bolt was so fast, I didn't even have time to react. But Kane did. Instead of attacking Genesis with his dagger, he held it up and reflected the black magic using the large stone in the hilt. If she'd been a demon, he would've sent it straight back to her, but instead he aimed it off in the distance away from Zoe and the Goddess.

Genesis stumbled a few feet to the right, trying to break Kane's hold. It was enough that Zoe was out of the line of fire. My white witch magic curled up from my depths and instead of battling the magic she was unleashing on Kane, I focused on her and whispered, "Bind her."

Six separate streams of magic shot from my fingers, each latching on to a different part of Genesis's body.

"What the—" she started as she tried to jerk backward.

But a rope of power wrapped around her mouth, effectively gagging her, while four of the others clasped around her wrists and ankles.

The black magic streaming from her hands started to fade to just barely a whisper of power.

"More, Jade. Cut her off," Kane said, steel in his tone.

Genesis bucked against my magical bindings. Her eyes turned jet-black as she glared in my direction. Then a tendril of her dark magic slipped under the band that was gagging her. The stream shattered and she sucked in a hard breath. "You stupid bitch!" She opened her mouth, and a torrent of evil escaped from the depths of her soul.

Shadow after shadow of broken spirits flowed from her, each of them screaming a high-pitched cry of agony. All the ones she'd fed off of over the years. I recoiled in horror, unable to even fathom such a terrible existence.

They flew around Genesis in a whirlwind of energy until finally Genesis broke free of my hold. My magic slammed back at me. A sharp pain hit me right in the gut and I cried out as I doubled over, gasping for air.

"Get back!" Kane stepped in front of me and raised his dagger, using the stone to shield us from the spirits.

I fell to my knees, unable to stay upright, and peered at the spectacle in front of us. Zoe wasn't moving from her shackled position behind Genesis. I wasn't even sure she was still alive after the Goddess had stolen her essence. God, what if she didn't make it? That would be three people we'd lost in a matter of days.

My heart got caught in my throat. But then anger took over. The world was too full of selfish, power-hungry beings. And immortals like Genesis were the worst kind of awful. She literally had the world at her feet, and it wasn't enough. I couldn't stand by and let her sacrifice one more innocent.

I leaped to my feet in front of Kane, ignoring the pain in my gut, and shot bolt after bolt of magic at the spirits shielding

Genesis. One by one they each slowed and faded away into the shadows, leaving nothing between me and the Goddess.

If anyone had ever asked me if I thought I could take a Goddess down, I'd say no every time. But right then, the conviction filling my heart said otherwise. I wouldn't let her go after one more person. Wouldn't let her get a chance to take Pyper again. Was willing to die before I'd let Pyper's spirit turn into one of the creatures controlled by the Goddess.

With the broken spirits out of the way, I tapped into all the fear and rage and horror of the last few days and focused my energy on targeting the Goddess. "Genesis," I called.

Her head snapped up and her big black eyes stared right at me.

"Eat this." White-hot magic burst from me and flowed straight at her head.

The Goddess did as I commanded and opened her giant mouth, sucking down everything I had to give. I stood there, feeding her all my power, every last bit of strength I had until my muscles started to give out. I fell to one knee and gritted my teeth, calling up the remaining power from the depths of my soul.

One last bubble of magic left my fingertips, and I fell forward onto my hands, utterly empty.

"Jade!" Kane called and lifted me up by my shoulders. He held me, both of us watching Genesis's body glow bright with my magic. Her eyes shifted from black to white and then back to black as she howled in obvious pain.

"I have to finish what I started," I gasped out.

"No, Jade. You've done enough," Kane said into my ear.

I shook my head. "No. She'll never stop. Please. Let me go."

"I can't. You've used too much."

I glanced up at him, desperately pleading with him. "I have to. I can do this. Trust me."

His worried gaze glanced from me to her and back again. "Here," he said and placed my hand on his heart. "Take what you need."

"Are you sure?" My breath came in short, desperate gasps.

"I'm sure."

My fingers dug into his flesh as I concentrated on his energy engulfing me. I knew him so well, had been in tune with him for so long, it was second nature to meld into his emotional energy. Except that wasn't what he was telling me to do. No, I was to take some of his power.

"You got this," Kane said.

I wasn't so sure, but when I glanced back at Genesis, my white magic was just starting to fade. If I didn't act now, I'd lose my chance, and everything I'd done would be all for nothing.

"Take it!" Kane demanded.

And with his words, I felt the first twinge of his power merge with mine. It was enough. Kane's power flowed effortlessly into me and churned in that place just below my heart, mixing with mine. My power jolted and suddenly I was alive with it. With one hand on Kane and the other outstretched in front of me, I called, "*Finis!*"

Nothing seemed to happen for a moment. Then my body bowed and everything left me in a whoosh. In the next second, the Goddess's mouth dropped open as she gagged. Her hand came up to her neck, her eyes bugging out and she choked on nothing.

*That's it, die, Goddess*, I thought with vengeance. *Die!*

A disturbance filled the air in the form of an ominous rumble, followed by light shooting from her center, her eyes, her mouth, until she literally exploded apart and vanished into nothing.

Sparkles of light floated down around us as I slumped against Kane.

"You did it," he said softly. "She's gone."

I nodded, so tired I wasn't even able to speak.

Kane brushed his fingers over my forehead. "You did good, love."

I sighed into him just as my eyes landed on Zoe. "Oh, God." I let go of Kane and moved toward her.

"Wait," Kane said.

I paused and glanced back at him, swaying on my feet. "Why?"

"We don't know what kind of condition she's in."

"There's only one way to find out." I held my hand out to him and together we made our way over to the fallen girl. "Her shackles are gone," I said as I stared down at her. "How?"

"It was probably Genesis's magic. You demolished her and any of her lingering magic."

"Good." I kneeled. "Zoe?"

The girl didn't move. She was very pale and her skin was clammy.

I glanced up at Kane in panic. "We need to get her out of here."

He bent and picked her up.

"Is she breathing?" I asked.

"Barely. Let's go." Kane and I clasped hands and a second later we were standing outside of Bea's compound. We were on the sidewalk outside the main gates. Her house was the carriage house behind a larger family home in the garden district. Because we had Zoe with us, we couldn't shadow walk right to the front of her cottage due to her wards. No one who hadn't already been granted access could get that close. Which was why her place was one of the safest in the city.

I waved my hand in front of her locked gate, and it opened

immediately. Her security was set to let certain people in at all times. I was one of the lucky few.

By the time we rounded the corner to Bea's cottage, she was already standing on her front porch. She ran to us. "What happened?"

"Jade destroyed the Goddess," Kane said matter-of-factly.

Bea raised a curious eyebrow. "All by yourself?"

I shook my head. "Kane helped."

"No, I didn't." Kane strode up the steps and waited for Bea to open the door. "Zoe's in bad shape."

Bea nodded. "I can tell. Take her straight up to the guest room. I'll be up in a second with healing herbs."

After my impressive display of magic, my body was barely cooperating. As soon as I crossed the threshold, I shuffled to the sunflower couch and collapsed.

"Your power's getting stronger," Bea said as she opened one of her living room cabinets.

"Hmm?" I curled into myself, my eyelids suddenly very heavy.

"Destroying a Goddess isn't something you could've done on your own a few months ago."

"I told you, Kane helped." I yawned and snuggled into the cushion.

"Well, whatever happened, I'm proud of you."

I met her kind eyes and felt warmth spread in my chest. "Take care of her," I said as I closed my eyes. "Bring Zoe back."

"I'll do my best, Jade."

I nodded, barely registering the words. Sleep was already claiming me.

# CHAPTER 25

*J* woke the next morning with a start and bolted upright, blinking in the bright light.

Kane rolled over and placed a hand on my thigh. "What is it?" he asked sleepily.

The familiar red hibiscus bedspread came into focus. My shoulders relaxed as I slumped against our headboard. We were at home in our own bed. Glancing down at myself, I took in the green silk nighty and frowned. "Kane?"

"Hmm." He tugged me back down and slipped an arm around me. "What is it?"

"How did we get here? And how did I end up wearing this?" I tugged the hem of my lingerie.

One of his eyes popped open. He flicked his gaze to the clock and groaned. "It's not even seven yet."

"Kane." I pushed on his shoulder. "Wake up. What happened with Zoe? Is she okay?"

He pressed a hand to his head and then turned his gaze on me. "Bea's taking care of her. You passed out hard, so I decided to not wake you up. A cab brought us home, and I carried you inside. That was…" He paused and looked at the clock again. "Hmm, less than four hours ago."

Goodness. I must've been dead to the world. "I don't remember any of that."

His eyes closed again and his arm tightened around me. "I'm sure you don't. After you fell asleep on Bea's couch, you were restless and seemed upset. So Bea cast a spell to really put you out."

"What?" I bolted upright again. "And you let her?"

He peered at me. "You don't trust Bea?"

"It's not that I don't trust her, it's just that… Crap." I slid out of the bed and stood in the middle of the room, my hands on my hips. "What if something else had happened? What then?"

Kane heaved himself up on a sigh. "Then I imagine she would've cast another spell to wake you up. But really, love, what do you think was going to happen while you were at her house?"

"I don't know." I stomped into the bathroom and shut the door. He knew how much I loathed being spelled. Hell, it had taken months for me to even come around to the idea of taking Bea's healing herbs. But to be put under by a spell after everything that had happened? It was unconscionable.

The floor tiles were cool under my feet as I stepped into the shower and adjusted the water to scalding. But instead of going through my morning routine, I just stood there, seething.

After a few minutes, the shower door opened, and Kane poked his head in. "Is it okay if I join you?"

The fact that he was asking meant he knew just how upset I was. On any other day, he would've just slipped in and wrapped his arms around me.

The apprehensive look on his face softened me and the anger slowly started to fade. "It's fine."

The door shut softly as Kane stepped up behind me. Without saying a word, he grabbed the shampoo and went to work on washing my hair. He took his time massaging my scalp and by the time he was done, I was putty in his hands.

"I'm sorry, pretty witch," he said softly as he brushed his lips over my shoulder. "I was worried about you and wanted you to get some rest. It's been a rough few days."

I turned in his arms and gazed up at him. Those wise chocolate-brown eyes were full of so much love, my heart melted all over again. "I know you were just trying to take care of me."

He nodded and brushed a lock of my wet hair over my shoulder. "Yes, I was."

"I might have a small problem with control when it comes to spells and magic." I gave him a whisper of a smile.

"A small one?" He grinned.

"Shut up," I said without any heat. I probably was irrational when it came to my stance on being spelled. It wasn't like I ever hesitated to spell anyone when I thought the person could help me. I was pretty sure my resistance was leftover PTSD from when my mother had gone missing during a routine spell when I was just fifteen. Of course, it turned out she'd been abducted by a demon and her spell hadn't been the problem at all. But I was still scarred. "I'm aware I have issues."

Kane shook his head. "Not any we can't work through." Then he dipped his head and claimed my lips with his. The kiss started out slow and sweet, but quickly escalated to hot and desperate. Before I knew it, he had me pressed against the shower wall, his hard length grinding against me. "I want you, Jade."

"I'm already yours." I hooked one leg around his hip and guided him to my center. A low moan reverberated from the back of his throat as he slowly entered me.

Our eyes met, and then in one swift movement, he lifted me. My legs automatically locked around his waist as he showed me exactly how much he loved me.

~

I WAS LEANING against the counter in the kitchen, sipping a chai latte, when Kane strode in clutching his phone. "We're all set. Lailah's meeting us in the angel realm in ten minutes."

After taking one last gulp of my tea, I set the cup on the counter and took his hand. "Chessandra knows we're coming?"

"Yes. The invitation should be here any moment now." We were headed to the angel realm to relay our news of the demon, the Goddess, and the status of the shadows. While we were there, we planned to bring Pyper back with us. With the Goddess destroyed, the threat to her life was gone.

Kane and I moved to the living room and waited. The ticking from the clock on the wall filled the silence and only seemed to get louder the longer we waited. My knee bounced involuntarily as nerves took over.

"Relax, Jade. Everything's going to be fine," Kane said mildly as he updated the club's Facebook page. Charlie had gone back to her apartment this morning, but before she'd left, the pair of them had decided to reopen the club as soon as possible. Tonight was the night. Kane was posting a two-for-one drinks special. An emergency crew had already been called in to clean up and repair any damage.

"You don't know that," I said. "The angels do whatever's best for them and no one else."

"But what would they want with Pyper? She's just a regular person."

I shrugged. "I'm just trying to be prepared is all."

"You're worrying too much." He put his phone on the end table and turned to me. "The angels—"

The bright light of the angel calling filled the middle of the room.

"Time to go," I said and together we stepped into the light.

The world blurred and an instant later we were standing in a completely white room decorated with rich gold and deep plum accents. The rug was a checkered pattern of gold and plum, while the white couch was adorned with plum pillows. A gold tapestry hung on the wall above the couch.

"Good morning." Chessandra's voice came from behind us.

We turned to find her sitting at a gold antiqued desk, wearing a sleek white suit. Her hair was slicked back and makeup applied perfectly. She should've been the height of sophistication, except no amount of makeup could hide the large circles under her eyes and the fatigue lining her face. She hadn't fared well the last few days either.

"Have a seat," she said.

Kane and I glanced at each other and then sat in a pair of white winged-back chairs.

"Good morning," I said, wondering where we were. Usually we met with her with the council present or in the room just off the dais. "New office?"

She took a sip of what appeared to be tea. After replacing the cup on her desk, she sat back, folding her arms over her chest. "These are my private quarters."

Kane and I shared a confused look.

"I want to hear what you have to say before I pass it on to the council." She flipped a notebook open and grabbed a pencil. "I assume you're here with positive news?"

Kane leaned forward. "The shadows have been restored, and the demon who was tainting it has been destroyed. We've prepared a report. Lailah will submit it once she arrives."

The high angel raised one eyebrow. "What about the Goddess who was stealing spirits?"

"Also destroyed," Kane said.

I watched him with interest. I hadn't realized he'd already talked to Lailah about a report. No doubt they'd kept the details to a minimum. Kane wouldn't want Chessandra to know about his connection to the demon. Hell, I didn't want her to know. The less she knew about our lives, the better. Trust was a hard thing to come by when it came to the angels.

"And our missing angel? Have you found her?"

Kane shook his head.

"We haven't seen her at all," I added.

Chessandra scowled. "The mission isn't complete until our angel comes home."

I tilted my head and really studied her. I'd never seen her so rattled...not even when her own sister had been trapped in the void world. "Excuse me, Chessandra," I said, trying for my most respectful tone. "As upset as we are that an angel has gone missing, I'll have to respectfully remind you that protecting and/or tracking angels is not in our contract. Of course we will do what we can to help, but you have to understand we're completely in the dark here. We don't even know her name."

Chessandra stood and narrowed her eyes at me. "Her name is Avery, and you will find her or I'll keep your medium here indefinitely."

Medium? What was she...oh. The memory of Pyper communicating with her mom in our guest room came rushing back. She wanted to keep Pyper? She couldn't be serious. "You have no right to keep Pyper here," I said coldly.

"I can do whatever I please, witch. You're the one who put her in my care, were you not?"

I opened my mouth to argue further, but Kane shook his

head slightly, indicating for me to drop it for the moment. He frowned at her. "You said Pyper is a medium?"

She dropped the notebook on her desk and stalked across the room. Stopping in front of a large gold-framed mirror, she gestured to it. "Your little friend has been invaluable for helping us resolve some unsolved mysteries."

Chessandra flicked a switch, and the mirror turned to glass.

Inside was an identical room to the one we sat in, only two large cabinets stood against the wall and a stack of files covered the desk.

And then there was Pyper. She was sitting in a swivel chair, appearing to talk to herself.

# CHAPTER 26

$\mathcal{K}$ ane walked over to the glass and peered at Pyper. She seemed perfectly at ease, as if she was talking to a good friend.

I shifted my attention to Chessandra. "Her mom showed up the other day. I thought it was a onetime thing. Can she really see other spirits, too?"

"Her guides showed up about an hour after she arrived."

"What are guides?" Kane asked.

I already knew but let Chessandra answer in case there was something I wasn't aware of.

"The spirits who talk to her about other spirits. They keep her safe and call on the ones we seek answers from. It's all very standard." Then she frowned at us. "You've never met a medium before?"

"I have," I said. "One of Aunt Gwen's friends is one. But she's not particularly accurate."

Chessandra nodded. "That happens. It all depends on the guides. Some of them are unreliable."

I moved to stand next to Kane and pressed my hand against

the glass. Being a medium wasn't a bad thing necessarily, but it did mean she'd be much more tied into the supernatural world. And considering the amount of evil that already seemed to find us, I wasn't convinced this was a good development.

"How reliable are Pyper's guides?" Kane asked.

"So far, very." Chessandra retreated to her desk and sat again as she rummaged through a file on her desk.

I eyed her. "How did this happen?"

She glanced up at me and raised an eyebrow in question.

"I mean—" I strode back over to stand in front of her, "— why is she a medium? You said her guides showed up about an hour after she got here. Why?"

Chessandra gave me a look that could melt iron. I actually felt myself shrinking away from her.

"Ms. Calhoun, if you're implying we did anything to the human to alter her mental state, I very much take offense. But to answer your question, the other soul she's carrying appears to have been a medium at some point. The gift has transferred to your friend."

Oh, whoa. That wasn't what I'd been expecting at all.

"I want to talk to her," Kane said as he joined me.

Chessandra pulled a piece of paper from her file. "Fine. Just as soon as you sign this." She handed it over to Kane and then stood with her hands on her hips, waiting.

Kane glanced at the document and scowled. "Neither of us is signing this."

"You will if you want to see your friend again. Otherwise, I'll just keep her here indefinitely. She's certainly being useful."

Kane handed me the contract. I glanced down and noted it was an exchange agreement. Pyper for the missing angel, Avery.

"You can't do this!" I cried and crumpled the paper in my fist.

"Who says?" Chessandra's demeanor was cold as ice. "I'm the high angel. I can do anything I want."

"Not exactly," Lailah said from behind us. "There are some checks and balances even in the angel realm."

I spun and caught sight of Lailah, and to my surprise Drake, my biological father, was standing behind her. What the hell was he doing here? I was too angry to deal with anyone, let alone the father I'd never known. Putting him out of my mind, I focused on Lailah. Thank the gods she was here. Since she was a low-level angel, Lailah knew their laws a lot better than I did. We needed someone on our side.

"Lailah," Chessandra said coolly, then she nodded to Drake, who glided to his mate's side. "Chessandra." Lailah nodded to the angel. "I hear you're trying to make a deal with the Rouquettes regarding my charge."

"If you're referring to the human, then you heard correctly." Chessandra stared Lailah in the eye, her gaze hard and unapologetic. "However, since the human's soul is no longer in danger, she's no longer your concern."

"Then I'm afraid I need to step in. You see, since she's still harboring a second soul, a magical one at that, she *is* in danger. If you recall, the body is really only built for one, and eventually she'll either absorb the intruder or expel it. If she absorbs it, the effects can be unpleasant at best. If she expels it, the soul will be lost to our cause." Lailah pulled a file out of her bag and waved it at Chessandra. "I have a proposal I think might suit our needs."

Chessandra glared at Lailah. "I'm not interested in your proposal. The human stays here while my shadow walkers search for my angel."

I clutched the contract harder and then threw it at Chessandra's desk. "I'm tired of your ultimatums," I said, my tone low and controlled. "Why do you have to manipulate everyone to get what you want? Have you ever thought of just asking if we'd help?"

Kane stiffened beside me. We'd been to Hell once before, and it was the last place I ever wanted to go again. But we'd have to consider going if we hunted for the angel. And I'd do what I had to in order to make sure Chessandra didn't use Pyper as a pawn.

"Chessa?" Drake asked hesitantly. "What's going on here?"

She shot him a shut-the-hell-up look, but he didn't let it go.

"What are you asking them to do?"

Her fists clenched and then she leaned in and lowered her voice. "I'm trying to work a contract for an exchange—the lost angel for the medium we've been watching over."

Drake turned to me. He held my gaze for a beat longer than was comfortable, but I refused to look away. Was he really willing to send his daughter into Hell? If so, I guess I knew where we stood.

Turning away from us, Drake put a hand on Chessandra's back, and this time when he whispered I couldn't hear a thing.

But when Chessandra pulled away, she scowled at him. "You're pulling the father card? Seriously? You barely know her."

Anger flared to life over my father's features. "She's my flesh and blood, Chessa. And I'll not stand by and let you send her to Hell. I don't care if you are the high angel. It's not going to happen."

Whoa. Shock hit me hard, rendering me momentarily immobile. That was the first time I'd seen him do anything to stand up to her in regards to me. A tiny bit of gratitude blossomed inside me. Chessandra was right, we barely knew each other, but the fact that he was taking a stand in my favor to keep me safe was more than I'd ever thought possible.

Chessandra seethed beside him but didn't answer his

outburst. She just picked up the phone and barked, "Bring the human to me."

Lailah inched closer to me and whispered, "Whatever I say, go along with it. Got it?"

I glanced from Kane to Chessandra and Drake and then back to Lailah. She widened her eyes with insistence.

I wasn't sure that was something I could promise, but I'd try. "Okay."

The door swung open, and in walked Pyper. Chessandra's assistant popped in just long enough to nod to her and then shut the door again.

Pyper's eyes lit up at the sight of us. "You're back already."

Kane pulled her into a hug. "How are you?"

She smiled up at him. "Fine. A little busy shuffling paperwork." An irritated expression claimed her face as she glanced at Chessandra and Drake. "But other than that, I'm good."

I reached over and squeezed her hand. "We heard you picked up quite the gift."

A small smile claimed her lips and her eyes softened. "Yeah. It's been…interesting."

"You can tell us about it later." I wanted to whisk her away from this place as soon as possible. Hadn't I told Kane that nothing was free with the angels? Trusting them to keep their word was impossible.

"Ms. Rayne," Chessandra said to Pyper. "We're having a disagreement about what shall be done with you now that the Goddess has been eliminated."

"Disagreement," I muttered under my breath. "That's one way of putting it."

Drake shook his head at me in warning. He looked very much like Lailah had just a second ago. I bit down on my tongue to keep from lashing out again.

Pyper glanced at me and then Kane. "You did it! I'm safe?"

I nodded but kept my gaze trained on Chessandra. I appreciated Drake's insistence to not force us to make a deal with the high angel, but all I really cared about at this moment was getting Pyper home safely. Chessandra was crazy if she thought we were going to leave Pyper here while the angels used her as their personal medium.

"No," Lailah said, her tone sympathetic. "Not quite. You're safe from immediate danger, but as I'm sure you're aware, you still have that second soul. As long as it's with you, your soul is in danger of being pushed out, or if it melds with yours, there's a good chance of insanity."

Pyper and I both gasped. I stifled mine while Kane put his arm around Pyper's shoulders and pulled her to him. "We're not going to let that happen."

Insane? I had no doubt that was a real possibility. My heart ached and I longed to be back at The Grind with Pyper making lattes and only worrying about how big the next rush would be.

"Stop being so melodramatic," Chessandra ordered as she glared at all of us. "Her soul is not in danger while she's in the angel realm. We are the keepers of souls, remember?"

"But she can't live her life here," I said. She'd end up a slave.

"She can and she will." Chessandra picked up the crumpled contract and held it out to me. "That is, unless you agree to my terms."

My insides heated as anger welled up inside me. The heavy-handed good-for-nothing piece of—

"No," Drake said and plucked the paper from Chessandra's hand. "I forbid it, Chessa. If you try to force her to do this, that's it. I'm done."

Holy shitballs. He'd just given her the ultimate ultimatum. And they were mates. Fully committed, magically bound.

Chessandra looked like she'd been gut punched. Then she steeled herself and straightened her shoulders. "How dare you question me in front of others."

Drake's nostrils flared. "And how dare you disregard anything I have to say in the matter of the safety of my daughter."

The raw anger that sparked between them was almost too much for me to take. Had I not been holding on to Kane, I likely would've been knocked on my ass.

Drake took a deep breath and stepped back, ending the standoff. "What would you need in order to let Jade off the hook on this one?" he asked, his tone much more even keeled.

"You already know the answer to that," she snapped. "I need someone willing to search for Avery...anywhere."

"I'll do it," Lailah said. "I'll take on the responsibility of finding the lost angel."

"What?" I stared at her in horror. "You can't. You do know she could be in Hell, right?"

"I'm aware." Lailah gave me a sharp look. "I'm also much more qualified to find the angel than you are. But..." She took a step forward and peered at Chessandra. "I need you to release Pyper. She doesn't belong here. And since she's my charge, I'll look after her."

Chessandra eyed her suspiciously. "Why would you do this? You know the risks of Hell as well as anyone. I don't understand your motivation."

Lailah stepped back and slipped a hand into Pyper's free one. "Her soul was assigned to me. It's my job to take care of her. I also happen to have experience with summoning angels from Hell. If I ever want to move up in ranks from lower-level angel, I'm going to need some impressive marks on my resume. I know I can do this. And I'm willing. I'll sign the contract that says I'm responsible for Avery and am willing to be sanctioned if it's determined I'm not doing my due diligence in locating her."

Everyone was silent as the implications of what she'd just said sunk in. Lailah was putting her career on the line for an angel she'd never met. Or was she doing it to protect us? She *had* said to go along with whatever she'd said. I just prayed she had a plan.

Chessandra looked over at Drake. An unspoken communication passed between them. Finally she gave Lailah a short nod. "I'll have my assistant draw up the contract."

"No need. I have one right here." Lailah flipped open the file in her hand and passed it to her. She'd been planning this all along. I gaped at her.

Chessandra grabbed it from her, clearly displeased to be making this deal in front of all of us. Still, she seemed to buy Lailah's explanation and she was getting what she wanted: someone to find her lost angel.

Chessandra picked up a pen as she read the contract. When she finished, she nodded. "Looks agreeable."

"Just one more thing," Lailah said before Chessandra could sign.

"You're pushing it, angel," Chessandra said through clenched teeth.

"It's about Pyper's extra soul."

The high angel raised her gaze to Lailah's. "What about it?"

"Jade and Kane rescued a young woman, Zoe, who'd had her soul stripped from her and sacrificed to the demon. Right now, she's just a shell of a person. I'd like to request we transfer Pyper's extra soul to Zoe."

I clasped my hand over my mouth so I wouldn't say anything to ruin whatever Lailah was up to. But I'd watched Genesis strip the woman of her spirit. I hadn't known if her soul was there or not, but without her spirit, she wouldn't be a whole person.

Lailah shot me a warning glance.

I dropped my hand and tried for a neutral expression.

Chessandra and Lailah held each other's gazes until Chessandra narrowed her eyes and then gave a short nod. "I'll see what the practitioners can do."

Lailah's shoulders relaxed for the first time since she'd entered the room as Chessandra signed the paperwork.

The high angel waved a hand, and the bright light shone once more. "The medium will stay here until we can complete the soul transfer. Lailah, after you retrieve your soulless human, we'll talk to the practitioners." She barely glanced at me and Kane. "You two are free to go. You'll be informed of your next assignment."

Kane and I gave Pyper a quick hug. "We'll see you in no time," I said, putting on a brave face. Soul transfers were a bitch. I'd shared mine for a while with another angel. When the angel council decided to give my soul to her, the pain from the failed transfer had been hell on earth. I only hoped since Pyper's soul was intact, the transfer wouldn't be as awful for her as it had been for me.

But Pyper saw right through me. She hugged me hard. "I'll be fine. Don't worry about me."

I let out a sad chuckle. "Never gonna happen. Just hurry home."

"I'll do my best."

When she released me, she reached for Kane and the two clung to each other for a long moment.

Drake moved out from behind the desk and stood in front of me. My mouth went dry as I looked up into his light green eyes. I wasn't sure what to say. He'd just stood up for me at great personal risk. But I didn't have to say anything at all, because he pulled me into a hug and whispered, "Take care of yourself."

Then just as quickly, he let me go, and I stood there watching him walk out of the room.

"Jade?" Kane said from beside me.

I slipped my hand into his. "Yeah?"

"Let's go home."

I nodded and without looking back, he tugged me into the light.

# CHAPTER 27

*K*ane and I sat together on the loveseat in our living room, while Duke, the ghost dog, had claimed one of the oversized chairs. Kane was sprawled across the cushions, and I was lying half on top of him. But there was nothing sexy about it. We were both too exhausted to move. And too relieved to care about anything.

Lailah was taking care of Pyper, the shadows were restored, and Kane had his demon hunter power back. As long as the Brotherhood didn't call or Chessandra didn't issue another order, we were free to do nothing for the foreseeable future.

"I'm not going to ever get up from this spot," I said into Kane's chest.

"Never?" Kane asked.

"Nope."

"Works for me." He ran his fingers through my hair and tightened his hold on me.

I sighed, snuggling into him. My eyes closed and my body relaxed for what seemed like the first time in days. I felt my body and mind floating off into the sweet oblivion of sleep…

And then the doorbell rang.

"Ugh." I stayed still for a moment, willing whoever it was to go away. But then Lailah and Pyper's faces flashed in my mind. What if they were back already? I pushed myself up, but Kane's arms tightened around me.

"No. You were never getting up again."

I laughed and gave him a soft kiss.

"Hmmm."

Then I tickled him.

"Hey!" His eyes opened and he glared at me as I strolled to the door. "Not nice."

I smiled at him. The doorbell rang again as I pulled the door open.

"Oh, sorry!" Mati said with a little wave. Vaughn was standing just behind her, clutching a small notebook. "I wasn't sure you were home."

"We just got in." I held the door open for them. "Come on in."

Kane swung his feet to the floor and rose to greet them. "Hey, man." He held his hand out to Vaughn. "Good to see you."

"You, too." Vaughn glanced around. "Is there a place we could talk? I've got something I think you might want to see."

"Sure." Kane led us all to the kitchen.

"Have a seat," I said. "I'll get drinks."

"Thanks, Jade." Mati touched my arm lightly, and a small tingle of her sex witch energy sparked into me. "Oh, oops."

I laughed. "Don't worry about it." Her little zap had actually perked me up a bit after my sluggish afternoon on the couch.

The three of them sat at the table while I busied myself with the sweet tea.

"I found this in the archive while doing some research for you." Vaughn handed Kane the small notebook. "I think you'll find it interesting."

Kane raised his eyebrows, but then opened the book.

I placed two iced tea glasses in front of Mati and Vaughn before leaning over Kane's shoulder. "Whaddaya have here?"

He glanced up at me, his face set in concentration. "It's a family tree. See this?" He pointed to a name near the bottom.

"Do you know him?" I sat beside Kane and pulled the book over just a smidge to get a better look.

"Yes." Kane glanced up at Vaughn. "Where did you say you found this?"

"In the archives…ah, in Maximus's office. I don't think it's information that's spoken about much."

"Why? It's just a…" My eyes focused on the oldest name on the diagram: Malafent the Demon. His name was connected with an unnamed witch. I traced the line all the way to the one Kane had fixated on: Winters Rouquette, his great, great grandfather. I lifted my gaze and stared at Kane. "You're the direct descendant of that demon."

Kane glanced at Vaughn and then nodded. "It appears so."

"Dayla says that's why the demon had been able to taint the shadows," Mati said. "She says since you're always in and out of the shadows, he was able to sense your energy and latched on to it."

I shivered. "But why now? We've been walking the shadows for months."

Mati shrugged. "Probably because now he's an incubus when before he wasn't. He didn't have anything to take before."

"Jesus," I said under my breath.

"Right?" Mati gasped out. "This world is nuts."

Vaughn slipped his hand over hers and smiled at her. Then he sobered and returned his attention to Kane. "I thought you'd want to understand why this happened. That's why I brought the book. You should also know that this means you're probably a lot more powerful than you even know. With a direct line, you probably have untapped resources."

"That's not necessarily good news." Kane handed the book back to Vaughn.

"No," we all agreed at the same time. Chuckling, we walked Mati and Vaughn to the door.

"Thanks for bringing this to my attention." Kane held out his hand to Vaughn once more.

The other incubus glanced down, but then pulled Kane into a quick bro hug. "No problem, man. Take care of yourself."

Mati and I grinned at each other.

"See you at the next girls' night?" Mati asked.

"Seriously?" The thought of embarrassing myself in front of the Coven Pointe witches again was slightly terrifying, but I would like to form a more solid relationship with them.

"Sure. Dayla likes you, even if she doesn't act like it."

I gave a half shrug in a sure-why-not motion. "Okay, then."

"I'll be in touch." Mati winked and then the pair disappeared out the door.

"GUMBO OR ITALIAN?" I asked Kane, holding up two takeout menus.

"Gumbo." He was lying on the bed, his hands clasped behind his head, staring up at the ceiling, his expression troubled.

All the enthusiasm for food vanished as I watched him. We'd already known he had to have been descended from a sex witch and incubus pairing, but to see the direct line to a demon had totally unnerved him. I couldn't blame him. Knowing about the connection and seeing it in writing were two totally different things.

I dropped the menus on the dresser, crawled onto the bed, and rested my head on his shoulder. I didn't say anything, though. There was nothing to say.

"I feel like I just found out I harbor evil or something," he said.

"You don't." I caressed his chest with my fingertips. "I'd feel it."

I felt him relax beneath me as that realization hit him. "I guess that's true."

"No need to guess. It is true." I lifted myself to stare down at him. "I know you already know this deep inside your gut, but where you come from matters to no one. The only thing that matters is who you are now."

He didn't acknowledge me with words, but his hand did tighten around my arm.

"And I happen to think you're one of the good ones...so there."

Kane chuckled at my childish words, wrapped his foot around my leg, and then flipped me over so he was hovering above me. "And I love who you are, pretty witch."

"You'd better."

His eyes glinted as he lowered his lips, stopping just millimeters from mine. "It's going to take me a few hours to show you."

My breath caught and I stared up into the desire filling those lovely eyes of his. My body responded the way it always did when he looked at me like that. "Kiss me," I breathed.

"Gladly."

He covered my mouth with his and just as our tongues met, the goddamned doorbell rang again.

"Son of a...! Shoot." I blew out a frustrated breath.

"We could just stay in here," he said and rolled off me.

"No we can't. And you know it." We were still waiting on Pyper and Lailah.

"Yeah, okay." He pushed himself off the bed and disappeared.

I took a moment to straighten my clothes and then followed him. But when I got to the living room, I stopped dead in my tracks. "Mom? Gwen?"

"Jade!" Mom exclaimed and ran to me, her dark hair flying behind her.

Gwen grinned at me from the doorway. Duke was sitting in front of her, his tongue dragging on the floor in excitement. His head swiveled to the side when Gwen shifted, revealing my ex-stepfather, Marc. He'd raised me until I was seven, when my mother had forced him to leave due to a difference of opinion on how much to tell me about my magical abilities. Marc had been ready to train me from day one. Mom had wanted to keep me in the dark until I was eighty. The last I'd heard, the pair of them weren't even on speaking terms.

Mom caught me in a hug. "We were so worried."

"I'm fine," I said, baffled. "What are you doing here?"

"We missed you." Mom let go of me and waved to Marc. He took her hand and twined his fingers between hers.

I raised an eyebrow at them. "Something you want to tell me?"

"Well…" Mom smiled almost shyly this time. "Yes, actually, and we wanted to do it in person." She glanced at Kane. "I hope you don't mind our intrusion. We did get a hotel room, so we won't be in your way."

"They did," Gwen clarified as she nodded at my parents. "I didn't."

"Good," I said and bypassed everyone to wrap her in a hug. "'Cause my guestroom has your name written all over it."

Gwen winked. "That's kinda what I thought. I figured if it was in use, I'd just go to your apartment."

I laughed. Gwen knew me too well.

Marc wrapped an arm around my shoulders and squeezed me. "It's good to see you, kiddo."

"You, too, Dad." I smiled up at him, loving that I could call him that. "All right, everyone. As much as I'm thrilled to see you, maybe someone wants to fill me in on what's going on?"

Marc let go of me and moved to Mom's side. She beamed up at him, her eyes sparkling with more happiness than I'd ever seen. She practically glowed with it.

Love radiated off them in waves. And I knew what was coming before Mom even took her next breath.

She held her left hand out, showing off the large princess-cut diamond ring. "Marc and I are engaged. And we want to get married at your house in Cypress Settlement."

My lips twitched and then slid into a slow grin. "I can't think of a better place."

# CHAPTER 28

With Duke at my feet, music blared from the iPod dock as Kane, Gwen, and I watched Mom and Marc sway to a sappy love song in our small backyard. "How long have they been seeing each other?" I asked Gwen.

"Just a couple of months." She placed a napkin over the bib of her overalls and then bit into one of my chocolate cream cheese cupcakes. Her curly gray hair bobbed as she nodded her head in satisfaction. "Dang, Jade. I forgot how good these are."

"I know, right?" I broke a piece of the cupcake off and popped it in my mouth. "Two months? Isn't that a little fast to get engaged?"

She shrugged. "They were married for almost seven years. It's not like they don't know each other."

"True. But a lot has happened since then." Like the fact that she'd kept me from him, lied to me about who my real father was, and then spent fifteen years in purgatory. They might have a few issues to work out.

"Try to be happy for them, Jade," she said gently. "They've

both lost a lot of years. Sometimes it's better to just live than to be cautious."

Her words made me glance at Kane over her head. He was staring at me with an odd expression and then he nodded. "She's a smart lady, your aunt."

I turned to look at my parents, caught the love shimmering through them, and said, "Yes, yes she is."

THERE'S nothing worse than waiting for something when you have no idea how long the wait is supposed to be. It had been twenty-five hours since we'd left Lailah and Pyper in the angel realm. And I'd taken to pacing.

"Jade, you're not helping," Gwen gently chided.

"I can't help it."

"Do you want to get out of here? Go get lunch maybe?"

I shook my head. "No. I need to be here when they get back. But you should go. Take Mom and Marc out. Get gumbo and hurricanes. Have some fun."

"Gumbo?" I heard Marc say from the other room.

"Yes," I called. "Go eat. No need for everyone to wait around here with us."

"What do you think?" I heard him ask my mom. Then there was a giggle.

Oh, jeez. *Please go*, I silently pleaded.

Gwen laughed and touched my arm. "Don't worry, we'll get out of your hair."

"Thanks."

Ten minutes later, the three of them were off for a day in the French Quarter while Kane and I settled in for the wait. But just as we started a movie, the front door burst open.

"What did you forget?" I asked absently, fiddling with the volume.

"Just my manners," Pyper said as she flew across the room and landed on the loveseat in between the two of us.

"Pyper!" I let out a happy squeal and wrapped my arms around her at the same time Kane did. The three of us sat there in a hug for a long moment, laughing and crying. Well, Pyper and I cried. Kane didn't.

When I finally let go, I fixed my gaze on Lailah, who was standing in the middle of the room, shaking her head at us.

"I told you I'd take care of her," Lailah said, smiling.

"And so you did." Pyper beamed at her. "And thank you."

"Best soul guardian ever." I got up and gave Lailah a hug. She stiffened, but when I didn't relent, she finally hugged me back.

"That wasn't so hard," I teased, "now was it?"

She rolled her eyes at me. "No. But don't get used to it."

"I wouldn't dream of it." I tugged her over to the two chairs that faced the loveseat. She sat in one, and I sat in the other. Kane and Pyper were across from us. "Okay, now tell me everything."

Pyper's smile fell and she glanced away. "Can we maybe talk about it later?"

Every instinct in my body screamed to demand that she give us the details, but I refrained. She'd tell us when she was ready.

Kane frowned in her direction, but didn't push her either.

"Of course," I said, "But first, are you okay?"

"Yes, I'm totally fine. I just don't want to relive the experience right this moment, if you know what I mean." She wrapped her arms around herself and shivered.

"I do. No explanation necessary." No doubt the soul extraction had been painful. The last thing I wanted to do was make her talk about it. So I turned my attention to Lailah. "How about you? Are you going to tell us what that was all about when you took responsibility for that angel?"

Lailah shrugged. "I'm Pyper's guardian. I couldn't let Chessa keep her in the realm."

"And?" I raised my eyebrows expectantly.

"What makes you think—"

"Lailah. No one puts their life on the line and willingly goes into Hell unless they have a damned good reason. Now spill it."

She grimaced and then sighed. "I needed a reason to have access to Chessandra and everything she's been up to. She's been doing strange things for a while now. First she tried to close the demon portal and ended up causing her sister to get trapped in the void world. Then she sent a bunch of angels into the shadows all at once, which isn't the way things normally work. And worse, I believe she ordered Avery to check on the shadows when she knew it was dangerous. All of this was done without informing the council. She's been going rogue, and I want to know why."

"You think she's engaging in some dirty dealings?" I asked, taken aback.

"Maybe. I don't know. What I do know is that she's keeping a lot to herself. Not to mention there's been some really strange demon attacks on angels in the last few months. Ones that seem completely random. My gut says something's off. And I'm going to investigate before something worse happens."

We all stared at her, not sure what to say. It was no secret I wasn't Chessandra's biggest fan. She was a bully and cold-hearted, but I always assumed she was that way for the greater good. But what if she was just an angel all out for herself and willing to roll around in the mud to get whatever she wanted?

"This is extreme fight club, obviously," she added.

"Understood," I said. Pyper and Kane nodded their

agreement. The information would never leave this room.

She stood abruptly. "I need to get home and then get to work. Pyper, let me know if you need anything or feel anything odd at all. I'll be around."

"Sure." Pyper walked Lailah to the door. "Thanks for everything."

Lailah smiled. "My pleasure."

"That was…interesting," I said after she left.

"And frightening," Pyper added as she took her spot next to Kane. "I get the feeling Lailah thinks Chessandra's dealing with demons."

Kane leaned forward. "Well, if she is, you can be damned sure we'll bring her down."

I couldn't imagine what kind of epic battle we'd have to engage in if Chessandra turned out to be one of the bad guys. But Kane was right—if she was dealing in evil, we'd take her down one way or another.

"Jade?" Pyper called.

"Yeah?"

"Can you come sit over here for a minute?" She was smiling like she had a secret.

"Sure."

Kane patted his lap and held his arms out to me.

I slid onto his lap and wrapped my arm around his shoulders. "Okay. What's up?"

Pyper was staring at the chair Lailah had been sitting in, and after a moment she nodded. Turning back to us, she said, "So, about this medium thing…"

"Is it true?" I asked, intensely curious. "Can you still see spirits now that you're back to only having your soul?"

"It's true. And yes, my guides are still with me. I'm told that since I've invited them into my life, they'll be there as long as I wish."

I met Kane's eyes and saw the same awe I felt reflected back at me. "That's cool."

She nodded. "But I have something cooler for both of you right now."

Kane gave her a curious look. "And what might that be, Pyps?"

"Mamaw is here," she said. "Right over there."

Kane and I both stared at the chair across from us. The look on his face went from mildly interested to heartfelt and gutted. "Mamaw?" he asked.

"Yes." Pyper positively glowed with happiness. "She wants you to know you picked a good wife and she can't wait for grandbabies to watch over during the night."

"Grandbabies?" I blurted out.

Kane grinned at me. "I'm certainly willing to practice."

Pyper cut her eyes to Kane. "Mamaw says if you're gonna be disrespectful, she's gonna smack the back of your head."

I laughed, and Kane sobered.

"She's really here," he said.

"Of course she is. I said she was, didn't I?" Pyper patted his arm. "Don't worry, you'll get used to it."

He shook his head. "No, I don't think so." Then he gazed at the chair she'd indicated his grandmother was occupying. "Damn, Mamaw, I miss the hell out of you." The words came out hoarse and full of emotion.

Tears filled Pyper's eyes, but she laughed. "She's cursing you for making her cry. And she says she misses your hugs most of all."

That rendered Kane speechless.

I bent and whispered in his ear, "You do give the best hugs."

"And Jade?" Pyper added.

"Yes?"

"Mamaw says she knows you'll take care of her boy and that she loved your wedding. Especially the minister."

Laughing, I nodded toward the chair. "I'm very glad you were there. Kane missed you."

"I'm always here when you need me," an older wobbly voice said from the direction of the chair.

I let out a small gasp as Kane's head shot up. "Mamaw?" he asked.

Pyper shook her head. "She's gone now."

"But I just heard her. You did, too, right?" he asked me.

"Yes. I did."

Pyper stood and smiled down at us. "It was her gift to both of you." She bent and gave Kane a kiss on his cheek and then did the same to me. "I'm going home now."

I caught her hand. "You can't. You just got back."

She moved to the front door. "I can. And I need to. All I want is a hot bath and my own bed."

"Take care of yourself, friend," Kane said.

"You, too." Pyper blew us a kiss and slipped out the front door.

I stared down into the face of my overwhelmed husband. "Looks like it's just you and me for now."

His arms tightened around me as he buried his head into my neck. "I can't believe I heard her."

I stroked my hand through his hair. "She loves you."

He shuddered a tiny bit at my words. Then after a moment he started laughing.

"What's so funny?"

He looked up at me. "I was just wondering how often she's here watching us."

"Oh, jeez. Don't go there."

His grin widened. "She's gone now. Pyper said so."

"Stop. That's not right."

"She did ask for grandbabies." He waggled his eyebrows at me.

I shook my head. "If you think—"

His lips caught mine and the next thing I knew, he had me wrapped in a powerful kiss. Everything left my mind except him and the incredible connection between us. Power flowed from him to me and filled me up, made my heart almost burst from joy. And when he pulled away, I whispered, "I love you, Kane Rouquette."

"I love you, too, Mrs. Rouquette." Then he picked me up and without any more words, he took me to our bedroom and laid me on our bed. "You're the most incredible thing I've ever seen," he said, carefully unbuttoning my cotton shirt.

I said nothing as I watched him undress me.

When he was done, he stepped back and eyed my naked body. "Gorgeous."

I smiled up at him. "Your turn."

His eyes glinted as he pulled his shirt off and then pushed his jeans down his hips.

"Glorious," I said when he was finally finished. Long and lean and muscles everywhere.

"You haven't seen anything yet," he murmured, lowering himself over top of me, his lips finding my collar bone. I turned my head to give him access to my neck and noticed the small potion bottle sitting by itself on my nightstand.

It was the same one I'd seen at Bea's shop. The fertility potion. For some reason, seeing it didn't strike me as odd at all, even though I knew neither Kane nor I had put it there.

And as Kane's lips moved gently over my skin, for the first time in my life, I started to wonder what it would be like to have a child. To my surprise, a peace settled over me and a longing I'd never felt before took up residence in my chest.

There was no denying it. I wanted Kane's child.

# DEANNA'S BOOK LIST

**Witches of Keating Hollow:**
Soul of the Witch
Heart of the Witch
Spirit of the Witch
Dreams of the Witch
Courage of the Witch
Love of the Witch
Power of the Witch
Essence of the Witch
Muse of the Witch
Vision of the Witch
Waking of the Witch
Honor of the Witch
Promise of the Witch
Return of the Witch
Fortune of the Witch

**Witches of Befana Bay:**
The Witch's Silver Lining

### Witches of Christmas Grove:
A Witch For Mr. Holiday
A Witch For Mr. Christmas
A Witch For Mr. Winter
A Witch For Mr. Mistletoe
A Witch For Mr. Frost

### Premonition Pointe Novels:
Witching For Grace
Witching For Hope
Witching For Joy
Witching For Clarity
Witching For Moxie
Witching For Kismet

### Miss Matched Midlife Dating Agency:
Star-crossed Witch
Honor-bound Witch
Outmatched Witch
Moonstruck Witch

### Jade Calhoun Novels:
Haunted on Bourbon Street
Witches of Bourbon Street
Demons of Bourbon Street
Angels of Bourbon Street
Shadows of Bourbon Street
Incubus of Bourbon Street
Bewitched on Bourbon Street
Hexed on Bourbon Street
Dragons of Bourbon Street

### Pyper Rayne Novels:

Spirits, Stilettos, and a Silver Bustier
Spirits, Rock Stars, and a Midnight Chocolate Bar
Spirits, Beignets, and a Bayou Biker Gang
Spirits, Diamonds, and a Drive-thru Daiquiri Stand
Spirits, Spells, and Wedding Bells

**Ida May Chronicles:**
Witched To Death
Witch, Please
Stop Your Witchin'

**Crescent City Fae Novels:**
Influential Magic
Irresistible Magic
Intoxicating Magic

**Last Witch Standing:**
Bewitched by Moonlight
Soulless at Sunset
Bloodlust By Midnight
Bitten At Daybreak

**Witch Island Brides:**
The Wolf's New Year Bride
The Vampire's Last Dance
The Warlock's Enchanted Kiss
The Shifter's First Bite

**Destiny Novels:**
Defining Destiny
Accepting Fate

**Wolves of the Rising Sun:**

Jace

Aiden

Luc

Craved

Silas

Darien

Wren

## Black Bear Outlaws:

Cyrus

Chase

Cole

## Bayou Springs Alien Mail Order Brides:

Zeke

Gunn

Echo

# ABOUT THE AUTHOR

New York Times and USA Today bestselling author, Deanna Chase, is a native Californian, transplanted to the slower paced lifestyle of southeastern Louisiana. When she isn't writing, she is often goofing off with her husband in New Orleans or playing with her two shih tzu dogs. For more information and updates on newest releases visit her website at deannachase.com.

www.ingramcontent.com/pod-product-compliance
Lightning Source LLC
Chambersburg PA
CBHW030327200626
46816CB00006BA/1952